Next of Kin

Sue Welfare

Next of Kin
Copyright © Sue Welfare 2015

ISBN 978-1514652077

Published by Castle Yard Publishing 2015

" *... the greatest trick the Devil pulled was convincing the world there was only one of him.* "
David Wong.

For Phil, Jake and Daisy-Dog

To Cathy
with all good
wishes

Sue

Next of Kin

Sarah

The detective hands me a photograph and I turn it towards the light so I can see it more clearly. I can feel him watching me, watching my reaction. He wants me to be shocked, but I'm not shocked I'm relieved.

The image is brutal. Raw. I know what it is straight away; he is looking out of the photo, eyes wide, but what catches my attention are the things around him. My marriage certificate under an outstretched hand. There's a stain on it, the same size as my fist, shaped like a flower. It's mahogany brown, although I don't remember spilling anything on it. It takes me a moment or two to realise that it has to be blood. And now, looking more closely, I can see that there is blood on everything, little droplets on letters, splashes on the papers, and smeared over the receipts and the bills and the dark stain under his head is not a shadow.

I hand the photograph back and the detective slides it into the folder amongst the others, back where it came from, carefully, and then back on the table, back in its place. I've looked through them all: photographs of the house, the box file and the biscuit tin and then alongside each one, the contents all set out inside evidence bags, all numbered, all neatly arranged, evenly spaced: passports, photographs, letters and bills. Lots of envelopes and my mobile phone.

Inside the room it is very quiet and still. There are windows running all along the wall, high up, so that you can't see out, but I can hear the muted voices of children playing in a school somewhere close by. Dust motes spin in a shaft of afternoon sunlight. The lights on the recorder glow red. Time seems to have slowed in here. I'm tired and my eyes feel heavy.

'Did you plan to kill him, Sarah?' the detective asks. He sounds as tired as I feel. There is a woman beside him, another detective I think, but she just sits there and says nothing.

I look up, surprised by his voice, and I'm about to say no, to deny it, but the words catch in my throat.

They are both listening now. Both waiting.

Chapter One

Sarah pushed open the door to the sitting room and peered into the gloom. Turning her head, she shouted. 'Ryan, how many times have I told you not to smoke in the house? It reeks in here. Can you get yourself down here and help me get tidied up? That woman is coming to look round at half ten.'

She was across the sitting room in half a dozen strides, padding over the bare boards and the colourful rugs, pulling open the faded velvet curtains and pushing up the sash window to let in a trickle of colder, damper air. Turning she could see the remnants of a long evening in scattered around the room, empty pizza boxes on the coffee table, controllers for the Xbox, dirty mugs, empty beer cans and discarded trainers. Someone had used one of the mugs as an ashtray; it was full almost to the top – but what stopped Sarah mid-stride was an awareness that there was someone else in the room, someone asleep on the sofa under a duvet.

'Ryan,' Sarah shouted, her eyes fixed on the shape on the sofa. She recognised the duvet, it was the one from the bedroom upstairs that she was hoping to let to the girl who was coming round for a viewing. It was new. There was a damp looking brown stain that had spread up from the floor and made its way across one of the corners.

'Get in here, *now!*'

She heard his footsteps and started speaking before he was in the room. 'What the hell do you think you're playing at? I spent all day yesterday cleaning the whole place from top to bottom. On my day off. That's the new duvet, Ryan.'

'I know, it's all right, I can explain,' he said, holding his hands up in a show of surrender. 'Keep your hair on. It won't take long to clear up. Ten minutes—'

'You promised me, Ryan. And who the hell is that?'

The sleeper stirred and grunted.

'Woody, he's sound as a pound,' said Ryan, scratching his head with both hands.

'What the hell is that supposed to mean?'

'I was going to tell you about him.'

'Tell me what? I'm out working and you've got your friends round here drinking and messing the place up? Do you take me for a complete idiot?'

'Of course not. He's a good guy – he's—'

Sarah's voice cut across his. 'I don't care what he is. I don't want your mates crashing round here, do you understand?'

'Yeah, all right, just slow down, will you. I thought you wanted to rent the spare rooms out.'

When Sarah didn't answer Ryan nodded towards the figure on the sofa. 'There you are then. Woody's your man; he's got money.' He made a gesture, rubbing his thumb and forefinger together. 'Minted,' he mouthed.

'Really? In that case why is he sleeping on our sofa?' Sarah said, making a show of gathering up the rubbish.

'He's a student.'

Sarah rolled her eyes.

'No, hang on, wait a minute. He's doing his MBA.' Ryan lowered his voice. 'Listen, Sarah, he gets an allowance from his old man. He's rolling in it and he really needs somewhere to stay, like yesterday.'

The figure under the duvet stretched, making sounds of waking and then very slowly Ryan's friend pushed the cover down. Woody wasn't at all what Sarah was expecting. He was Asian, nice looking, bare-chested and probably in his late twenties. He blinked and rubbed his eyes. For the first time Sarah took in the pile of neatly folded clothes on one of the side tables, the brogues paired and parallel together on the floor, the sports jacket hung over the back of a chair.

Ryan grinned. 'Woody. You old dog, how're you feeling, mate?'

Woody grimaced. 'A little delicate.' And then, seeing Sarah, he said, 'I'm so sorry. It was late and—' his voice was low and even and without any discernible accent.

Ryan's grin held. 'And you were slaughtered, man. The Woodster is new to the demon drink, aren't you, mate?'

'Do you have to talk like that?' snapped Sarah.

'For god's sake lighten up, will you?' Ryan pulled a face, and when she didn't reply, snapped right back. 'What? We just had a few beers, that's all. There's no law against it. And Woody needs a place to stay, don't you?'

The young man nodded and sat up. He was nicely made, muscular with a hairy chest and broad shoulders; Sarah made the effort to look away.

'Ryan told me that you have a room to let?' he said.

'That's right we do,' Sarah said.

'I would be interested, seriously and Ryan is right. I can afford the rent,' he said and then, as if suddenly aware of his bare chest, gathered the duvet up around himself.

'Why don't Ryan and I go in the kitchen and you can get yourself sorted out,' said Sarah, waving towards his clothes. 'Come through and we can discuss the room when you're ready. It'll be easier to talk in there.'

Woody nodded. 'Thank you,' he said, his voice smooth as silk. 'I won't be a minute.'

11

'Take your time,' Sarah said and closed the door behind them.

Ryan and Woody

While there was no one up on their feet cheering the nag on, there was a sense of growing anticipation and tension in the room. Almost all eyes in the betting shop were fixed on the bank of screens that ran along the back wall and the images of a phalanx of horses careering around the racecourse at full stretch, their great necks working, their long legs eating up the distance, mouths straining against the bits, the jockeys up in the stirrups, heads down, backsides skyward.

The sound was turned down; on other screens there was football and other races but the main event was this horse race; two furlongs from home and the favourite was being hunted down by the 100-1 outsider.

There was a warm, anxious, excited, sick feeling in the pit of Ryan's stomach. He tried hard to control his breathing, stay still and stay calm, but he couldn't stop himself from chewing on his bottom lip, his fists clenching and unclenching as the horses thundered on towards the finish line. The betting slip for this race was tucked into the top pocket of his tee shirt. Out of sight but not out of mind.

In the last few hundred yards the two horses tore themselves away from the pack, legs a blur.

'C'mon, c'mon,' Ryan murmured under his breath; they were so close, so *very very* close now. It looked as if the favourite might just hang on and take it. Fleetingly, Ryan thought that he should have taken the teller's advice and backed the outsider each way, not used his last fifty quid for an on the nose bet, first past the post. But where was the fun in that?

Where was the buzz? He'd got a solid tip and this meant that when his horse came home he could pay Darryl off and Neil too, have a few beers, sort out his bills with maybe a bit over to give Sarah. A little something to keep her off his back. If it came in. No, when it came in, *when.*

The outsider dug in and was still coming on strong, still closing. Ryan's instinct was to close his eyes but he fought it with every breath. He needed this horse to win and it would; it would. If he could just keep his nerve. He knew it. He could feel it in his gut. This was the moment that things changed. The point where things turned around. He just needed to see that horse cross the finish line, after all this was a rock solid tip. Rock solid. The rush of the adrenaline coursing through his bloodstream was making him dizzy.

The favourite was still just holding the outsider off, fighting back, digging deep. The contender dug deeper, deeper – they were neck and neck now. The breath was caught up in Ryan's throat, hard and dense like cotton wool.

The outsider suddenly seemed to find a renewed vigour, an extra something and pressed for home, but the favourite wasn't done yet and hung on in there, and seemed to stretch out, struggling to find a little more, a little more. Ryan hung on to his breath as the two horses raced full bore down towards the line, not a hair's breadth between them. The yards vanished under the unheard thunder of their pounding hooves. Fifty yards out, forty – the outsider gave one final push for home.

'Come on, come on,' Ryan called, oblivious now to the men around him. The camera had moved in for a close-up of the two horses. 'C'mon,' he said again, on an outward breath. 'Don't let me down, don't you dare–'

It was almost as if the horse heard him. It flicked its ears and a split second later stumbled, cartwheeling the jockey off over the top of its head and onto the grass.

'No, *fuck, no!*' gasped Ryan, the win and the money slipping through his fingers. His gut clenched as the favourite crossed the line, the 100-1 shot was close behind him - riderless now - while the rest of the field came up thundering in behind.

There was a moment's beat, a moment's taking stock and then Ryan pulled the betting slip out of his top pocket, crumpled it into a ball and dropped it into the bin.

No one else moved. He breathed out hard, trying to suppress the desire to punch something. Five grand, five fucking grand. Gone. Lost. It would have seen him good, seen him home clear, seen him ahead for the first time in weeks, months.

Ryan let his shoulders slump forward, no point in hanging around now, probably better to go home just in case Darryl or Neil dropped in on their way home from work wanting to know if he had their money. They wouldn't be chuffed to find out he had spent what he owed them and more beside on half a dozen bad bets.

As Ryan turned, an Asian guy playing the slots close to where he was standing, raised his eyebrows and pursed his lips, nodding his head in little gesture of solidarity, or maybe commiseration. The guy was in his late twenties, maybe a bit older, and looked out of place in the bookies in his tweed jacket, button down shirt, corduroy trousers and Buddy Holly glasses. As their eyes met, all his ducks lined up and the machine started to play a metallic fanfare and punch out pound coins into the tray, the word *Jackpot* flashing on and off the screen in garish lights.

Ryan smiled grimly and shook his head while the machine kept on churning the coins out with steady a chunk, chunk, chunk. At least someone was winning.

The guy, bending down now to stem the tide, looked up and flipped him a pound coin. 'There you go. You look like you could use a beer,' he said.

Ryan looked down at the coin in his palm and laughed; a pound wasn't going to get him very far. He'd seen the man there before, feeding the machines, which sat in a line in the bookies' window. He always seemed to be in a little world of his own, pound coin in, press the button, hold and nudge, and nudge again, the play accompanied by the annoying quack-quack-oops of failure and the little fanfares of triumph. They had never spoken before.

'Cheers, man, but it's not a beer I need so much as a horse with four good legs,' he said, and reached over to hand back the coin. 'Thanks anyway.'

The man waved him away. 'Keep it, it might bring you some luck.'

Ryan snorted but pocketed the money. 'Let's hope so. I need to be getting back. I said I'd help clear the house up.' Usually Ryan wouldn't have said anything and wondered why he was now, maybe it was the pound, maybe it was that the guy seemed kind. Maybe it was because it was raining outside and he'd be soaked to the skin the minute he stepped through the door. Maybe because his luck was shit and for a moment he wanted it all to stop.

Ryan looked at the rain coursing down the betting shop window. He wondered why he hadn't noticed it before, and hesitated. It was tipping down, water running down the gutter like a river. Perfect; soaked, cold, broke and with a long walk home.

The machine was still spewing coins. 'Nagging wife?' the man asked.

Ryan shook his head, still staring out into the

rain. 'No, it's my sister. We've got someone coming round tomorrow to see about renting a room. I said I'd give her a hand to clear the place up.'

The man from behind the counter was heading their way with a plastic tub. 'You want to put the coins in here? I can change them up for you if you like. We can always do with change,' he said.

The Asian man nodded and started scooping piles of coins into the little bucket. Ryan watched idly; it was something to do rather than head off into the rain.

'I'm looking for a room,' the man said, without looking up

Ryan nodded. 'Right.'

'No, really. The sooner the better really. I need to get out of the place I'm in.'

Ryan nodded again. 'Maybe I can help you. You like the machines?' he asked casually.

'I do today. But I'm not much of a gambler really. They're fixed odds. I'm in it for the long game,' he said.

Ryan had no idea what the man meant. 'Slot machines?' Ryan asked.

'No, that's a side-line. I'm just passing the time. Picking my moment. I'm planning bigger things.'

'Me too,' said Ryan, half-heartedly.

He had come in to the betting shop with two hundred and fifty quid burning a hole in his pocket, a clutch of solid tips and a plan to be sensible and bet each way right up until the last horse. The 100-1 shot had just been too much of a temptation to resist, after what had proved to be a shit afternoon and a run of losers. He'd been convinced the outsider was going to be the one that turned his luck around.

'Most of my friends call me Woody,' the man was saying, extending a hand.

Ryan took his hand and shook it. 'Ryan,' he said.

'Fancy nipping next door and grabbing a drink. Help me celebrate?'

Ryan considered the idea. Walk home in the rain or bum a couple of drinks off a nerd in a tweed jacket? No contest really, but it didn't pay to look too eager.

'Better than going out in that,' the man added, glancing towards the door.

'Maybe just a half, then,' Ryan said grudgingly.

Woody indicated that Ryan should lead the way. Outside, despite the rain, Mill Road was still busy; it was lined with little shops selling everything from vintage clothes to spicy falafel and Vietnamese vegetables, and was the place foreign students headed for to buy a little taste of home. There was a pool hall and Chinese supermarket and a Cajun café tucked between a guy who sold hookah pipes and a place that sold spices and herbs, that, when the wind was in the right direction, flooded the air with mouth-watering smells. This end of the road was the betting shop and across the way the pub.

Ryan had always liked Mill Road. He'd never got around to travelling, missed out on all that whole gap year shizzle. Mill Road, he thought, was probably the closest he'd ever get to exotic places, although today the air smelt not of spices but of laundry and diesel fumes.

The pub on the corner was as close as Ryan had got to a local; it wasn't flash but it was comfortable, not done up to be something it wasn't, which was a proper working man's pub with sport on the TV, a couple of slot machines, decent beer and a good line in basic pub grub. More than that it was far enough away from where he lived to keep Sarah off his back.

'So do you live round here?' Woody asked, as they waited for the barman to notice them. This time of the afternoon the place was almost empty, the man was on his own, nipping in and out, clearing up, and refilling the shelves, so it took them a while to get served.

Ryan shrugged. 'Maybe half an hour's walk away, not that far, but there's a bus.'

'Handy.'

Ryan laughed. 'Seriously. It's not that far. And it's a nice area.'

'The place I'm in at the moment isn't. I'm looking for somewhere else.'

'You serious about that?'

Woody nodded. 'Yeah. The room I've got at the moment is a bit out of the way and a bit rough, you know what I mean?'

Ryan nodded. ' Yeah,' he paused. 'The thing is we, that's Sarah, we need—'

Woody held up a hand to stop him. 'References, deposit, someone who can pay on time and pay every month?'

Ryan nodded. 'She's a bit of a stickler.'

'Nothing wrong with that.'

The barman finally came over. Woody encouraged Ryan to order first, insisted he had a pint, ordered an orange juice for himself, and then paid. 'I'm doing my MBA,' Woody said, handing the barman a crisp new twenty. 'I've got references and my parents are bank rolling me while I'm over here studying. I get a regular allowance, and I need to be away from where I am, and I'm happy to pay for an upgrade.'

'Right,' said Ryan, nodding thoughtfully, as he took a mouthful of beer, sipping away the foam. He was parched. The lager was sharp and cold and for a moment Ryan thought that maybe the gods had smiled on him after all, recompense for the failure of his dead cert. 'Well, we've got a couple of rooms,' he said. 'Nice rooms. Clean.'

Woody nodded enthusiastically.

'And it's a nice area. On the other side of Jesus Green. You know, the park? Off Victoria Road.'

'Is there any chance I could come round and have a look at it?'

Ryan nodded. 'Sure, when do you want to come round?'

'The sooner the better, really.' Woody picked up a menu from the bar. 'I'm starving, do you fancy grabbing something to eat?'

Ryan shrugged; he was flat-busted broke, the truth was that food sounded like a great idea but he certainly wasn't going to order something he couldn't pay for. He was hoping that there was something in the fridge when he got back. Maybe Sarah had been shopping. Sometimes she brought home leftovers from the restaurant where she worked in the evenings.

'Cottage pie and chips,' Woody was reading aloud, working his way down the menu. 'Lasagne.'

Ryan's mouth watered. He hadn't eaten all day, and hadn't realised just how hungry he was. Better take it easy on the booze. It must have showed, because Woody grinned, and said, 'Don't worry, my treat, mate. 'He tapped his jacket pocket. 'Jackpot, remember? Now are you going to tell me about this room? And what about your sister, what's she like?'

In the end, a few of pints later, they decided to grab a couple of take-away pizzas and pick up a few more cans from the off-license on the walk back to the house. As they headed through the wet streets, the pavements glittering under the street lights, Ryan found himself telling Woody about the money he owed to Darryl and Neil – not that he intended to, but Woody had a way with him, a way of listening and asking questions as if he was genuinely interested.

As they climbed the steps up to the front door and

Ryan rifled through his pockets to track down his keys, Woody said not to worry, why hadn't he said something about the money before? Woody could lend Ryan the cash no problem, no problem at all, he could call it a sub on the rent or something. Ryan had a problem getting the key into the lock; he hadn't realised quite how drunk he was.

Chapter Two

In the kitchen the following morning, Sarah was plugging in the kettle.

'He's a good bloke,' said Ryan, pulling out a chair and sitting down at the table.

'And you know this *because*?'

'Because I've seen him around, you know, about.'

'When you say *around*, what does that mean exactly?'

'Just about, you know, *around*.'

'No, I don't.' She looked at Ryan. 'You're twenty-three, don't pretend to be some moronic teenager. I'm your sister, not your mother. You said that you would help me keep this place going. You promised me you'd pull your weight and so what do you do? You're out nearly every night on the beer, and you're way behind with your share of the bills. I shouldn't have to keep asking you for money, Ryan. You need to grow up. Pay up. I'm sick of it.'

'All right, all right. I am helping; you just don't notice all the things I do.'

'And what would they be? Tell me. What are they, all these things that you're busy doing?'

'Come on, Sarah, ease up. This is not about me. Woody does need a room.'

'Where did you meet him? Down the pub? The bookies? You met him down the bookies, didn't you?'

Ryan winced as if she had slapped him. 'No.'

'The last thing we need in here is another one of your gambling cronies.'

'Don't, Sarah,' said Ryan, holding up his hands to deflect her. He could swing between being a boy and a man as it suited him. Now he was all man. 'I know what you're going to say. And you have to believe me; I didn't know Billy was a thief. I wouldn't have

21

brought him back here if I'd known what he was like. It was a mistake. Years ago. One mistake. All right? Everyone is entitled to make a mistake once in a while. Oh but no, I forgot, not me, because I'm talking to little Miss Perfect here, aren't I?'

'You've had more than your fair share. I caught him going through Mum's things.'

'That must be five years ago, Sarah,' Ryan protested. 'Five years. And how many times do I have to tell you; I didn't know he was like that. I thought he was a good bloke. Sound.'

'Sound as a pound?'

Ryan stared at her, jaw working.

'Like Woody?' she pressed, just in case there was some chance, some faint chance, that he had missed the point.

Ryan sighed. 'There's no way I can win, is there? You never let me off, do you? Never let me forget. Woody's straight as a die. He's doing an MBA. His parents are minted and they're bank rolling him while he's studying over here. He just likes a little flutter now and then, that's it, and that's all. They all do. He told me – he's a good bloke.'

'Who do?'

'The Asian guys. They're all in there playing the machines and having a few quid on the horses here and there. It's a cultural thing.'

Sarah stared at him.

'It is – you can ask him if you want. It's the only fun they can have, no booze, no drugs, no women. It's the truth, Sarah. Honest.'

'Until you got hold of him and gave him beer?'

Ryan rolled his eyes heavenwards. 'C'mon, Sarah, give me a break. He's a grown up. Woody's his own man. He can make his own mind up, and he didn't have that much. He told me he likes a drink now and then. Anyway, I've told him he can stay here for a couple of days if he wants to. He's been having trouble with his landlord and some guys at his place. I didn't think you'd mind. We've got the room.'

'How much do you owe him?'

Ryan shook his head. 'Will you just shut up. Nothing – nothing. All right?'

Sarah had heard it all before. 'How much?' she repeated.

'I just told you.'

And so she waited. Just looking at him. Ryan wasn't good with silence. After a minute or two he crumbled. 'Okay, okay. So he offered to help me out of a hole, so I owe him a few quid, but I'm good for it. You know that. He knows that too. So don't go getting all self-righteous on me, Sarah. It's fine. Marty owes me a hundred for the paving I did for him last week and Ben said he can use me on the tools next week. I just needed to sort Darryl and Neil out, just a couple of hundred and Woody said it wasn't a problem.'

'You can't keep doing this, Ryan.'

'I don't *keep* doing anything. It's just this once. And it's fine. Just lighten up, will you, nobody died.'

Behind her, Sarah heard Woody cough.

Ryan grinned and waved him in. 'There you are. Come on in. Do you want a cup of tea, mate? Or coffee?'

'I'm so sorry, I didn't mean to interrupt.'

'You're not interrupting, is he, Sarah? Do you want tea?' Ryan asked again. He trailed a finger along the canisters on the shelf. 'Earl Grey, green or just plain builders', we've got it all here, haven't we, Sarah? Wide tastes, every palate catered for.'

He was showing off.

Woody hesitated. 'Ordinary tea will be just fine, thank you. If it's no trouble.' He was plainly uncomfortable.

With a forced cheeriness, Ryan took a mug off the draining board and dropped a bag into it. 'It's no trouble at all, is it, Sarah?'

What could she say? Woody seemed polite and deeply embarrassed at having walked in on them. 'No, it's fine; I'll make the tea if you like,' she said. 'Ryan, can you go and clear the front room up before that woman gets here?'

'Sure, not a problem,' Ryan said with false cheeriness and, stuffing his hands into his sweatshirt pockets, sloped off.

Woody didn't look at all like the kind of person Ryan usually mixed with or brought home; he was dressed in a sports jacket and checked viyella shirt, tucked into cords, and worn with finely tooled brogues. Everything looked slightly too big for him as if he was wearing his big brother's clothes. He glanced around the kitchen, shifting his weight from foot to foot, seemingly nervous and self-conscious.

They both started to speak at once. 'Ryan said—' Sarah began.

'—About the room,' Woody said. They both stopped at the same time. He gestured towards Sarah. 'I'm so sorry, after you.'

Sarah shook her head. 'No, please. I insist.'

'Ryan is a good man,' Woody said.

'I know exactly what Ryan is. And he owes you money,' said Sarah.

Woody shrugged. 'I'm sure I will get it back. He said I will have it by the end of this week.'

She laughed. 'Well, good luck with that. I would be very grateful if you didn't lend him any more, Woody. Ryan's not good with money.' She dipped the tea bag in and out of the mug, pressing it with a teaspoon. 'Milk, sugar?'

'Milk and two sugars please.'

'Are you really interested in seeing the rooms? Or

24

are you just saying that to get Ryan out of trouble?'

Woody grinned and shook his head. 'No, not at all. I am genuinely very keen to see it.'

'What's the problem with where you're living now?'

'The house is okay, but there are a couple of young men living there. They're on the dole, they're trouble-makers, into all kinds of things, I suspect. One in particular.' He paused. 'He is making my life difficult. It's not like this, not a family home. I prefer a quiet life, and they like drinking, and swearing, drugs too I think, women. They're very loud. Sometimes I think they are doing it on purpose to upset me, banging around outside my door, shouting and singing and swearing. They bang on my door sometimes and one of them jostled me in the hallway. He said afterwards when I threatened to go to the police that it was just a joke, you know, all good-humoured, but that isn't how it felt.

'My landlord was not very sympathetic when I told him about it. He's a good man but I think he is afraid of them too. They make me nervous. I'm finding it difficult to study.'

'You know that Ryan lives here, don't you?' Sarah said, handing him the tea.

He smiled. 'Ryan's not like them. Not at all. They're trouble. Really.'

'Okay. Well if you are serious, the room is eighty-five pounds a week, first month in advance, which includes your share of the bills. Shared kitchen. Lodger's fridge...' She nodded to the one she had hauled home from the Sally Army. 'No overnight visitors, you can have a TV in your room, and use the washing machine in the utility room. We haven't got a tumble drier but there's a line in the garden. And there's Wi-Fi; we split the bill for that between us, and you can't use the landline for overseas calls.'

He nodded. 'It all sounds fair enough.'

'If you want to leave your tea on the table for a couple of minutes I can show you the rooms if you like,' Sarah said.

Woody nodded, and got to his feet.

Together they made their way out of the kitchen and up the stairs, Sarah talking as they went: 'There are two rooms, one is in the attic up at the top of the house,' she said, as they reached the landing. 'That's the biggest, and then there's this one on the first floor. Oh and I'll need references.'

'Not a problem. What do you do?'

Sarah glanced back over her shoulder. 'Me?' The question took her by surprise.

'Yes. Ryan didn't say. Are you two married?'

'To Ryan?' Sarah laughed. 'No. Ryan is my brother. No, I'm single.'

'And so this is your house, yes?'

'Yes, well, we own it between us. We were left it by our mother; it's a couple of years ago now.'

Woody nodded. 'I'm so sorry for your loss. Ryan tells me that he is a builder.'

'That's right. He's a labourer, but don't be fooled. He could have done anything he wanted to do, anything, gone to Uni – anything. Mum wanted him to be an engineer. He's really clever. He's just bad at focusing on anything. Anyway, this is the room,' Sarah said, as she pushed opened the door.

All the rooms in the big Edwardian semi had high ceilings and tall windows. Today the sunlight was streaming in, spilling over the mellow sanded boards. The first floor bedroom was almost square. Sarah had painted the walls cream and hung two big mirrors to make it feel bigger and more airy. There was a double bed, a desk and chair, and a rug in dark green to match the curtains. By the window, in the little bay, was an armchair and coffee table, and there were bookcases lining the walls under the sill. In the alcoves either side of the fireplace were built-in cupboards with more shelves and aerial sockets for a TV. The double bed was bare except for the two pillows that matched the duvet downstairs.

Woody made an appreciative noise. 'It's very nice,' he said, walking over to the window and pulling aside the net curtains. 'And Ryan said you've got a garden too?'

Sarah nodded. 'Yes. That's just the bit along the side, there's more at the back. My mum loved gardening. I think it's one of the main reasons she bought the house in the first place, although I'm afraid gardening skipped a generation. It's all I can do to keep the lawn mowed.'

'Nice to have though,' he said, still looking through the window. 'Maybe I could give you a hand with it?'

Sarah laughed. 'Are you serious?'

He nodded. 'Yes of course. I enjoy gardening,' he said.

'Oh okay, well that would be great. Do you want to go and have a look at the other room now?'

Woody nodded.

Sarah directed him back out onto the landing and to the next flight of stairs, which led up into the loft space. The stairs were narrower and steeper here, rising up to the tiniest of dogleg landings. 'I think that this used to be where the servants lived. If you'd like to go up first, I'll follow you,' Sarah said, inviting him to lead. 'It's a bit tight space wise, and I wouldn't put too much trust in the handrail.'

He laughed. 'Okay, good to know. I'll remember that,' he said, as he climbed the stairs and pushed open the door into the attic room.

'Oh yes, this is nice,' said Woody. The attic room ran the whole length of the house and was bathed in sunlight from the two dormers set into sloping the ceiling. The bed was up against the chimneybreast but there was still plenty of room for a small sofa, a desk and chair and bookcases.

'Are they both eighty-five pounds a week?'

Sarah nodded. 'Single let.'

'Of course. I think I prefer this one. More room up here. It's perfect.'

'I'm happy to hold it for you for a couple of days if you like,' Sarah said. 'And if you decided you want it I'll need four weeks rent in advance and two references. There's a fee for drawing up a tenancy agreement and a five hundred pound refundable security deposit.'

Woody nodded. 'That shouldn't be a problem.'

'And for the first three months we're both on a week's notice. You know – if it doesn't work out. So...'

'So, I'd still really like it if you're happy to let me have it. You didn't tell me what it is that you do?' he said, moving over to the window to take a look at the view out over the garden and neighbouring houses.

'Me? I work in a nursery, with plants that is, not children.'

'Didn't you just say you weren't very good with gardens?'

Sarah laughed. 'I'm not. I'm not sure what Ryan's told you about the family, but Mum was really ill and I had to come home to take care of her, and she used to work there.'

'In the nursery?'

Sarah nodded. 'Yes. She worked there for years. I started to go in to help them out when she couldn't manage any more – offered to go in and cover her shifts. In the end they took me on to do her job. I sometimes think they did it as a favour.'

'I'm sure that's not true.'

Sarah reddened. 'I'm sorry, Ryan didn't tell me your real name?'

'So sorry, it's Mustapha Sid Ahmed.' He stepped back towards her and held out a hand. His skin was smooth and cool and dry as parchment. He smiled. 'I appreciate it's a bit of a mouthful. Woody is easier. Most people call me Woody.'

'And you prefer it? I mean I don't mind what you're called...'

He nodded.

'Okay. How long have you been in the UK? If you don't mind me asking.'

'No, not at all. Just over a year.'

'Your English is fabulous.'

He grinned. 'Too much TV I'm afraid. And of course it's the language of commerce and my parents both studied in the UK; my father is a complete Anglophile. He's very envious that I'm over here.'

Sarah

A uniformed female constable is standing just inside the door to the interview room. She looks bored. She makes a point of not meeting my gaze when I look at her. The detective makes a note of the time on a form in front of him.

'Why don't you tell me what happened, Sarah?' he says. His tone is conspiratorial and gentle, as if I'm a child. 'Just tell me in your own words. We can take as long as you want. All right? I just need to make sure that you understand that these are very serious charges.'

'Yes. I understand,' I said.

He smiles, as if I have done something clever.

They've taken all my clothes away and given me a paper jump suit but I was so cold, my teeth chattering, that in the end they found me a tracksuit and a pair of canvas beach shoes. Everything is far too big; my feet keep slipping out of the shoes, making me shuffle like an old lady.

'You're sure, Sarah?'

I nod.

'Can you say yes or no for the benefit of the tape, please?'

'Yes,' I said, 'I understand that these are very serious charges.'

'Good,' he says, moving his chair in a little closer and indicating that I should do the same. He has a manila file alongside him. It's open. 'And are you sure you don't want a solicitor? We can arrange for someone to represent you if you want.'

'No, I'm fine.' I say. Which is a stupid thing to say because I am anything but fine.

The chair is heavier than I expected and scrapes across the floor as I try to lift it.

'So, are you okay?' he asks, when I'm settled.

I nod.

'Good.' He slides a photograph across the table towards me.

'When did you first meet this man?' the detective asks.

'When my brother, Ryan, brought him home.'

'And he needed a room?'

'Yes, his name is Mustapha Sid Ahmed. Although we always called him Woody.'

He nods and hands me another photograph. 'And what about this man?'

I shake my head. 'I don't know who that is,' I said.

I'm hoping that the detective will believe me and then it occurs to me that I don't really care anymore what he believes or understands, or even, really, what happens to me now, because it is finally all over and, and he is dead, and I am free, and nothing can touch me now, and nothing can be worse than where I've been. Nothing. But that doesn't stop the detective from talking because he doesn't know that I know.

'How did Mustapha Sid Ahmed, Woody, seem when you first met him, Sarah?'

'He just seemed pleasant. Personable. Interested in me.'

'In a flirtatious way?'

'No, not at all.'

'But he was an attractive man?'

'Yes, but he asked me questions about me and my life, work and stuff. It felt more like he was just being friendly rather than coming on to me. He struck me as someone who was naturally quiet, studious.'

'So what did Woody do after you had shown him around?'

'We agreed that he would rent the attic room and he asked if he could move in straight away.'

'And you said yes?'

'I didn't really see any reason not to.'

'You didn't think it was strange?'

'No, not really. He seemed plausible, and he said he had the references for the place he was currently renting. And he kept saying that he was nervous.'

'Nervous? Nervous about what? Did he explain?'

'Yes, although he wasn't really specific just that he was afraid of someone at the house where he was living and the sooner he could move out the better.'

'Did he mention Farouk at this stage?'

'He didn't mention anyone. He just kept saying that he wanted to move out as soon as possible and that he could bring the money round later that afternoon.'

'And you needed the money?'

'Yes, I needed the money. Money's always been

tight even when Mum was alive. And then when she died she left Ryan and me the house, but it's in trust until Ryan is twenty-five. I know she meant well but it's made things really hard. We couldn't sell it. We couldn't let it. It's lovely but it was a bit of a millstone at times. The last few months, before we decided to take in lodgers, things had been really tough. We had to try and find a way to make the place pay for itself.'

'When you say "we"?'

'Ryan and I, although I suppose I mean me really. Ryan's the kind of person who can just stick his head in the sand and ignore things.'

'Have you any idea why your mother tied the house up like that?'

'Ryan has always been a bit of a handful, especially after Dad died, and I think she was hoping that having a proper home, somewhere to live, a base, would make it easier for him, that, and not getting his hands on a chunk of money till he was a bit older and he was mature enough to use it sensibly if we decided to sell it.'

'But that tied you up too?'

'Yes, but it's a big house and it wasn't for ever. We've got plenty of room. And I love Cambridge. It's such a beautiful city, and there's plenty of work here.'

'But you had to give up your course, your life?'

'I'm not saying it wasn't hard but it was the right thing to do. I'm glad I did it. And I thought that I could always go back. Like I said, it wasn't for ever.'

'And what about Ryan?'

'For him too, but he has always had a problem sticking to things. Anyway, Mum thought it would be better for him if he had a proper base, some roots.'

'So Ryan shared the house with you?'

'No, not exactly. He had the basement flat. Mum had had it converted before she got sick. She planned to let it out as a way of making some money or to live in the flat herself and rent out the house. I mean I could see that it made sense. Her pension she used to say, but then, when she died, Ryan thought it would be better if he lived down there. So that he could be independent.'

'But he still came up into the main house?'

'Yes, he was always in and out. He still saw it as his home.'

'And you didn't object to that?'

'No.'

'No?'

'Well, yes and no. Sometimes. It's a big place for just me on my own, but he used it like a hotel. Letting his friends come round, letting them stay over. We're always falling out about keeping it tidy; he just leaves stuff all over the place and I work full time.'

'Remind me what you do again?'

'I work at Fuller's Nursery out on the St Neots Road, and then I do a couple of nights a week at Vincentis on the market square, sometimes as a waitress, sometimes in the kitchen, depends what they need.'

'Always busy?'

'I suppose so, but someone has got to keep on top of the bills. I don't mind doing my share but sometimes it feels like I'm doing it all, I am always tired.'

'And what about Ryan?'

'He picked up an odd day here and there, but nothing regular. It makes things hard if you can't be sure how much money is coming in. I feel like I'm always trying to play catch-up with the bills, and he didn't see the household bills as being anything to do with him. Behaving like he was still the baby of the family – you know – the youngest child, the dependent one. It drove me crazy.'

'Which was why you decided to take in lodgers?'

'It seemed like a good idea, the only way really. I thought it would give us a regular income. The house was too big for us, and Cambridge is full of people looking for somewhere decent to live. Taking in lodgers seemed like the only practical solution unless Ryan got himself a regular job.'

'You didn't think of renting out the basement?'

'Ryan didn't want to give it up.'

'Okay. But Ryan was paying for the bills on the basement flat?'

'Sometimes.'

'Sometimes?'

'Like I said he wasn't very good with that sort of thing. I've had to bail him out a few times when they threatened to cut his electricity off. And his phone. It was why letting the rooms seemed like a perfect solution.'

'Okay, so you let Woody rent the room. And then what happened?'

'He brought the deposit round that first afternoon, just like he said he would. In cash. Then Ryan borrowed a van from someone he works with and they went round to collect his things from his old place, and he moved in.'

'And did you check Woody's references.'

'No. I mean yes. I did check them.'

'So which is it, Sarah? Yes or no?'

'He showed his references to me and they seemed to be fine, but I didn't ring them up and check them out, if that's what you mean.'

'And can you remember who his referees were?'

'One was his course tutor – I think.'

'And the other?'

34

'I'm not sure now. I think it was some sort of college liaison officer for overseas students.'

'But they were both for Mustapha, both for Woody?'

'Yes, of course.'

'You're sure of that?'

'Yes. His name was on both of them.'

'Okay. And did you rent the other room? The room on the first floor?'

'Yes, to the woman who came round at half past ten; as soon as she saw it she said she would have it. I mean, it was a lovely room.'

'And her name was?'

'Anna. Anna Dunkley. She's a nurse at Addenbrookes; she seemed really nice. She hadn't long split up with her boyfriend and was looking for somewhere to live as a stop gap till she got herself sorted out.'

'And did she give you references and a deposit?'

'Yes, I'd already told her the terms of the let.'

'Okay. So, in the course of one day you had two new lodgers who would be paying you nearly seven hundred pounds a month, and you had the month in advance, and their deposits.'

'Yes.'

'That must have made things easier for you. Made you feel better?'

'It should have. I mean it did; it was a relief. I banked the money. I'd already told Anna that she could pay me by bank transfer and she was happy about that.'

'And what about Woody?'

'He said he wanted to pay in cash. He said it made things easier for him.'

'And was that a problem, Sarah? I mean, he did pay presumably?'

'Yes, sometimes.'

'Sometimes?'

'Ryan—'

'—your brother?'

'He would ask Woody for a sub on his rent.'

'Often?'

'Quite often. At least that is how it felt.'

'Okay. And did that make you angry?'

'Yes, of course it did. Angry and annoyed and sad, I suppose. We've got a whole list of things that needed doing to the house as well as the regular bills. The windows need replacing, everything needs updating – the cooker, the boiler, the bathroom and kitchen. Ryan wasn't contributing, he was just taking. Like always. Sorry, but that's what it felt like. While she was ill Mum had let the place go; she couldn't help it, but there is so much that needs doing. So yes, we needed the money and I just started to get things sorted and get ahead, and then there was the thing with Anna.'

'The thing?'

'They'd been there two or three months. Anna and Woody.'

Chapter Three

It was a bright sunny Sunday morning. Sarah, cheered by the sunshine, hadn't long been home from the nursery. She'd slipped off her shoes and left them outside in the porch, and was padding about in her bare feet, making proper coffee and slicing bread that she had picked up from the Italian deli on the way home. The coffee smelt good, and the smell, along with the thought of hot buttered toast and apricot jam, was making her mouth water.

She turned on the radio to catch the news. Through the open door she could hear the birds twittering in the garden; it was one of those glorious early summer mornings that make your heart sing.

And it was early – on Sunday mornings in the summer Sarah went in before the nursery opened to tidy up the outdoor areas and water all the plants and shrubs so that everything was fresh and perky for the customers. Sometimes she drove, but today she cycled in. It was something her mum had always done and Sarah had just carried on. Spring and summer Sundays were the nursery's busiest day. Sarah usually worked three weekends out of four but this week, as she had pulled a couple of extra shifts during the week helping to unload deliveries, her boss had given her the day off. So, once the tidying and watering was done she had hurried home.

It was a rare treat and the day stretched ahead of her, clean and empty and full of promise.

Anna, who had just got in from a night shift, leaned in around the kitchen door. 'Sarah, can I have a quick word with you?'

'Sure, come on in. Would you like some coffee? I've just made fresh.' Sarah lifted the pot in invitation. 'And I'm about to put some toast on if you'd like some.'

'No, thank you.'

'You sure? There's plenty?'

Anna nodded. 'This is a bit difficult. The thing is, Sarah, someone has been in my room.'

Sarah turned round, good mood stalling. 'Really? Are you sure?'

Anna nodded. 'Yes, I am. I think it happened last time I was on nights as well, but that time I wasn't certain, I was tired and thought maybe I'd made a mistake, but this time I *know* someone's been in there.'

Sarah set the coffee pot down on the counter. 'Oh god, Anna, I'm so sorry. What's missing?'

Anna sighed. 'There's forty pounds that I'd left on top of the bookcase, and some of my jewellery has gone as well.'

Sarah stared at her. 'And you're certain?'

Anna's expression hardened. 'Of course I'm certain. I wouldn't be telling you if I wasn't. I locked my door last night before I went on shift and left two twenty-pound notes on top of the bookcase. When I came in this morning they were gone, and so was the watch my parents gave me for my eighteenth birthday, a pair of gold earrings, a couple of silver bangles. I think you need to call the police, Sarah. And if you don't then I will.'

Sarah nodded, feeling her joy draining away; she was now flustered and wrong footed. 'Of course. I'm so sorry. I don't think anything's been taken in here. I was out too last night. I was working at the restaurant – I should check.' She glanced round, anxiously. 'I've got no idea who could have done this. Are you sure you've looked?'

Anna's voice was tight, controlled. 'Of course I've looked. I didn't just assume my things had been stolen.'

'No, of course not. Okay. And your room was locked, you said?'

Anna nodded. 'I always lock it when I got out, especially after the last time.'

'Okay,' Sarah said, more as a place marker than a real reply while she tried to work out what her next move should be.

She glanced round the kitchen, thinking things through, going through a checklist in her head: the front door was locked. She'd unlocked the back door first thing that morning when she went out, and locked it up after her. Glancing round Sarah took in the details; the TV was still there; there was a pile of change and her iPod on one of the counter tops, along with the radio and the microwave. Easy pickings for any opportunist burglar. By contrast, Anna's bedroom on the first floor had been locked and was hardly an obvious target. Whoever it was had to have walked through the house and yet had left all this stuff behind. It made no sense at all.

'You didn't give anyone else a key?' Sarah asked.

Anna raised her eyebrows. 'No,' she said flatly. 'Why would I?'

'Do you mind if I just go and ask Ryan and Woody if they heard anything or let anyone in last night. As far I know no one's been in here but us, but the boys might have had some friends round. I'll just check.'

Even as she said it an icy feeling tracked down Sarah's spine, and she could see that Anna had already had the same thoughts and arrived at the same conclusion.

'Help yourself to coffee. I'll be back in a minute. If they don't know anything then we'll ring the police,' Sarah said, trying to sound supportive and more confident than she actually felt. 'I'm sure we can sort this out.'

Anna nodded but said nothing.

Sarah opened the back door and hurried round to the basement steps that led to Ryan's flat. The curtains were closed tight. There were dead flies trapped in grey webs between the glass and the fabric, and carrier bags of empty bottles and cans stacked up in the light well beside the stairs and under the cellar windows. Sarah walked past it every day but today she noticed how neglected and squalid it looked. There were hundreds of dog-ends stubbed out in the flowerpots that once upon a time her mum had filled with bright red geraniums and Marguerite daisies. It looked seedy and unkempt.

Sarah knocked. There was no reply. 'Ryan, are you in there?' she called, knocking harder this time. 'Ryan?' She knocked again.

'Of course I'm here, for fuck's sake, where's the fire?' he called. She could hear him unlocking the door and sliding the chain aside, jerking the door open over something on the floor that hindered its progress. 'What do you want?' he said, words slurred and sleepy. He was wearing a grubby towelling robe and screwed up his eyes against the light. 'It's Sunday morning. I'm having a lie-in for god's sake.'

Sarah glanced past him into the flat, not altogether sure what she expected to see. 'Have you got anyone in there?'

'You mean like one of my scuzzy little mates or maybe a woman?' he said grimly, rubbing a hand over his chin. 'No, I'm here all on my lonesome, thanks for asking. Now, if you don't mind and you're done checking up on me I'll be getting back to bed.' He made as if to close the door.

'Wait, Ryan, I need to talk to you.'

'What is it this time?'

He hadn't shaved. His hair was a mess. He looked about fourteen. Some days it made Sarah feel tender that he still looked so young, but today it just made her angry. 'Were you in the house last night while I was at work?'

'Yeah, you know that I was. You saw me before you went out. Me and Woody were in the sitting room watching a film. Why?'

'Did anyone else come round while I was out?'

'No. What is this about exactly?' He held up his hands in surrender. 'Or do I need a note to have people round now? If it's about smoking in the sitting room it was just one and I opened the—'

'Someone broke into Anna's room last night.'

'What?' he said, sounding surprised, and then Ryan stared at her and sighed. 'Oh yeah right, and that would have to be me, wouldn't it? I mean I'm just bound to steal stuff from the lodger. Good old untrustworthy Ryan.' He held out his hands in front of him, wrists together. 'So are you going to book me now or take me down the station?' All sarcasm and annoyance.

'No, no that's not what I'm saying. I just wanted to know if you had invited anyone else round while I was out?'

'I already told you. There was just me, Woody, a few cans of beer, some DVDs and the Xbox.' He went to close the door again. She wanted to ask him why he didn't invite Woody downstairs to the flat, why did he have to watch DVDs upstairs when he had his own place? But she already knew the answer. He was staking his claim, making sure she was never under the misapprehension that the whole of the house was hers alone.

'She's going to call the police,' Sarah said before he had chance to shut her out.

'Well let her, because I didn't take anything. All right? She probably left whatever it was somewhere, or forgot where she put it or dropped it. How do you know she's not the one lying?'

'Please, Ryan. We need to talk about this.'

'Why? Why the fuck do you have to talk to me about it? It's because you think it was me who took whatever it was, don't you?' he snapped. 'Hey? Tell me? Don't you, Sarah? Why don't you just come out and say it? No? Well, let me say this nice and clearly so you don't misunderstand me. I haven't touched anything of hers, all right? I never have and I never would. I may get myself into a muddle with money from time to time but I didn't take it – you hear me? She thinks she's better than me, better than us, you know that, don't you? She's a stuck up bitch. She barely even nods when she sees me.'

'Have you seen yourself in the mirror lately? I wouldn't nod to you if you weren't my brother. You look like a tramp most of the time. And while we're on the subject of money you need to stop subbing off Woody. We need that money for the bills and to get the place sorted round.'

'You mean *you* need it.' He sounded petulant.

'How many times do we have to go through this? You know what it costs to run this place. It's a money pit. The council tax, water, the heating, electricity? The boiler is shot. The windows need doing, the roof, the electrics – everything needs updating. We need to sort it out if we're going to sell it for a half decent price. I can't do it on my own, Ryan. I need your help.'

'Yeah, yeah, yeah, so you keep telling me.' His face contorted into a sneer. 'Who'd got you pegged as a martyr? Oh yes I remember, giving up everything, packing in college, running home to look after Mummy – that would be Saint Sarah of Cambridge.'

She stared at him, barely containing her fury and a desire to slap him hard, hating what she could hear in his voice.

'You resent me for that? For putting my life on

hold so that Mum had someone to look after her?' she said incredulously.

'Only when you come out with all this holier than thou crap, Sarah.'

She stared at him in disbelief. 'What am I supposed to do?'

'Get off my case. We're stuck with this for another two years and then we're both free. Okay? We can sell up, be out of here. You can go back to college, sail round the world, join a convent. I don't give a flying fuck what you do, but meanwhile get off my back, all right?'

'Okay, please just stop asking Woody for money.'

'It's not your money and he's my mate not yours.'

'Oh for god's sake just grow up, will you?' snapped Sarah, finally losing her cool. 'Yes, we can sell up in a couple of years and for me it can't come fast enough, but meanwhile things needs paying for now, right?'

'Like I would ever be able to forget,' he said, pushing the door to on her. Just as it was about to close he said, 'And before you ask me again, no I didn't steal any of Anna's stuff, okay?'

Sarah stared at the closed door for a second or two, struggling to regain her composure, finally turning away and hurrying back up to the house.

Anna was still there waiting in the kitchen. Sarah made an effort to smile, wondering how much she had overheard. 'Ryan didn't see anything and no one else was here. I'll just nip upstairs and have a quick word with Woody.'

Anna had her arms crossed over her chest. 'To be honest, Sarah I don't care who it was who took my stuff. I just want the watch back. I don't even care about the money. Am I making myself clear?'

Sarah nodded. She suspected from her expression that Anna had already made up her mind about who had stolen her things.

43

'Ryan said—' Sarah began.

'I don't really care what Ryan said either. And I'm giving notice. I'm moving out as soon as I can. I can't stay here.'

Sarah nodded. 'No, of course not. Obviously. No, I completely understand and I'm so sorry. Let me just go and have a word with Woody.'

Anna nodded. Her expression said, *As if that will make any difference.*

Sarah didn't really think it would do any good speaking to Woody but she wanted to be away from Anna and her accusing looks, which even though she hadn't taken the money or the jewellery made her feel guilty.

Sarah hurried up to the attic and had barely knocked before the door opened. Woody was already up and dressed in his trademark cords, a baggy checked shirt tucked into his trousers, his hair damp. He was carrying a book and wearing oversized glasses tipped up onto the top of his head. 'Good morning, Sarah. How are you?' he said.

'I'm fine, thank you. I'm really sorry to disturb you so early on a Sunday,' she began.

'Not at all. I was only working. Is there a problem? Do you want to come in?' he asked, waving her inside with this hand. Sarah shook her head and instead told him about Anna.

When she was done, Woody sighed. 'I'm so sorry. I didn't see anyone come in. There was only Ryan and me here. We watched a film. Some space war epic. Is there anything I can do to help?'

'I don't think so. Anna's already said she is going to move out.'

He nodded. 'That's a shame. But I'm sure you can understand how she feels. You have to feel safe where you live. I felt the same way at my last place; there are some things you can cope with but not others.' He paused. 'Maybe someone left one of the outside doors unlocked. Someone could have crept in. We had the volume up pretty loud on the TV.'

Sarah shook her head. 'I don't think so. It doesn't make any sense. And her bedroom door was locked. Why go up to Anna's room when there is a TV and things in the kitchen, money, the radio, my iPod...'

'Ah,' Woody said. He didn't need to say anything else. She could see what he was thinking. 'Would you like me to come down and talk to her, try to sort things out?'

'And say what?' she said grimly. 'Sorry, that was rude of me, Woody. It was a kind offer. Thank you, but no. I'll sort it out. She said she doesn't really care about the money, but the jewellery had sentimental value.' Sarah sighed. 'It's about trust, isn't it? As well as feeling safe.'

Woody nodded. 'It is,' he said. 'And I'm sorry.'

She looked at him; both of them knew they were apologising for Ryan.

Sarah

'So what happened after the incident with Anna?' asked the detective. He was sitting back in his chair now, long legs stretched out in front of him, and fingers steepled across his belly.

'I went downstairs and I rang the police. It took them three days to come round and then it was just basically to give us a crime number so we could claim on the contents insurance. By that time Anna had already found somewhere else to stay and moved out, so I gave them her new address so they could take a statement. I don't know if they did or not. We never heard anything else from them. Anna went to stay with a friend till she could find somewhere. I gave her the forty pounds back.'

'Because you thought Ryan had taken it?'

'I hadn't got any proof.'

'But you suspected it was Ryan?

'Yes, I couldn't see how it could be anyone else – and he was the only one who knew where the spare keys were.'

'And where were they?'

'In the kitchen. On a hook.'

'So not exactly hidden?'

'No, not really. Although there was more than one key on the ring and several key rings. But the thing is that Ryan knew which ring it was on and which key it was.'

'So you were more or less certain that Ryan had stolen the money and the jewellery?'

'It was hard not to come to that conclusion. I'm not proud of that, but he was so difficult. I took all the keys upstairs after that, locking the door after the horse has bolted, you might say, but it made me feel a bit better knowing that only I knew where the keys were.

'Then about a week later I came home from work and Woody was waiting for me in the kitchen. I told you I work in the restaurant two or three nights a week? It depends on how many people they've got booked. Anyway the manager had texted me at the nursery asking if I could come in and do an extra shift for them, so I'd just come in from work and was on the turn around. You know, quick shower, change of clothes and then I was going back out again.'

'So you were in hurry?'

'Yes. Yes I was.'

Chapter Four

'I need to show you something,' Woody said, as Sarah opened the back door and dropped her bag onto the kitchen table. He was sitting at the kitchen table, looked serious, uncomfortable and had obviously been waiting for her to come home.

'Can't it wait? ' Sarah asked, not meeting his eye, using her toes to ease off the back of her shoes and shuffling them into the corner by the door. 'I'm not being rude, Woody, but I really need to be out in of here in half an hour. I have just about enough time to get cleaned up, get changed and grab a sandwich.'

'No, I'm sorry, I don't think it will wait,' he said.

Something about his tone stopped Sarah in her tracks and she looked round as if she might be able to spot what the problem was. 'Why, what is it? It's not the shower again, is it? I'll try and ring the plumber first thing tomorrow.'

'No. You need to come and see for yourself,' he said, getting to his feet. The legs of his chair scraped over the tiles as he got up.

'Can't you just tell me? I've really not got time.' Even though she was saying it, Sarah found herself following Woody outside into the garden.

'I was tidying up out here this afternoon and I found something that I really think you need to see,' he said. He sounded sad.

'Did you break something? I mean there's nothing precious out here, I'm sure it'll be fine.'

Just before she'd gone to work Woody had popped downstairs to say he had a couple of days off and would she mind if he made a start on the garden? He was thinking he would cut the grass and do some weeding, tidy up a bit, burn some rubbish, if that was okay.

Sarah had laughed. She didn't mind a bit, far from it, she was grateful. She knew he felt bad about not paying her all the rent and guessed that this might be his way of making amends. So, humouring him, Sarah slipped on a pair of flip-flops and headed outside after him. It was easy to see where Woody had been. Two of the flowerbeds had been dug over, the lawn had been mown and the clippings raked up into a heap. In one corner by what had once been the vegetable patch, a pile of last year's leaves and rubbish was smouldering in a brazier.

Slightly bemused, Sarah fell into step as the two of them headed across the lawn to the shed, or at least what was left of the shed. The corrugated roof had fallen in some time over the winter. The door was trapped open by the weight of the tin sheets, held down and wedged ajar to reveal a crush of tools and flowerpots, sun-faded paper sacks and weathered cardboard boxes. Just inside the door, sheltered by the fallen roof, stood a newly sharpened rotary lawn mower, a spade, fork and a rake. Woody reached inside, past the tools into the jumble of boxes and bags and pulled out a red fabric bundle. Looking uncomfortable he handed it to Sarah.

'I don't understand,' she said, turning it over. 'What is it?'

'You need to look for yourself. I found it when I was trying to get the lawn mower out.'

Sarah turned it over in her hands. It was an old tee shirt, wrapped tightly around something hard – maybe not just one thing though, the core of the bundle moved and gave as Sarah very carefully unrolled it.

Inside was a tangle of necklaces, a lady's watch, a couple of pairs of earrings, and some silver bangles. Sarah felt her heart lurch. She turned the watch over. On the back were engraved the words, *'To Anna on your 18th Birthday - With all our love, Mum and Dad xxx.'* Sarah stared down at the jewellery in her hands and then looked up at Woody.

'This is Anna's and this...' she said, the words catching in her throat, as she pulled out a locket on a tangled chain from amongst the rest, '...this is my mum's and I think those are too.' She picked out a pair of diamond studs. 'They were in the jewellery box on my dressing table. I didn't even know they had gone.' She felt sick.

Woody said nothing.

'This is Ryan's tee shirt,' said Sarah quietly.

Woody looked as if he was in pain. 'I'm so sorry, Sarah. I wasn't sure whether to say anything or not. But I thought you ought to know.'

Sarah nodded. 'Thank you,' she muttered. 'I'll talk to Ryan and then I'll get these back to Anna.' She sounded brisk, matter of fact, while the pulse thundered in her ears.

'Some one could have taken his tee-shirt,' Woody began, glancing back towards the house. 'It would be easy enough to take it from the washing line and then hide the things in here. Maybe they were coming back for them when the coast was clear – maybe—'

Sarah's expression stopped him. 'That doesn't make any sense, and you know that, Woody,' she said. 'If someone had taken the money and jewellery then why didn't they just take it away with them? Why bother hiding it? Unless of course they just wanted it out of the house, somewhere safe where no one would look until it was safe to get rid of them.'

Woody looked downcast. 'Maybe he didn't know how to sell it?' I can't imagine what he was thinking,' said Woody, embarrassed. 'I know that he's not good with money, but I never imagined that he would—'

'It's all right,' said Sarah, holding a hand to silence him. 'And you're right. We shouldn't jump to conclusions. I'll deal with it, but please don't lend Ryan any more money, is that clear? And keep your room locked. I don't think he would steal from you but who knows. I've got the spares in my room now.'

He nodded, although from his body language Sarah wondered if Woody was going to say something else, but in the end apparently he thought better of it.

'So where exactly did you find this?' she said.

Woody look embarrassed. 'I was going to burn some of the leaves and I've got some rubbish that needed burning as well so I was just pulling out some old newspapers to get the fire started.' He nodded back towards the chaos in the shed. 'I managed to get the mower out and there it was under that pile of papers. Just slipped inside, into the top of one of the boxes. It was pure chance that I found it at all. And now I wish I hadn't.'

Sarah could feel the tears welling up in her eyes. 'It's not your fault,' she said thickly. She looked past him into the shed and then shook her head. 'I can't do this,' she whispered, almost to herself.

'It might not be Ryan,' he said.

Sarah stared up at him, wishing that she believed him. 'Who else could it be?' she said miserably, feeling the tears welling up. 'Who else? Tell me, Woody.'

'Don't cry. Come inside,' said Woody, catching hold of her arm. 'I'll make us some tea.'

Sarah let him guide her back into the house. The door to the basement flat was closed, all the curtains pulled tight shut, a scatter of rubbish bags and bottles still stacked up around the door.

'Do you want me to talk to him?' asked Woody, catching the glance. 'I don't mind. Maybe it would be easier coming from me. I'm his friend. Maybe he'd listen to me?'

Sarah stared at him and then shook her head. 'No, he is my responsibility, and anyway I think he's working, doing some paving today. I'll catch him when he gets in.'

'I thought you said you had to go to work?'

'I did but I'm going to call in sick.'

'Are you sure?'

Sarah nodded, her fingers closing tight round the bundle. 'I've got to do something, haven't I? I just can't pretend it didn't happen, that you didn't find it.'

Woody nodded. 'If you need me...' he let the sentence hang.

Sarah smiles, grateful. 'Thank you.'

Sarah heard the van pull up at around half past six and, taking the tee shirt and the jewellery, she waited for a couple of minutes to let him get inside and then went downstairs to Ryan's flat. She caught him at the door just as he was fumbling around in his pockets for his keys. The sun had bleached his hair, he looked tanned and fit and happy. He looked up as she picked her way down the steps behind him.

'Hi, what're you doing? I thought your text said you were going to be at work tonight?' he said.

'I was but something's come up; I wanted to have a chat.'

'Oh okay, sure come on in,' Ryan said brightly, shouldering the door open as the key turned. 'You'll have to excuse the mess.' He grinned. 'I'm thinking I really ought to get myself a cleaner. How are you fixed? Or do you want me to come upstairs? I'll just grab a quick shower. I was wondering, is there any chance you could cut my hair? I could do with a bit off the back and off the fringe.' He grabbed a handful.' Just maybe take the ends off?'

When they were little their mum had always cut their hair. Since she had gone Sarah had taken over the job. Ryan was happy and tired and Sarah was reluctant to embark on the conversation that she knew she had to have with him. She had been nearly six when Ryan was born, and when he was little she had loved him so fiercely that she thought she might die. She didn't want him to be a liar or a thief, she wanted him to take all the clever bright funny things that he was and be more than this, be more than the bundle of jewellery she was holding in her hand. He was worth so much more; all her love for him was worth that alone.

'So, do you want me to come up later?'

'No, here is just fine,' she said, following him inside. The air in the basement was heavy and stale, thick with the scent of frying, damp washing and the smell of sweat and old trainers.

'Do you want some tea?' he asked, opening the fridge, pulling out a carton of milk and sniffing it speculatively.

'No, thanks. I'm fine.'

'So to what do I owe the pleasure, then? If it's about the money I've had off Woody then don't start, okay? I've got it here. Cash, two hundred and forty quid; you can have it now if you like.'

Sarah nodded. 'That would be good.'

He slipped his hand into the back pocket of his jeans, pulled out a fold of notes, counted out some, and dropped them onto the table. 'There you go. Do you want to sit down?'

'No, not really.'

He eyed her up; cooler now. 'So what is it? If it's about the rubbish round the back door I promise I'll sort it out tomorrow. And I've got a couple more days' work next week too. Don was saying he might be able to find me something a bit more regular. Maybe even on the books. I told him to sign me up. Show me the way. You know, like a proper job?' Ryan laughed. 'You sure you don't want a drink? I've got a beer here somewhere; it might be a bit warm though.'

Sarah set the tee shirt down in amongst the chaos on the kitchen table and picked up the money.

'What's that?' Ryan asked, tucking the rest of the notes back into his pocket.

'I think you probably already know.'

Ryan shrugged. 'No, I don't. Why would I?'

She looked at his face. Oh he was good. 'Ryan, please, don't do this,' she said.

'Don't do what? I don't know what it is. Something I'm meant to have lost or spoilt or put in with white wash, what?' He picked up the tee shirt. It fell open as if he really didn't know what was wrapped up in it. Clever, very clever. The jewellery spilt out onto the table, clattering down in amongst the bowls and the mugs and the bottles of sauce.

He looked at Sarah. 'For fuck sake, what's all this? Is it some kind of joke?' His good mood had evaporated. 'This is my tee shirt.'

Sarah nodded. 'I know.'

His expression darkened. 'Oh right, I get it. Here we go again. I know where this is going, Ryan the thief, Ryan the liar. Ryan who can't be bloody trusted,' he growled. 'That's what you think, isn't it?'

'I don't want to think that, Ryan, but how else do you explain it?'

'I can't explain it. I don't need to explain it. I've never seen any of this stuff before.' He stopped and looked closer. 'Hang on, those are Mum's earrings, aren't they? You think I'd steal jewellery that belonged to Mum? Where did you find all this stuff?'

'Woody found it in the shed.'

'Okay, well I can't remember the last time I was anywhere near the shed. I have no idea how it ended up there. Do you understand?'

53

Sarah nodded.

'You don't believe me, do you? You think I put it there, don't you?'

'How else could it have got there?'

'I don't know, and if I'd stolen it why did I hide it? Why didn't I sell it or pawn it. Why hide it, Sarah? It makes no sense. Have you talked to Woody about it?'

'Woody?' said Sarah.

'Yeah. I'm assuming this is Anna's stuff that got stolen. I wasn't the only one in the house that night, you know. Have you asked him what he knows about it? What he was doing? Did you get around to accusing him?'

Sarah stared at him; the thought hadn't crossed her mind. 'No of course not.'

'Why not?' Ryan snapped.

'You mean Woody, the man who you're always telling me is minted, who you're always borrowing money off? Why would he steal someone else's money and jewellery? Tell me that? You told me yourself he's as sound as a pound.'

Ryan ran his hands back through his hair and then gestured towards the jewellery. 'It wasn't me, all right? You have to believe me. I don't know anything about this stuff or how it got in the shed. I really don't, Sarah. Someone else must have been here. And I'm serious about Woody, what if he is having people round when we're out, you never know.' Ryan was gabbling now, looking for another way out.

Sarah nodded. 'You're right. I will ask him. I'm going to take the things round to Anna's tomorrow.'

'And say what?' Sarah could see she had his full attention.

'That I found it in the garden. Ryan.' She paused. 'But this is the last time I'm going to lie for you. I can't cover up for you if you break the law, do you understand? This has got to stop. I don't care what you tell me. You need to turn your life around, get a grip – sort it out, before it's too late.'

He slammed his fist down on the table, the shock of the blow making Sarah jump as cups and bottles tumbled over, a glass crashing to the floor. And then he looked up at Sarah, his face a mask. 'For god's sake, I already told you that I didn't do it, didn't I? What does it take to make you believe me? Some of this is Mum's stuff. I just said I wouldn't take Mum's stuff, surely you ought to know that?'

Sarah said nothing. She wanted to believe him but the problem was that Ryan lied to her all the time. She gathered the jewellery back up into the tee shirt and rolled it up; the truth was, however much he protested, however much she hated it, Sarah didn't believe a word he had said.

'I promise you it wasn't me,' Ryan said as she was leaving. 'I'll show you. I will.'

Sarah nodded and went back upstairs. She had heard it all before.

Sarah

'You say that you'd heard it all before, Sarah? What do you mean?'

'When Ryan was, I don't know, nine maybe, he got caught shoplifting in the local newsagents. Mr Patel, the man who owned the shop, rang my mum up. He knew my dad was sick and he didn't want to involve the police if possible or upset my mum any more than necessary. At the time I think we were all stunned, but it kind of made sense of lots of things that had been happening at home at around the same time, money had been going missing, my pens and things, some of my mum's oddments – just knick-knacks mostly, ornaments, costume jewellery. The thing was that Dad was really ill and it was

only a matter of time. Maybe by then he'd just got a couple of months left, I can't remember exactly, but I remember he was at home, downstairs in the front room of our old house, and there was Mum nursing him, up all hours of the night, sorting every out, trying to keep it all together. Mr Patel didn't press charges because he knew Mum and Dad. Mum said she thought it was Ryan's way of dealing with the stress. His reaction to Dad being ill and the centre of attention; and that he was attention seeking, finding a way to make people take notice of him.'

'It was a long time ago.'

'But it wasn't the only time. When Mum was first diagnosed with cancer, Ryan and a couple of his mates stole a car. Stupid. I wanted to kill him. We'd got enough on our plates without anything else happening, and there he was off joy riding.'

'So you had good reason to suspect that Ryan may have taken the jewellery from Anna's room? You didn't have a problem with believing that it was Ryan?'

'I didn't say I didn't have a problem with it. I hated it. He's an adult now, not a child anymore. He's got no excuse for it. I didn't want to believe it; I didn't want him to be a thief and a liar. I felt like he had betrayed me, betrayed us.'

'But you took the jewellery back?'

'Yes. The next day on my way home from work. I told Anna that I'd found it in the garden shed; I told her about my mum's stuff being in there too. I could see that she didn't believe me, but you could see that she was glad to get her things back.'

'Okay, and was this around the time that you first met Josh Phillips?'

'Yes, I was working at the nursery, with my friend, Anessa. We were sorting out a delivery of plants when he came in. I can't remember what he

56

wanted now. He just sort of stopped and looked at me and then he grinned, and Anessa pointed at him and said, 'I think you've got an admirer.'

'You're smiling, Sarah.'

'I know. I'm sorry, I can't help it. It felt like rain after a long drought. Josh was a breath of fresh air. I laughed and said maybe he was looking at her, and she said, "No way". And then he came over and we just started talking. It just seemed so easy. I can't remember what we talked about now, exactly, and then he told me he was a garden designer, and Anessa said she would leave me to help him – at which point I told him I was rubbish with plants. I think he thought I was joking.'

'And he asked you out?'

'Kind of. I'd only gone in for a half day to help Anessa with the delivery so he said he'd come back when I was finished and take me out for lunch. I said I'd cycled in, so he put my bike in the back of his truck.'

'And you just went with him?'

'I know, I suppose it was crazy but yes, it felt okay. It felt good. It had been a long time since anyone had looked at me.'

'I find that hard to believe, Sarah.'

'Okay, maybe it was a long time since I'd looked at anyone.'

'But you looked at Josh Phillips?'

'Yes I did. I really did.'

Chapter Five

'God, this is so nice. What did you say it was again?'

Josh grinned. 'I've got no idea. Some sort of goulash, I think. You have to take potluck here. It's always the same. They do three starters, three main courses and three desserts.'

Sarah spooned the last chunk of meat into her mouth. 'The same three things?'

'No, always seasonal. And the food's always been really good every time I've been in. I eat here a lot. '

'I can see why,' she said, tearing a hunk of bread from the newly baked loaf the waitress had set down in the middle of their table.

They'd taken the window seat in a little café in an alleyway a stone's throw from the market square. The cafe was squeezed in between an upmarket dress shop and a place selling second hand books. It was long and narrow and set with bench tables, and it was busy. Most of the tables were full, full with people sharing with strangers, tucked in elbow to elbow. At the table next to them a group of Chinese tourists were busy taking pictures of each other.

Josh smiled and, leaning in closer, wiped something from her chin. 'There we go,' he said. 'That's better.'

'Gravy?'

He nodded.

Sarah blushed. His touch made her feel hot, and she giggled. 'Thank you. Sorry, I was ravenous.'

'You're welcome,' he said. 'Do you live locally?'

'Not that far away, in Maudsley Terrace. It's just off Victoria Road. Other side of the river to Jesus Green?'

Josh nodded and mopped up the last of the juices from his own bowl. 'I think I know where you mean.

To be honest I'm just getting my bearings.' He glanced up at the day's special, written on a blackboard above the counter. 'Do you fancy a dessert?'

She nodded. 'Sounds like a good idea.'

They ate treacle tart and drank coffee, talking and laughing while the other diners moved around them almost unnoticed.

'So where do you live?' Sarah asked, spooning the froth from the coffee into her mouth.

'I'm renting a cottage in Cottenham at the moment. It's nice, small. A mate of mine, Andy, runs a landscaping and garden design business, and he asked if I wanted to go in with him.'

'And are you going to go in with him?'

'Yes, or at least I'm seriously thinking about it. At the moment he's got more work than he can handle. I'm giving it a year. See how we get on working together. I'm already bringing in work – so we'll see. So far, so good. I'm enjoying it.'

'We'll be seeing a lot more of you then?' Sarah said, conversationally.

Josh smiled and leaned in close, holding her gaze. 'I hope so.'

Sarah felt her colour rising. 'I meant at the nursery.'

Josh grinned. 'Oh right, yeah. And there too.'

Their plates were empty, their coffee finished, but it didn't seem like either of them wanted to leave.

'I really ought to be going,' said Sarah finally, pulling her purse out of her handbag.

'My treat,' he said, taking out his wallet.

When she began to protest, he said, 'Don't worry, you can get it next time.'

Sarah grinned. 'So, there's going to be a next time, is there?'

'I hope so.'

'Okay, you're on,' she said.

Reluctantly, Josh got to his feet. 'I'm going to go and look at a garden this afternoon. I know it's a bit of a busman's holiday but don't suppose I can persuade you to tag along, can I? Dry shade; I'd really value your opinion on the planting.'

'I'm not sure.' Sarah was hesitant, not wanting to seem too eager.

'It's also only about a five minute drive from here.'

'I already told you I'm genuinely rubbish at gardening.'

He grinned. 'I can't say I haven't been warned then, can I?' He held out a hand to help her off the bench and she took it, enjoying the sensation of her hand in his.

Sarah

'So am I right in thinking that you re-advertised the second room, the room that Anna had rented, at around the same time as you first met Josh Phillips?'

'Yes. I think so. More or less.'

'And how did you advertise the room?'

'On Gumtree and a couple of other websites. I'm not great with computers but I've got a laptop. I didn't think we'd have a lot of trouble letting it again. We'd had lots of interest first time round and I couldn't be sure that Ryan would stick to what he'd said about not subbing off Woody. I wanted to be sure that there was regular money coming in.'

'Okay. And what about Ryan? How did he react when you said you were trying to find someone else to take the second room?'

'When I tried to talk to him about it he said that I didn't have to do it. He told me that he would sort things out, and that he was going for an interview for a proper job; that he would show me that he

could be the man. That he wanted to sort stuff out – turn things around.'

'And that's what he said, "Be the man". I'm not sure I understand?'

'It's what my mum used to say to him after Dad died, when he started to kick off or there was something important that she wanted him to be good for. "You have to be the man now, Ryan". I think she was hoping that it would make him feel important, make him toe the line.'

'Right, okay, and so when he said that to you, you assumed Ryan meant what exactly, Sarah?'

'That he would step up, get himself a regular job. He'd done it before when Mum was in hospital. At least eventually he did when Mum had a word with him. I thought that maybe the thing with the jewellery had shaken him up. Being caught more or less red-handed.'

'And so did it?'

'It seemed to, at least to begin with. He started paying money towards the bills regularly, not always his full share, but most of it. He seemed different. He was working most weeks. And he cleaned himself up.'

'And so did you have any takers for the second room?'

'A couple of people came round, but then Ryan came in one afternoon and told me that he'd got this project sorted out – some sort of big contract – and that we'd be all right, that we wouldn't have to let the other room.'

'And you believed him?'

'Not really but he kept on about me needing to learn to trust him. To let him prove himself.'

'So you gave in over renting the room?'

'Reluctantly. I suppose I wanted to give him the benefit of the doubt, even then. Although I did try to persuade him that it would be much easier for both of us if we had another lodger – it would take the pressure off – but he was adamant. He said he hated having strangers living in the house. But I wasn't so sure. He'd had a couple of regular jobs over the years but they'd never lasted that long, although this sounded more promising, like he was working with people he'd worked with before.'

'Do you know who they were?'

'No. He didn't say. He was defensive – said he didn't want me jinxing it for him. And to be fair I'd been really hard on him in the past.'

'Seems to me justifiably so. But you wanted to believe him this time?'

'Yes, like I said I was hoping that maybe that thing with the jewellery had shaken him up. And Ryan was different, more confident, more like the person he had been before Mum died, and then he bought a van. It was nothing special but it seemed like a turning point.'

'Did you ask him where he got the money for the van?'

'He told me that he'd picked up a decent cash job.'

'And you believed him, did you, Sarah?'

'Honestly?'

'Honestly.'

'No, at least I wasn't sure what the truth was, but I decided not to ask him, in case – I don't know – I suppose it was all going so well. I didn't want to upset him and I didn't want to know if it wasn't. And even though he can be an idiot, Ryan could be really clever when he wanted to be, and he was an adult even if sometimes he doesn't behave like one.'

'Okay, and so then what happened?'

'I tried to persuade him that we should take another lodger in anyway. I know he didn't want to do it but it would mean for the first time in god knows how long that we'd have some spare money, but Ryan said no. He was adamant. He liked it as it was with just me and him and Woody, and in the end, to be honest, I just couldn't be bothered to argue. Life settled down.'

'When you say settled down, Sarah, what do you mean by that exactly?'

'Ryan was going to work every day. I started to see Josh regularly.'

'And was Ryan okay about that?'

'Yes, I think so. I didn't really ask him. And my friends at work were really pleased. Anessa was over the moon. She was always trying to fix me up with people. I'd been on my own a long while.'

'And Woody?'

'What about him?'

'Did Woody seem jealous or upset that you'd started seeing someone else?'

'No, not at all. Why should he? He was my lodger not my boyfriend and I didn't really see Woody that much. He was mostly out or upstairs in his room, or at college.'

'And did he have friends. Bring anyone home?'

'No. Never. Not that I'm aware of.'

'Did you think that was odd?'

'Not really. I mean I assumed he had friends on his course but he kept himself to himself most of the time. He was quiet, didn't say very much. He didn't strike me as very outgoing.'

'Okay, and did you?'

'Bring friends home? Sometimes, Anessa came round once in a while, but to be honest I work all sorts of odd hours and I've never been someone who has had a lot of friends. My dad being ill meant I was different from other kids and I didn't bring people home because Mum had enough on her plate. Then, after we moved, I didn't really get to know anyone; I went to college, and then Mum was sick, and I had to come home. It was always disjointed, I hadn't got a lot of time for a social life. Most of my friends were from work.'

'So you were lonely?'

'No, not really, I'm used to being on my own.'

'But you were seeing Josh?'

'That's right, and it felt really good. Things had finally started to come right. Things were settling down into a nice routine. Like I said, Ryan was working regularly.'

'And what about Woody?'

'I just said. He went to college; I hardly saw anything of him. In lots of ways he was the perfect lodger. And I don't want you to get the wrong idea about what it was like in the house then. It wasn't all doom and gloom. I felt like we'd finally turned the corner. It felt good. We were talking about having a party. If we were all in the house at the same time we'd eat together, share the cooking, watch a film on TV together. Like a family.'

'Okay and then what happened?'

'Josh offered to help me clear the garden up. We were planning to take the shed down and build a terrace with some slabs that someone had asked him to get rid of. So we could have somewhere to sit, and stand a barbeque. He'd got the truck and the tools. I was hoping Ryan might give us a hand too.'

'Okay.'

'Anyway, Josh and I made a start and took the roof off the shed – we put all the debris, the corrugated roof and things we couldn't burn, into his truck. And then he handed me out some bin bags, but nothing that I remembered putting in there – they were full of all kinds of stuff.'

'When you say stuff? What sort of things do you mean?'

'Letters, clothes, old books.'

'And they weren't yours or Ryan's?'

'No.'

'And there were letters?'

'Some, quite a lot to Mustafa – Woody – and some others too, mostly official looking government documents which were addressed to someone called Farouk Holbein. And they were all addressed to Woody's old address.'

'The Kirby Road address?'

'Yes.'

'And were there many of these letters?'

'Quite a lot.'

'How many is quite a lot, Sarah?'

'I'm not sure now. Some were junk mail. But there were at least a couple of dozen, maybe more for Woody, maybe half that for Farouk. Some of them were official looking and I was worried that they were important and that Woody didn't realise. I knew he had been getting rid of things because I'd seen him out in the garden burning rubbish in the brazier.'

'Did you ask Woody about the bags and the letters?'

'Yes, when he came in that night. I'd cooked for everyone. I'd made a curry, and I'd saved all the letters and put them in the kitchen just in case he wanted them, or they were something important.'

'Did Woody know that you were planning to take the shed down?'

'No, I don't think so. I mean we hadn't deliberately kept it from him I just can't remembering telling him directly. I suppose I assumed that he must have heard us talking about building a terrace.'

'So what did he say?'

'About the letters? Nothing much. He said they

were just rubbish, that he kept getting the same letters over and over again from University and from various government agencies, and he'd already answered all their questions, sometimes more than once and that he had been told to ignore them.'

'Didn't that strike you as a bit odd?'

'No, not really. Haven't you had that? We had the same thing when Mum died. Woody told me that he'd rung them and they had told him a lot of the letters were computer generated and to ignore them if he had already replied. He said he was going to burn them because they had personal details on them – addresses, all sorts of numbers, his passport details, his bank account.'

'You're frowning, Sarah; was there something else?'

'Yes, I noticed that a lot of the letters hadn't been opened, and that did strike me as odd.'

'And what about the post for Farouk?'

'Woody said he had found them in amongst his mail when he was sorting things out to throw away. He told me that he had been planning to burn all the other rubbish when he had a chance, letters included.'

'And what about Farouk's mail?'

'I think – although I didn't ask him – that he planned to burn those too. Farouk was the man at the last flat that had given him trouble. He told me the reason he moved was that he was afraid of him.'

'So did Woody explain why he had Farouk's post?'

'He said that he'd gone back to pick up his mail from the pigeon hole at his old place and that there must have been some of Farouk's mail in there with it.'

'Okay. And he didn't think to take it back, or just

leave it there rather than bring it home and burn it?'

'He told me that he didn't want to hang around, that Farouk was bad news. So Woody had gone in and out really fast and hadn't bothered to sort the post out while he was there.'

'And you believed him?'

'Yes, why wouldn't I? Anyway I said if he wanted I could drop the letters off on my way to work one morning. Just stick them in through the door.'

'And Woody agreed to that?'

'He said that would be great if I didn't mind doing it, but that he didn't want to put me to any trouble. He just didn't want to run into Farouk.'

'He said that, Sarah? That he didn't want to run into Farouk?'

'Yes.'

'Okay. So Woody told you that Farouk was violent?'

'Not directly, like I said he just seemed very nervous of him.'

'But you weren't?'

'Why would I be? I didn't know who Farouk was and he didn't know me. I couldn't see me taking the post back was going to be a problem. I just planned to put it through the door, not go in or anything.'

'So what happened when you got to the house?'

'The landlord was there painting the windows. I told him that I had some mail for Farouk, and he took it for me. I couldn't really see a way round explaining what I was doing there; there were quite a lot of letters.'

'And did you mention Woody?'

'Only in passing. I told him that Mustapha, Woody, had picked up some of Farouk's mail by accident, and that I was returning it. He seemed relieved.'

'Can you explain what you mean by relieved?

Relieved that the letters were back?'

'No. I think he was relieved to know that Woody was okay. His landlord said that Woody was a nice man – a good tenant – and that he had been concerned when he had left in such a hurry. He said he hadn't been in contact, and hadn't seen Woody since he'd left. He sounded genuinely concerned.'

'Did you mention that Woody was frightened of Farouk?'

'No.'

'And did you give Woody's old landlord your address so that he could forward any mail?'

'No.'

'Did that not occur to you?'

'Yes. I did think about it, but I was worried that Farouk might find out where Woody was living.'

'Okay, Sarah, so are you suggesting that Farouk posed some kind of threat to Woody?'

'I don't know. I just know what Woody had told me.'

'And so at that point Farouk was still living in one of the flats at the Kirby Street address, then?'

'I don't know, I didn't ask, but I suppose I thought he must have been because his landlord took the letters in for me.'

'Okay, Sarah. So tell me about Woody. What was he like as a tenant?'

'There's not a lot to tell, really. I barely noticed he was there most of the time. He paid his rent on time. He went out most days, from just after eight often until quite late. And when he was in, if he wasn't with Ryan watching DVDs or playing on the Xbox, he was in his room. I didn't see much of him. I think he stayed out the odd night but I didn't ask him about that. He kept himself to himself.'

'And did you know he was in the UK on a student visa?'

'I didn't. I hadn't really thought about it. Ryan told me.'

'When did he tell you?'

'I'd been out with Josh to the cinema. By that time we were seeing each other regularly. I'd invited him back for coffee. I was just making it when Ryan came up from the basement and said that we really needed to talk. I could see it was something important.'

'He was agitated?'

'Yes, anxious – he's my brother. I could tell that something was really worrying him.'

'And Ryan was happy to discuss his worries in front of Josh?'

'No, Josh took the hint.'

'And left?'

'Yes.'

'Just like that?'

'I don't think he wanted to go but he could see Ryan wanted to talk to me alone. He said he'd ring me when he got home. And if there was anything I needed just to give him a call – he's a lovely man. He wanted to make sure that I was okay.'

'Were you sleeping together by then?'

'What business is that of yours?'

'I wouldn't ask you if it wasn't relevant, so please can you tell me? Were you having sex with Josh, Sarah?'

'No. Although I think we had both thought that night the coffee would lead to something more. I think we were both expecting him to stay.'

'And Ryan coming in interrupted you?'

'I suppose so. Not directly, but after a few minutes it was pretty obvious Ryan wasn't going to go and he wasn't going to talk in front of Josh. So we didn't have a lot of choice really. Josh was okay about it.'

'So why was Ryan so anxious?'

'He told me that Woody's visa was going to run out when he'd finished his course and that he didn't want to go back to Pakistan. Ryan was really concerned about it – upset.'

'Okay. And how did you feel about that?'

'I'm not sure. It struck me as being odd, I suppose. I mean I could understand it was unfortunate but I didn't see how it really affected us. I know that Ryan was his friend and I could understand him being upset. I suppose I knew that Woody liked living in Cambridge – in the UK – but I couldn't really see why Ryan thought it was such a big thing, so big that he had to come and tell me about it like that.'

'So it seemed strange?'

'Yes. And then Ryan said he was worried about the contract he was working on. Although I couldn't see at that point how the two things were connected.'

'So did you find out why he was worried about the contract, Sarah?'

'He just said it wasn't exactly what he had thought it was going to be, and that there might not be as much work as he had been led to believe.'

'And can you remember what you said?'

'No, not really, not word for word. I suppose I made the right noises – you know – take what there is, do what you can, not to worry, that kind of thing. I said we could always get another lodger in, like I'd said before. And that he was doing really well, so he should hang on in there, something else might come up. Like I said, I wasn't sure how it tied in with Woody at that point, but as far as Ryan was concerned the two things seemed to be connected.'

'But he didn't mention being in any kind of trouble?'

'No. Not then.'

'And did Ryan tell you that he planned to sort something out to help Woody stay in the UK?'

'No, but he did say that Woody needed both of us to help him.'

'And you agreed?'

'Well, yes, in principle. I thought he meant writing a reference or filling in some forms or something like that.'

'So then what happened?'

'Ryan seemed relieved.'

'And?'

'Josh suggested that he and I go away for the weekend together.'

'I thought you just said that Josh had gone home?'

'He had. He rang me while he was driving back to his house. I had more or less finished talking to Ryan by the time he rang. Josh said it was the only way we would ever get any real time to ourselves and he said he wanted the physical thing to be special not rushed. He laughed and said he didn't want our first night together being us upstairs and Ryan and Woody downstairs on the Xbox – I think we both needed a break away from work and things – and I think we both knew that this was it. You know. The big thing. The special thing. The thing we all wait for.'

'And what did Ryan say about you going away?'

'He had gone by the time I was off the phone.'

'So you didn't get a chance to discuss exactly what helping Woody might entail?'

'No. Not then. And to be honest I wasn't thinking about Woody or Ryan. I was thinking about Josh.'

Chapter Six

Sarah unlocked the door and stepped into the cottage, while Josh followed close behind her carrying a box of groceries.

'So what do you think?' he asked, as she looked around.

'Oh my god, it's lovely.' Sarah turned to him, grinning. Josh slid the box onto the counter in the tiny whitewashed kitchen and took her in his arms.

'I'm so glad you said you'd come. You deserve a break. We deserve a break. I've been looking forward to this for so long – just some time away together without my job or yours.'

'Or Ryan.'

'Or Woody,' Josh laughed. 'Finally just you and me. Us.'

'Us has got a nice ring to it,' Sarah said. She couldn't remember the last time she had spent any time away from home. It had to have been years since she had had a holiday, or even a night away. 'The cottage is so sweet – oh I love the boarded walls, like New England.'

'Small but perfectly formed,' he said with a smile. 'I'll take you on a guided tour in a minute.' He paused and took a breath. 'So, this is the kitchen,' he said, grinning, before pressing his lips to hers. Her whole body responded to his. It felt like they had waited forever to get to this moment.

'I've been thinking about you all week,' he said, as he pulled away.

'What about the rest of the tour?'

'Oh don't worry, we'll round get to that,' Josh said, and kissed her again. This time his kiss was more insistent and hungrier and she matched it.

'Do you think we should unpack the food?' she

mumbled, as his fingers struggled with the buttons on her jacket and hers with his denim shirt.

'Maybe we should,' he said, as her coat dropped to the floor. 'Maybe we should put the things in the fridge.'

'Maybe you're right,' she murmured, as his shirt joined it. 'We should do that.'

'Good idea,' he gasped, his lips on her neck and shoulders.

Sarah closed her eyes and drank in the feel of him as she ran her fingers over his muscular shoulders, across his broad hairy chest, her mouth watering, her pulse quickening, and then he kissed her again, his hands sliding up inside her sweater.

'Or we could do it later, maybe,' he breathed, between kisses. 'When we do the rest of the tour.'

'Good plan,' she mumbled, as he pulled the jumper over her head, kissing her neck, her collarbones, while his hands, his fingers, stroked and caressed every inch of her. She moaned with delight, every cell alive and glowing white-hot. It had been a long time.

'Do you want to go upstairs?' Josh asked breathlessly, as she undid the belt to his jeans.

'What and spoil the tour?' she laughed, as he lifted her up onto the worktop, alongside the shopping, his hands working their way up under her skirt. 'No, I think we should stay here. Let's not spoil the surprise. Save upstairs for later.'

She had been thinking about this moment all the way there, feeling slightly nervous as well as excited, wondering how it would happen, wondering how they would cross the line, and now they were and it felt so, so good and so easy. There was more kissing and touching and Sarah finally stopped thinking and let go, let herself float away into the sensations.

And then, as the kissing and the touching grew

more, more intense, more exciting she toed off her boots and helped him take off her tights and knickers.

'God, it's so lovely to be here,' Sarah said, to no one in particular, as Josh's hands slid under her thighs, and then there was a moment finding a condom, undoing the packet – and then he was pulling her down onto him and sliding deep inside her. Sarah gasped and cried out in sheer pleasure.

'You know that I'm falling in love with you, don't you?' whispered Josh.

'Me too,' said Sarah.

Later, when they were done, Josh lit the little wood burner in the tiny sitting room with its doll's house casement windows, and they curled up on the sofa under a blanket and watched the fire crackle and burn. 'Do you want to eat here or maybe we could go down the pub, or eat out, or we could go for a walk if you like?'

'I would like to do all those things. I want to do everything,' Sarah said, giggling, as she snuggled up against him, relishing the feel of his arm around her.

'And then we should maybe do the tour?' Josh said, with a grin, looking down at her.

'Sounds like a very good idea,' said Sarah, and didn't resist as he kissed her again.

The beach at Holme was deserted when they set out, wrapped up against the chill. Outside the thick walls of the cottage the day had turned wild and windy, and the beach, with its white sands, rolling dunes and whipping marram grass felt a world away from Cambridge, although it was less than two hours drive from the cottage.

The sea was steel grey under a matching sky, and kicking up great plumes of spray on the late evening wind. Sarah stayed tucked in close to Josh, hand in hand, arm in arm. They picked up driftwood and shells and talked a lot, their words carried along beside them on the stiff breeze. Sarah didn't want the day to end.

It was almost dusk by the time they made their way back over the dunes, walking down through the nature reserve, into the lane and back to the cottage. The cottage was a two up two down on the end of a row, tucked up in a narrow side street. Gulls circled and called overhead, and Sarah could smell the sea on the night wind. As they rounded the corner, in the distance she could see the lamps they had left on, lighting their way back, and as Josh put his arm around her and pulled her in close, Sarah realised that she hadn't felt this happy or this at ease for years. It felt like she had come home at last.

'I'm so glad you could come,' he said, as if reading her thoughts. 'I want us to remember this forever. When we're old and grey. When we can't remember anything else I want us to remember this.'

Sarah laughed and tipped her head up towards his, tasting the salt on his lips as he kissed her. 'You are such a romantic,' she murmured.

'Guilty as charged, M'lud,' he replied. 'Now let's hurry up and get back. I don't know about you but I'm famished.'

'I'll cook,' Josh said when they got to the cottage and he slipped the key into the lock. 'I was thinking maybe chilli and ginger prawns with some rice? What do you reckon? Is there anything you don't eat?'

'No, I pretty much like everything.'

'Good. Do you want to sort the fire out while I sort out supper?'

Sarah nodded, afraid if she said too much the spell might break. She knew that whatever it was she had been looking for, this was it, and as their eyes met, although neither of them said anything, she knew that Josh knew it too.

Sarah

'When we got home to Cambridge on Sunday evening Ryan was waiting for me, in the kitchen. He said we needed to talk and that it couldn't wait.'

'And so let me get this right; this was after the weekend away at the coast with Josh?'

'That's right. Yes. We'd just arrived back.'

'And where was your relationship with Josh at this time?'

'We'd been talking about moving in together.'

'He'd asked you?'

'We'd talked about it while we were away and on the drive home. Yes. We both wanted it, both wanted to be together. He told me that he loved me. I think we were both ready for the next stage of our lives. Moving in together seemed like a natural step.'

'Didn't you think it seemed a little quick?'

'No, it just felt right. I think you know when something is right. And I knew.'

'And had the two of you discussed when that might happen?'

'No, we hadn't set a date or anything, and we both agreed that it wouldn't be straight away – but not long. We both knew that that was the way it was heading.'

'And you planned that Josh would move in with you into the house in Maudsley Terrace?'

'Yes, well initially at least. We thought we might buy somewhere together later. Josh had been renting the place in Cottenham for six months and the lease was coming up for renewal. It seemed like an ideal time.'

'And he understood that your house was tied up for at least the next two years until Ryan reached twenty-five?'

'Yes.'

'And Josh was happy with your brother living downstairs?'

'I don't know that he was happy about it. But he understood that that was the way it was, the circumstances, and it wouldn't be forever. And it wasn't like Ryan was there all the time. He had his own place. And I thought if Josh was living there that Ryan might spend even less time upstairs.'

'And it was serious between you two?'

'Yes. I just said that.'

'Okay, so, according to your account, when you got back to Maudsley Terrace, after your weekend away, Josh went home and Ryan was waiting for you in the kitchen? Is that correct?'

'That's right.'

Chapter Seven

'Has Josh gone?' said Ryan, glancing round the kitchen.

'Yes,' said Sarah, sliding her holdall onto the table. 'He had to go round to pick up some paperwork and the plans from Andy's for a job he's got on tomorrow. Why, what's the matter?'

'We need to talk.' Ryan pulled out a chair and sat down.

'Okay,' said Sarah, taking out her dirty washing and a bag of shells. Sand scuttered across the floor tiles. 'I need to talk to you too, about Josh and me. Let me just get this stuff in the machine. Do you want to put the kettle on?'

'No, can you just leave that, Sarah, and sit down.'

Sarah laughed. 'Oh right. What, and you're going to deal with the laundry now, are you? Did anyone ring up about the room while I was away? I know you said not to, but I put it up on that new website to see what happened. Get a bed.com or something. It would be good if we could get someone else in that room this month, even if it is just short term. I know you don't like the idea but it would give us both a bit of breathing space.'

'Sarah. Please just sit, will you?'

She glanced across at Ryan. He was pale, dark-eyed and unshaven. She didn't want him to spoil her good mood, not after such a lovely weekend with Josh.

'Okay. So, what happened?' she asked, sliding out a chair and sitting down at the kitchen table opposite him. 'What's the matter? Don't tell me. You got fired?'

Ryan snorted. 'No, I didn't. I wish it was that simple. I'm in really deep shit, Sarah,' he said softly.

'I mean like the deepest shit I've ever been in in my life.'

Sarah looked at his face. He said nothing, instead he turned a salt pot round and round, sliding it back and forward across the top of the table between his finger tips.

'You can't just leave it like that, Ryan. What it is? What have you done? What's happened?' she pressed.

Ryan banged the salt down. It made Sarah jump. He pushed his fingers back through his hair. 'The job I was telling you about got pulled. I suppose I knew it was going pear-shaped but they kept messing me around, saying it was on, saying it was just a matter of time, a few days, a couple of weeks. Anyway I borrowed a bit of money on the strength of it, for the van, some tools, enough to bankroll the job properly, and to tide me over till it all got signed off.'

'Not again,' Sarah snapped.

'Please will you just be quiet and hear me out,' he said. 'The thing is I can't pay it back.'

'Oh Ryan, for god's sake, this is crazy. You've got to stop doing this. How many times—'

He glared at her. 'Will you just shut up? I need your help not a fucking lecture.'

'I can't keep bailing you out.'

'Sarah, please.' There was something grim and desperate in is voice.

'Okay, but this is the last time. You understand. I'm sure we can sort it out. I'll really push the other spare room. And you can always get more work. You've done it before, it'll be fine. How much is it?'

He looked up at her, eyes bright. 'I can't fix it. Not this time. Not like this. They're going to kill me if I can't get the money together, Sarah.'

She laughed. 'Don't be so melodramatic. What do you mean *kill you*? Don't be ridiculous, Ryan. How much is it?' She was deliberately brisk and no nonsense; annoyed that he had done this now, just when things were going so well, just when she had finally found her new start. Just when she was happy. Just when her life was back on track. How many times could he sabotage their lives? Sarah stared at him, waiting for him to say something. Trust Ryan to scupper her mood.

She glanced up at the clock; the truth was she was tired, certainly too tired to deal with Ryan and another of his crises. She had to be at work the next morning by seven. All Sarah really wanted was to get the washing in the machine, make a mug of tea, maybe have a bath, watch the TV in her pyjamas and then go bed.

When he said nothing, Sarah sighed and stood up. 'Look, I'm sorry, Ryan, but I've got things I need to do. People can't threaten you like that. If you don't want my help that's fine. I'm shattered. We can talk in the morning.'

'No, don't go. I do, I really do need you,' he said.

'Okay. How much do you want?' she asked, reaching for her handbag.

He didn't look up.

'How much, Ryan?'

She turned to say something else but the words dried in her mouth: Ryan's shoulders had slumped forward, any shred of bravado gone, and when he spoke it sounded as if he was close to tears. 'Twenty thousand pounds,' he said.

Sarah stared at him, the breath stopped up in her chest.

'What do you mean *twenty thousand pounds*, that's ridiculous, Ryan. How the hell can you owe anyone twenty thousand pounds, that's crazy. Who would lend you that kind of money? Are you serious? How the hell did you manage to borrow that amount of money?' The words tumbled out of her mouth, unhindered, unstoppable, full of outrage and shock and disbelief. 'How on earth did you think you were ever going to pay it back?' she said.

He looked up at her, eyes bright, face pale.

'The site I was working on, the main contractors said that they wanted me for this new contract they'd just taken on. They reckoned there'd be at least six months work, maybe more if the next phase went ahead – and the guy said they'd need me to provide a couple of other guys. It's why I needed the money. Why I bought the van. I wanted to show you I could do something, Sarah, be someone. This is your fault. I wanted to show you that I wasn't a waste of space, that I didn't steal things. You told me to get myself together. And I was doing it. I was. You told me to be the man.'

'Not by borrowing money. I didn't want you to borrow money, Ryan. I just wanted you to get a proper job. An ordinary job.' Sarah took a breath, trying hard to sort her thoughts out. 'So that's how you got the money to buy the van and all those new clothes and stuff? I thought you were working and getting yourself sorted out. I was proud of you. I thought it was finally all coming together. For god's sake. You haven't got a job at all, have you?'

'I did have. I did. First two or three weeks I was on the tools with a couple of the other guys with one of the big contractors and then they said they were looking for someone to tender for a job they'd got coming up. I thought I could do it and the contractor, Ted, reckoned he'd be able to help me out, get the tender worded right, help me sort out the rates and stuff, lend me any special gear I needed, and I'd give him a bit of drink for seeing me right. I mean it would've been ideal, but I needed a van and the right equipment before they'd even look at me. And then it all went to cock. Ted got pulled off the job for fiddling, and he was the one who hired me in the first place, so I was off the job too. And there was no way they were going to look at a tender from me without someone to back me up. I've been looking round for something else and doing some paving,' he said miserably. 'I've had a few days on the tools here and there. But they want their money back. All of it.' He looked up at her. 'You've got to believe me; I just wanted to pay my share, Sarah. That's all.'

Sarah shook her head, her pulse thready and frantic. 'That was all I ever wanted you to do, Ryan, just pay your share, get yourself together, get some regular work, be who you are. You didn't have to prove anything to me, you don't – just step up.'

He let out a throaty angry sob. 'That's what I thought I was doing.'

'Who the hell did you borrow the money from?' she asked.

'Some people that Woody knew. Friends of this guy Farouk who used to live at his old flat. In Kirby Street.'

'Farouk?' Sarah was confused. 'I don't understand. I thought Woody said that he was frightened of Farouk? I thought that was why he moved out in the first place?'

'I know, and you're right, but I was just talking about the new job and maybe getting this contract and needing a van and tools and all that, and how I couldn't really get this job without it, and Woody said that maybe he could help me out. He said that this Farouk guy is connected, and that maybe he could lend me some money. He was only trying to help. And I thought I'd be able to pay it back.'

'Are you mad? With what?' snapped Sarah. 'You can barely manage to pay your half of the bills. Where the hell did you think you were going to find twenty thousand pounds from, for god's sake? It's total madness.'

'I know,' he said. 'I know.' Ryan stared at her. It didn't matter that he looked fourteen or that he was so close to tears. She wanted to hit him. She was so angry and so worried and so bemused and horrified that he could have been so stupid.

'What were you thinking?' she said in an undertone. 'How were you ever going to pay it back?'

'When we sell the house,' he said. 'Woody arranged for me to meet this guy in a pub. He seemed okay. So I explained that I'd be able to pay the money back when we sold the house, and in the meantime I could pay them interest on the loan and he told me that that would be okay. That Woody had vouched for me. He said—'

'It's two years away, Ryan, if we can sell it.'

'I know and I told him that too. I explained everything. But he said it would be okay. They knew I was good for it and in the meantime I'd pay them what I could. Interest. Just to keep the loan ticking over.'

'So you talked to Farouk?'

'Not exactly. Me and Woody met this guy in a pub. He works for Farouk.'

Sarah shook her head.

'It was fine. I went back later on my own and he'd got the money. He said everything was sweet as long as I kept up the interest.

'So what changed?'

Ryan threw up his hands in despair and shook his head. 'I dunno. I lost the chance of the tender and I suppose I couldn't give them as much as I promised, but I was paying them; I was,' Ryan said, voice cracking with emotion. 'Every week. Everything I could spare. I just don't understand what happened really. Something changed. Like the rules changed.

'The guy I met in the pub came round to the site where I was working and told me that the deal was off and that they wanted the money back and that I'd got a month to get it to them. *A month.* And then yesterday morning he came round here. Him and this fucking great thug. A little reminder he said, just in case it had slipped my mind. Like I needed reminding.'

'They came round here?' said Sarah, glancing towards the back door. 'How the hell did they know where you lived?'

'I don't know. Seriously, I don't know. Maybe Woody said something, I don't know. They're going to kill me, Sarah.' His head dropped into his hands. 'I could see them eyeing stuff up. What am I going to do?'

Sarah picked up the phone. 'I'm going to call the police.'

'You can't,' he snapped.

'Why not?'

'What are you going to say?'

'I'm going to tell them that they threatened you.'

Ryan looked at her and laughed grimly. 'Right, and you think that is going to do any good? I borrowed the money, Sarah. I owe these guys, and even if they could do anything the police can't watch me twenty-four seven. And me grassing Farouk up to the law isn't going to help my case one little bit.'

Sarah sat back down beside him. Her chest hurt. 'Look,' she said after a minute or two. 'We'll have to find a way to try and sort this out, okay? Maybe I can go to the bank, maybe we can borrow the money against the house or something.' Even as she was saying it Sarah knew no one in their right mind was going lend her that kind of money. She barely earned enough to pay the outgoings as it was, and there was a part of her that was livid that Ryan assumed that this was something *she* had to sort out, which was when Sarah saw a subtle shift in Ryan's body language.

'What is it?' she said. 'What are you planning? Please don't do anything else stupid. What is it?'

'Not me. It's Woody; he said that he might be able to help.'

Sarah snorted. 'Really? He's helped you enough already, don't you think? What the hell was he thinking getting you tied up with this lot in the first place? *Was* he the one who told them where you lived?'

'I don't know, Sarah. And it's not his fault. Really. He's a good guy. He was trying to help me out, that's all.'

'So how can he help now?'

'They hadn't been gone more than a few minutes when he showed up. I was in a state. He wanted to know what the matter was, so I told him. He was really upset. He blames himself. He said Farouk was pretty heavy duty. I mean not that Woody needed to tell me that. I could see it from the boys he'd got working for him. I told him about them wanting the money back. And then he said that he's got savings and things and that his parents are loaded, 'Ryan said. He was animated now, excited. She could see that he had seen some sort of a way out of where he was that she couldn't.

'And so, what? He's going to lend you the money?' asked Sarah.

'Not exactly but he was saying he might be able to help.'

'I don't understand. Why? Does he feel guilty, because if he doesn't he bloody well should do. He knows the way you are with money. Why the hell did he suggest you borrow money off someone he was afraid of? It's totally crazy. And so much money...'

Sarah shook her head. 'I suppose it's stupid to ask if you've got any left?'

Ryan made a non-committal noise. 'I think he feels bad about it,' he said. Ignoring her question.

But there was something else. Sarah could see it in his face, she knew him too well to be fooled. 'What, Ryan? What is it?'

'He wants to stay in the UK.'

'I know that. You told me before.' She could see him struggling to find the right words or maybe the courage to say what was on his mind. 'What is it, Ryan, for god's sake just spit it out, will you?'

Ryan leaned back and lay his hands palm down on the table. 'Woody has said that he would let me have the money.'

'Okay, well that's good. If we can work it out then we can pay him pack when the house is sold.'

He looked up at her. 'It'll be too late then.'

'Too late? What do you mean? I'm not with you.'

'He'll be back home.'

'That's not a problem, we can still get the money to him. We can work it out.'

'I know, but he's desperate to stay in the UK. And he's got a solution. Just let me finish.' Ryan paused. 'Woody said that he would let me have the money if you agreed to marry him.'

Sarah felt her jaw drop. She stared at Ryan and then she laughed. 'What? Are you completely mad? What the hell. No! I'm not going to marry Woody – for god's sake, what is that, some sort of sick joke?'

Ryan's expression didn't change. Sarah's laughter faded and died.

'You can't be serious, Ryan. Oh come on. You can't sell me off so you can sort your life out. What are you thinking? I'm going out with Josh. We've been talking about moving in together – no – no you're mad. No.' She held up her hands to fend the idea off.

'Please,' said Ryan. 'Just hear me out. It would just be a piece of paper, that's all, nothing else. Just a formality so that he could stay here. And then he could apply for a visa so he can carry on living here. A right to remain. At the moment he hasn't got a leg to stand on. If he doesn't get it he'll just have to go home or risk staying on illegally and being deported.'

'That's not my problem. No, No – I can't, Ryan. I can't.'

'But it's just a piece of paper,' he said again. 'And what other way is there?'

'No. Just no.'

Sarah

'Did you talk to Josh about the situation with Ryan?'

'No, no I didn't say anything. Josh had got a job to do in Brighton for a couple of weeks, so he was going to stay down there in a B&B, and I didn't want to talk to him about it over the phone. When he asked me why I was so quiet I told him Ryan had lost his job and left it at that. He didn't press me. He wanted to talk about the future. Our future. Maybe I should have told him, it would have made things so much simpler later on, but I didn't. To be honest I didn't know what to say to him. It was crazy. I just couldn't believe Ryan had got himself into such a muddle.'

'Didn't it occur to you that Josh might be able to help?'

'No, I mean, I suppose so, but I didn't want to ask him.'

'But you could have talked it through with Josh.'

'I know but Josh is a good man. He is the kind of person who, if I had talked to him about it would have felt he had to do something to help me. He's like that. I didn't want to put him in that position. First of all I didn't want him anywhere near Farouk. And I was ashamed, embarrassed. '

'By Ryan?'

'By the money, the marriage, the whole thing. Ryan is a liability, a dreamer. He's always been unrealistic and self-centred; all he can ever see is what he wants and needs. And he doesn't care about how any of that affects anyone else. He had made me vulnerable and he couldn't see it. How could he even talk about something like that with Woody? I understand he wanted to turn things around, but why did he borrow the money to take on a six month contract? This is a man who found it hard to do two days running at work, let alone six months. What was he thinking about?'

'Maybe he thought it was worth the risk.'

'He was so stupid. Twenty thousand pounds. How the hell did he think he was ever going to be able to pay it back?'

'So what did you do?'

'I did what I said I was going to do. I made an appointment to see the bank manager on the Monday morning.'

'And? '

'He took one look at my figures and my bank statements and said that he couldn't see his way clear to lending me any money against the house while it was in trust, and on my current income and outgoings he didn't feel I would be able to service a personal loan of that size. Not that I had thought he would but I had to start somewhere. It made me feel like I was doing something.'

'And so what happened next?'

'When I got home I asked Ryan if there was any way we could arrange to talk to Farouk or this man who had given him the money, meet up, maybe see *if they would give him some leeway, or some more time – but he just laughed and said they weren't that sort of people; you couldn't make an appointment and have a friendly little chat.'*

'And what about Woody, did you talk to him about his offer at this stage?'

'And say what? No. I didn't want to even see him, let alone talk to him. I couldn't bring myself to say anything to him, not after what he'd suggested to Ryan. I couldn't believe he had even suggested it. It felt like he was trying to buy us both. And I was angry. What sort of person offers to get married for money? I couldn't bear to look at him. As soon as he came in I went out or upstairs.'

'And Josh?'

'It was crazy, stupid.'

'What was?'

'The whole thing. It felt like I couldn't breathe. I left a message on Josh's answer machine and told him I was really busy at work, that there was someone off sick and that I had been asked to cover for them – and I avoided his phone calls. It was just to give myself some breathing space really, just to give me a chance to think about what we should do. And what I could say.'

'By we, do you mean you and Ryan, Sarah?'

'Yes, I suppose so.'

'So you were avoiding Josh?'

'Yes. And then towards the end of the week I got a phone call when I was at work at the restaurant.'

'From Josh?'

'No, from the hospital. They rang to tell me that Ryan had been beaten up. He'd been coming home from the pub after work. At least three men jumped him and dragged him into a side alley where they keep the bins. They broke his fingers, smashed his face up. Kicked him. It was so awful. He looked

89

terrible.'

'Are you okay, Sarah? Would you like a break? Maybe a glass of water?'

'No, no I'm fine. It's just – it was awful. Ryan was a mess. Just looking at him made me hurt. I went to A&E at Addenbrookes, but by that time they'd admitted him for observation. His face was such a mess. I tried to persuade him to tell the police who'd done it, and what it was about, but he wouldn't. He told them he had no idea who it was. The officer who came round to take his statement kept telling us that he was probably just in the wrong place at the wrong time. Crazy.'

'But Ryan told you what happened?'

'Eventually. He said that they'd told him next time they saw him they'd kill him and then they planned to come after me, and that he had two weeks to come up with the money, or else. And...'

'And there was something else?'

'Yes. They said they would burn the house down if that was what it took.'

'You sound as if you were resigned to it.'

'Resigned? What do you mean? How can you possibly say that? I wasn't resigned; I didn't know what to do or where to turn. All the things that have happened – I felt crushed and scared, and it felt like there was no one who could help. I've never done anything illegal in my life; I've not got so much as a parking fine. Can you understand what I'm saying? I wasn't resigned, I was frantic.'

'It's okay, just take a breath, calm down – I can hear what you're saying. So what did you do?'

'What choice did I have?'

'Didn't it occur to you to go and see the police yourself, Sarah?'

'No. Ryan was terrified about that. Terrified that I might do it off my own bat. He begged me not to tell anyone. He said if I split on them I'd only make things worse. I didn't know what to do. I've never felt so lost – or so trapped, or so scared.'

'So what did you do?'

'I went home to talk to Woody.'

Chapter Eight

Riding the bus way back from the hospital, Sarah kept glancing over her shoulder, just in case the men who beat up Ryan were there, just in case they were following her. Would they follow her onto a bus? Worse, would they follow her home? She glanced round at the faces; the boy in the hoodie, the man with tattoos, ponytail and a denim jacket with the sleeves ripped out, busy reading his newspaper, were they after her? Or the two men in tee shirts or the fat man in the scruffy suit? She tried hard not to meet anyone's eye, wishing she had asked Ryan more questions, like what did the men look like? How old were they? She kept her head down, willing herself small and invisible.

By the time Sarah got through the city the bus was almost empty, but she still couldn't shake the feeling she was being watched. When they got close to her stop, she got up and stood by the door so she could get off quickly. The driver had barely stopped before she clambered down the steps and headed for home, sticking to the middle of the path, keeping in the light till finally she got to her turning and then she upped her pace, taking one more long glance behind her, before she hurried along the road, ran up the path, slammed the front door behind her and slid across the bolts, top and bottom, her heart thumping like a drum in her ears.

Sarah stood for a few moments to catch her breath, pressing her back up against the solid wooden door, as if there might already be someone there on the other side, and that she could hold them back. She felt tired and lost, the scent of the hospital clinging to her clothes and hair.

After a minute or two Sarah took a deep breath,

slipped off her coat and hung it up on the hallstand before heading into the kitchen. Her plan had been to make a tea, settle herself, and then go upstairs to see if Woody was in, but it seemed there was no need. He was already in the kitchen. He had his mobile phone in his hand, and was standing by the sink waiting for the kettle to boil. She had a sense that he had been waiting for her to get home.

'So how did it go? How is Ryan?' he said, glancing over at her, before she had time to say anything. He hung up and slipped the phone back into his pocket. 'How's he doing?'

Sarah stared at him. Something about his expression unsettled her. 'How did you know about Ryan?' she asked.

'Sorry, it was me who took the phone call. The hospital rang here first. I was upstairs working. I hope you didn't mind me answering the phone. I was expecting a call. I gave them your mobile number. Do you want a tea?'

Sarah shook her head.

He dropped his teabag into the bin. 'So how is he?'

'Awful. His face is a total mess. I didn't recognise him when I went in. He's got god knows how many stitches, a broken nose – lost some teeth. Cuts, bruises, cracked ribs. They broke some of his fingers.' Sarah closed her eyes and made an effort to swallow down an unexpected flurry of tears. She didn't want to share this with Woody of all people, but who else was there that she could talk to?

'They said they're going to keep him for a day or two for observation. They're worried that there might be swelling in the brain. The doctor said he's lucky he didn't lose an eye. Or worse. Ryan's frightened, but he won't say anything about who did it.' Sarah met Woody's gaze. 'They could have killed him.'

Woody nodded.

'Why on earth did you have to introduce Ryan to people like that? You told me you were frightened of Farouk, and you know what Ryan's like. He's a complete disaster with money. How could they let him borrow so much?'

'Are you sure you don't want some tea?' Woody said. His voice was gentle, even, sympathetic. Sarah's shoulders slumped. Before she could say anything else he was switching the kettle back on, finding a mug. It unsettled her. She didn't like how proprietorial and how easy and at home he seemed to be in her kitchen. 'I'm really sorry about Ryan,' he said. 'I didn't think it would turn out like this.' He slid the biscuit tin onto the table and opened it.

'Will you just stop playing house? Sorry isn't enough,' Sarah said grimly. 'Sorry won't get Ryan out of this bloody mess. He won't go to the police. You have got to talk to him. You have to make him see sense and tell him to turn these men in. They're animals, Woody. You should see the state of him. They need locking up. I can't believe you set Ryan up to meet with them. They could have killed him.' The words came out on the edge of a ragged desperate sob.

Woody held up his hands. 'I know, I know, but trust me, Sarah, I'm not the enemy here. Really. I want to help if I can.' His tone was even, conciliatory. The kettle clicked off the boil.

'No? That's what it feels like. Why the hell did you introduce Ryan to your friends?' she sobbed, while he made the tea she didn't want and hadn't asked for.

'They're not my friends. They're Farouk's friends and I didn't know what Ryan was going to do, did I? He just told me that he wanted to borrow some money, that's all, I didn't ask him how much he wanted, and you'd said I wasn't to give him any more.'

'So what? You're saying that this is *my fault?*' Sarah snapped.

Woody pulled a face and then shrugged. 'No, I'm not saying that. I'm just telling you what happened.'

'We both know what happened, Ryan got beaten up over a debt he hasn't got a snowball's chance in hell of paying off. You have to go the police, Woody. Please,' she begged. 'Please, you know who they are. We can stop this before it goes any further. They've threatened to kill him. You have to ring them. Please.'

He smiled grimly and shook his head. 'That's not going to happen.'

Sarah stared at him; she felt cold and fragile and powerless. And nothing he was saying was helping.

'They beat him up, Woody. They said they're going to kill him. And he believes that they will if he doesn't do something.' Her voice quivered and finally cracked. 'And they said if he doesn't pay up there're going to come after me next. Burn the house down. Do you understand?'

He slid the mug of tea across the table towards her. 'And you think the police are going to be able to stop them?'

'Yes.'

He shook his head. 'Well, you're wrong. They can't. They can't watch anyone twenty-four seven. And what if the police bring them in for questioning and then lets them back out again, or if Ryan refuses to identify them or press charges? Then what happens? You're back to square one. And these aren't the kind of people you mess with.'

Sarah stared at him. 'So what are we going to do? All that money. I don't understand; how could he have been so stupid?'

Woody shrugged. 'I know. I thought Ryan wanted

95

to borrow, I don't know, a couple of hundred pounds, five maybe, at the most,' he said. 'I would have given him that. It would have been easy.'

'But I told you not to?'

Woody nodded. 'Like I said it would have been easy.'

'Well, it isn't easy now, is it? What the hell am I going to do?' Sarah sobbed, unable to hold the tears back any longer. '*What am I going to do?*'

She felt Woody's hand drop gently onto her shoulder. 'I'm sure that we can work something out,' he said, and something in his tone made her shiver. She looked up at him. He was smiling.

Sarah

'And then Woody insisted that I drank the tea he had made. He got me some tissues, and we sat down and then he said, "I know Ryan's talked to you about my proposition".'

'His proposition?'

'To marry him.'

'And are you sure that that is what Woody meant, Sarah?'

'Oh yes, I'm certain. He said, "If you help me then I will help you".'

'And by help he meant you marrying him?'

'Yes.'

'Did he say anything else?'

'More or less the same as Ryan had said, that if I agreed to marry him that it would only be a piece of paper. Just a formality, he said. And that it would save me.'

'Save you? Is that what he said? Didn't that strike you as an odd thing to say?'

'I suppose so, but I didn't really think about it till later. He just said we needed to make sure it stood

up to scrutiny. *People would need to believe it was the real deal. Not a sham. All I had to do was say yes and marry him and everything else could be taken care of.'*

'And you're certain that that's what he said? For the benefit of the tape could you say yes or no, please, Sarah, rather than nod?'

'Yes. I'm sure that that's what he said. All I had to do was marry him.'

Chapter Nine

'I can't,' said Sarah. 'I'm sorry. I just can't. Please, Woody, can't you just lend me the money? I'll pay you any amount of interest that you want and as soon as we sell the house I'll pay you back. Every last penny. Please, Woody. I'm not like Ryan. You know that your money would be safe with me. We can have a proper legal contract drawn up if you don't trust me. Can't we come to some sort of an arrangement?'

'I do trust you, and this is my arrangement,' he said, his gaze not leaving hers. 'We get married, you get your money and I get to stay here.'

'I can't,' Sarah said again, but this time she sounded and felt less sure, less certain. It was just a piece of paper said a tiny insistent voice in her head, a voice that sounded uncannily like Ryan's.

Woody shrugged. 'Okay. It's up to you. It's very simple. I can help you out, I can pay Ryan's loan off, but I won't wait forever. I need to know your decision by tomorrow.'

Sarah stared at him; she felt sick. 'Tomorrow? Why tomorrow?'

He smiled and drained his mug. 'Because time is running out for me too, Sarah. I have things that need sorting out, things that need to be arranged. Things I need to do.'

Sarah didn't know what to say. This was crazy. 'Okay,' she said after a moment or two. 'I understand that, but it's a lot to take in. I need to think and I need to talk to Josh about it,' she said. 'He needs to know what's going on. I just need to explain things to him and then we can maybe sort something out.' She was playing for time, trying to work out some other solution – surely there had to be one?

Woody's expression hardened and he shook his

head. 'You can't tell Josh about this. You can't talk to anyone about this. Do you understand? If you tell anyone then the deal is off.'

'What?' gasped Sarah. 'No, that's not going to happen. He needs to know what's going on.'

'You heard me. You can't tell anyone about this. Particularly not Josh. Do you understand?' His tone was hard and uncompromising.

'Why? Josh is my boyfriend. It would be easier to explain to him—'

Woody shook his head. 'Those are my terms. Take them or leave them.'

Sarah stared at him. It felt like someone had reached into her chest and was crushing her heart in their fist. This couldn't be happening, Sarah thought. It felt as if she had walked into someone else's life or onto the set of a soap opera. 'But I can't do that, Woody. I can't. I love Josh. He's going to move in here with me.'

Woody shook his head. 'No, he isn't, not if you want the money. Not if you want Ryan off the hook. My offer is very straightforward, Sarah. We get married and I will pay off Ryan's debt. That is it, take it, or leave it.'

During their conversation there had been a subtle shift in Woody's demeanour, the way he stood, the way he spoke to her. Sarah stared at him, trying to fathom what he was thinking, why he was doing this, and what had changed.

'I don't understand why you won't just lend me the money. I mean I'd have no trouble paying you back if you're just prepared to wait a while. Won't you at least consider it, please?'

Before Woody replied there was a knock at the front door. Sarah got to her feet to go and answer it.

'Wait,' snapped Woody, catching hold of her arm.

'It's all right; it's probably just Josh. I rang him on

the way back from the hospital,' Sarah said, shaking him off, but there was something in Woody's tone that stopped her from heading out into the hall. Her earlier fear seeped back like a chill and she stood very still. 'What's the matter?' she whispered.

Whoever it was knocked again, a little harder this time and Woody held a finger to his lips. Sarah stared at him, her pulse quickening. Neither of them moved, neither of them spoke. The knocking became louder and then louder still till it was a banging and a kicking and Sarah couldn't bear it and clamped her hand to her ears, terrified that the door might give way and break – and then what would they do?

'Is the back gate locked?' hissed Woody.

Sarah swung round and peered out into the darkness beyond the kitchen windows, trying to remember if she'd locked the gate before she went out to work, her heart starting to race now as the adrenaline kicked in. 'I think so,' she stammered. 'I'm sure I did.'

'Good.' Woody nodded.

Sarah reached across the table and grabbed her handbag.

'What do you think you're doing?' whispered Woody, as she started to search through it.

'I'm going to call the police.'

'Don't,' he said, holding up a hand to still her. 'It'll only make things worse. And they'll never get here in time. Just shut up and keep quiet.'

After a moment or two more the banging stopped. Sarah wasn't sure that the silence wasn't worse, and then someone shouted through the letterbox.

'No good you hiding, bitch. We know you is in there.' The voice was male, sing-song, taunting, streetwise.

'No point you thinking we can't see you, cos' we can. We know where you is. We know where you work, where you live, we know where you go,' said the man, his tone sounded as if he was teasing, and that the threat was some kind of a sick joke. 'We can get you anytime we want, any time we choose. Any time. You remember that.'

Sarah stood rooted to the spot, her hands clenched into fists, curled so tight that her nails dug into her palms. Woody lifted his finger to his lips again, as if there was any chance she was going to say something.

'You got two weeks, bitch,' said the man outside her front door. 'Two weeks and then we're coming to get you and that dipstick brother of yours. You hear what I'm saying? Two weeks and then you pay, one way or another.' With that the letterbox dropped.

And then it was quiet, all except for the beating of Sarah's heart, so loud now that she was sure Woody could hear it. When, after a few more minutes, she was sure they had gone Sarah up ended her bag onto the kitchen table and snatched up the phone.

'Are you totally crazy?' snapped Woody.

'No, no I'm not. I don't care what you say, I'm calling the police,' she said. 'This is my home.' Her voice cracked with emotion. Her hands shook. 'I can't live like this, they can't threaten me, they can't; it's ridiculous. I haven't done anything wrong.'

Woody grabbed her wrist. 'Don't. It'll make things worse.'

She spun round to confront him. 'What do you mean, *don't*? You can't tell me what to do. I'm being threatened in my own home by the same thugs that nearly killed my brother. How can it make things any worse if I get them arrested? Tell me.'

He didn't move. Sarah snatched her hand away and fumbled to unlock the phone, fingers trembling.

'I'll sort it out,' he said.

Sarah glanced up. 'How can you sort it out? Aren't

these the same guys who you were frightened of?'

He nodded. 'Yes, but I know them,' he said. 'I know what they're like. I know what they want.'

Sarah stared at him. 'And that's going to help?'

'I'll talk to them. If you go to the police it will make it worse. Promise me.'

'You keep saying that. If you know who they are why don't you just give the police their names and stop them? How the hell can it get any worse than it already is?'

'Believe me it can get a lot worse than this.'

'So what am I supposed to do?' she said. In her hand the phone screen shut down.

'Marry me,' Woody said. 'Please, Sarah. I will make sure that they don't ever come round here again. I promise you. Just say you'll do it. I'll make all this go away.'

Sarah laughed and then, when she realised that he was deadly serious, said, 'I don't want to marry you, Woody, I love Josh.'

Woody nodded and then took a piece of paper from his pocket and set it down on the table alongside the mug of tea.

'Let me know what you decide tomorrow,' he said, and turning away headed back upstairs.

'What if they come back?' she called after him.

'They won't,' he said, without looking round.

When her phone started to ring she almost jumped out of her skin. Sarah glanced at the caller id: it was Josh. She pressed the button to decline the call, hoping he would think she was still at the hospital, and then she texted him:

'Sorry. Can't talk now. Love, S x', she typed and then pressed send.

And then Sarah picked up the piece of paper that Woody had left and unfolded it. It was a cheque for twenty thousand pounds, unsigned, but made out in her name. Sarah dropped it as if it was on fire.

Sarah

'What did you do with the cheque?

'I left it on the table.'

'And do you know what happened to it?'

'No, it was gone in the morning.'

'So did you call Josh after your conversation with Woody?'

'And say what? No, I didn't. In the end I texted him again later just to say that I was okay, just tired and that I was going to go straight to bed.'

'And what did Josh do?'

'He texted me back to say that he loved me and if there was anything I needed or wanted all I had to do was call. And he wished me sweet dreams.'

'You didn't mention Woody's offer?'

'No, I didn't know what to say to him and Woody had made it crystal clear that I wasn't to tell anyone about our arrangement.'

'But you could have? The police, Josh – friends?'

'You weren't there. You say Woody's offer like I had some kind of a choice but it wasn't like that. It didn't sound like an offer; it sounded more like a threat.'

Chapter Ten

They could both hear the phone ringing. Sarah glanced over her shoulder towards the closed bathroom door but said nothing.

'Do you want to go and get that?' Ryan asked when it was obvious that whoever it was wasn't going to ring off. 'I don't mind if you want to go and answer it. I can manage in here now. Really.'

Sarah shook her head. 'No, you can't, and it's fine. A couple more rings and the machine will cut in. If it's important they'll leave a message. Are you ready?'

Ryan nodded. It was a few days later. The hospital had kept him in to make sure that he was stable: make sure his brain didn't swell, make sure that the damage to his eye wasn't permanent, not that Sarah had talked to him about that.

She had taken time off to drive to Addenbrookes and pick him up, helping him gingerly into the car, trying to strap him in without hurting him. He'd been home long enough to eat, long enough to say that he hadn't had a bath since the night he was admitted to hospital. Long enough to make Sarah's heart ache. There was so much she needed to say to him but it didn't feel like now was the right moment, although if not now, then when?

Climbing the stairs to the bathroom Ryan had moved like an old man. She had helped him off with his clothes, dropping the ones he had brought home with him, crisp with dried blood, grease and gravel into the dirty washing basket.

'Okay,' she said. 'If you're sure that you're ready. The water's not too hot. I'm just worried that it's going to hurt.'

Ryan laughed grimly. 'I'll be fine. Just go for it,' he said.

'Tell me if it's too much.'

'Don't worry, I will.'

He was perched on the edge of the bath, with a towel wrapped around his waist. Sarah stared at his body. It was hard not to, although she felt uncomfortable seeing him as good as naked. He was muscular, tanned golden brown from working outdoors with his shirt off. The last time Sarah had helped Ryan into the bath he had been a little boy, six, seven maybe, certainly not a man. But the sight of a mass of bruises and cuts offset her self-consciousness and discomfort. Ryan's body was a mess, a war zone.

Gently, Sarah peeled away the great wad of dressings from his shoulders and back, trying hard not to hurt him, trying hard not to cry, trying hard not to be angry or to scream at him for being so stupid. There was so much that needed to be said, but for the moment the screaming stayed on the inside.

Since Ryan had been attacked she had barely been able to sleep or eat or think about anything else; every thought, every moment of every day she found her mind being dragged back to Ryan, and Josh, and the money and the men banging on her door, and Woody and his proposition.

After all he was right, when it came right down to it; what choice did she have? How could she ever be safe again while Ryan owed so much? Sarah turned the thoughts over and over and over in her head, and when she was asleep she dreamt about it. In her dreams the men were banging on the door, breaking in through the windows, tearing up her home, setting fire to the house, beating her and far, far worse. She was exhausted.

Ryan gasped. Here and there the scrapes and grazes had wept and glued the fabric pads to Ryan's skin. He winced as she eased them off and dropped them into the bin.

'How're you doing?' she asked.

He nodded. 'I already told you I'm fine. I'm looking forward to getting into the bath.'

'Just a couple more to go,' she said. 'And I've put some salt in the water. As well as bubbles, not so much that it'll sting but it'll help clean the cuts and those grazes.' Sarah had left the big dressing across his lower back until last.

'Last time I put you in the bath you were about six,' she said, trying hard to keep the shock and the despair out of her voice. It felt like she had been looking out for Ryan all her life. It wasn't going to do either of them any good if she caved in now. 'Come on; let's get you in the bath.' She made the effort to sound bright and competent, as he got to his feet.

'That's it, just hang on to me, that's it, gently now, gently,' Sarah said, taking his towel as she tried to support him, trying to find a part of him that didn't look as if it might hurt, while all the while trying not to stare at the livid bruises, the angry purple patterns of trainer soles stamped into his skin, or the scrapes and the cuts. The expression of pain on his face made her flinch with him, as she helped him over the edge and took some of his weight as he lowered himself very slowly into the warm water.

'God, that feels so good,' he sighed, letting out a long slow breath as the warm bubbly water sucked him down. 'Oh yes, that is fantastic.'

'You'll be all right now?' Sarah asked, looking away. 'I won't be very far away if you need me, just give me a shout when you want to get out. And there's a plastic jug on the side there if you want to wash your hair or do you need me to do it?'

Ryan shook his head. 'No, I'm good to go now,' he said, letting himself sink even lower into a sea of bubbles. Sarah looked back at him as she picked the towel up and hung it up on the back of the door. 'I've put your robe on the chair,' she said. 'And I wondered, are you going to be staying in the house or are you going back downstairs? I could make up the spare room if you wanted me to?'

'I just want to get back to my own place really,' he said. 'Sleep in my own bed.'

In spite of everything Sarah was relieved that Ryan was back home. His face was a mess. His body wasn't much better, although his clothes seemed to have saved him to some extent. He looked tired and lost and vulnerable. The steam from the hot water had twisted his sun-kissed hair into ringlets.

'Downstairs, back in my flat,' he continued. 'I need to get some sleep, and get back to normal.'

Normal. What a joke. What was normal now, she thought grimly.

'Sarah,' he said, as she opened the bathroom door.

'Yes? What is it?' she asked.

'Thank you,' he said.

Ryan didn't turn round, his voice was low and even and she didn't know how to reply, so instead she turned to stare at him, but it appeared that Ryan's attention had moved back to his bath, he was tipping his head back, letting himself slide lower down in amongst the bubbles, looking as if he didn't have a care in the world.

Something flared white hot in her stomach. Thank you? *Was that all?* It felt like she had been dismissed. There were so many things that Sarah wanted to say to him, so many things that she didn't know where to start.

With the words all crammed up in her throat, Sarah hurried out onto the landing and downstairs, tears rolling down her face. *Thank you?* Did Ryan mean for the bath or for what she had agreed to do for him? Had he any idea of the position he had put her in? And worse still what choice did she have but to go through with what Woody was proposing if she didn't want Farouk's thugs to kill Ryan or for her to end up like him, or worse?

Sarah turned slowly and went back upstairs. When she opened the bathroom door Ryan was lying on the bottom of the tub, with his knees bent and his head submerged beneath the water. As she came in he exploded up from beneath the bubbles, sweeping the water back over his face and hair with both hands.

'For fuck's sake, now what?' he said, sounding annoyed. 'I'm fine, all right? I was just having a soak. I'll give you a shout if there's anything I want. Didn't I just say that? You can go and get on with whatever it is you do.'

'Whatever it is I *do*?' Sarah stared at him. 'You need to know that thank you isn't enough,' she said. 'Nowhere near. You have got no idea what you've done, have you?'

He looked heavenwards. 'Oh that's right, Sarah. I wondered how long the Florence Nightingale act would last,' he said. 'It'll be fine. It'll be okay, it's just a case of putting things right. That's all. Now are you going to get out and leave me to my bath?'

How had he got the nerve to be annoyed with her? How had he got the nerve to dismiss her?

'*Just putting things right*? Is that what you think? Just putting things right – what is that supposed to mean, Ryan? You're not putting anything right. You never do. I'm the one putting things right. I always end up clearing up your mess. If you are so keen to get the money paid off and keep Woody in the country why don't you marry him yourself? Go through a civil partnership, whatever it takes. If you're that keen to get him to give you the money and get these people off your back and he is that keen to stay in the country, why not? Why me, Ryan? Why have I got to do this, just tell me, will you?'

For a moment Ryan just stared at her open mouthed and then he laughed. 'Can you hear yourself? Are you crazy? Because it wouldn't work, Sarah, that's why. There's no way. No one who knows me would buy that I was gay, and if anyone seriously thought Woody was gay there is no way he could ever go home. Ever. No – it's not happening. Okay? The story needs to be credible. That's what Woody said.'

'The story?' She stared at him. 'You've discussed it with him?'

'Yes, of course I have,' said Ryan, squeezing a sponge of water over his chest, as if all this was the most normal thing in the world, and then his expression softened. 'Sarah, come on, you know I can't have sorted this out without you. I know what you're doing for me. But the bottom line is it's just a piece of paper, and a couple of years, that's all. No big deal. You get married, Woody gets his leave to remain, you get divorced. That's it.'

'For you maybe.'

He puffed out his lips. 'For you too if you could just lighten up. Don't sweat it,' he said.

She stared at him, furious, and for a moment Sarah realised that she wanted to finish off what Farouk's thugs had started, and then she turned away; it was a dead end, this road. No way out, but the path she was already on, unless she went to the police, and then god knows what would happen.

'It'll be fine,' said Ryan, slipping back under the water. 'Trust me.'

Sarah took a moment or two to compose herself, and with the pulse still banging in her ears she picked up the laundry basket and went back downstairs to the kitchen, struggling to find a way to distract herself. As Sarah started to sort the clothes, she picked up the house phone and pressed the key to pick up the voice mail, clicking the button that turned it on to speaker-phone so she could have both hands free and work while she listened.

'You have one new message,' said the electronic voice. 'Message received today at 11.20 am.'

Sarah did a calculation; it had to have been while she was out picking Ryan up.

There was a metallic beep and then the sound of Josh's voice. 'Hello, this is a message for Sarah Reynolds. Hi, Sarah, if you're there, can you pick up? I'm not quite sure what's going on at the moment.' He hesitated, making noises that echoed his uncertainty. 'I wanted to see if you were you okay? Can you call me? I've been round to the nursery and Anessa said you're taking a couple of weeks off. I wondered how Ryan was doing. If you need anything you only have to ring, you know that. I dropped by the house earlier but I couldn't make anyone hear, and your mobile goes straight to voice mail. The hospital said Ryan was out...' There was a pause and then he laughed. 'Sorry, this sounds like I'm stalking you. Can you please ring me? I just need to know you're okay. I realise you're probably up to your eyes – and if you need a bit of space at the moment, then that's fine – I understand – it's fine. Just let me know how you are, will you? I'll try again later.'

The sound of his voice was like an embrace. Sarah stood very still. There was a pain in her chest, along with the ocean of tears that threatened to overwhelm her. She closed her eyes, took a breath, and then – making a decision – set the linen basket down on the table, picked up the phone and started to key in Josh's phone number. It had been a mistake not to tell him what was going on. He needed to know. It would make things so much simpler if he was in the loop. If she could just see him. She missed him and, whatever Woody said, he deserved an explanation. She heard the ring tone.

'Would you like me to deal with him?' asked Woody.

Sarah jumped; she had no idea that Woody was in the house, let alone behind her or eavesdropping on her. Hearing him, she gasped and swung round, the phone slipping through her fingers and dropping to the floor as she turned. The phone's case smashed as it hit the ground, fragments skittering across the tiles.

'I'm so sorry,' he said. 'I didn't mean to scare you. Here, let me help.' Woody dropped to his knees to retrieve the broken pieces, gathering them up into a cupped hand. 'Were you were planning to ring him back?'

She nodded. 'I have to explain to him.'

He said nothing.

'And what did you mean, *deal* with him?' asked Sarah, not moving.

'Call him, talk to him. What did you think I meant?' And then he pulled a face and laughed. 'For goodness sake, Sarah, I've already told you. You made your decision. It's all over and done with. You're safe now. I've spoken to Farouk and he's called his thugs off. What happened to Ryan wasn't my fault.'

'Or mine,' said Sarah.

Woody said nothing.

'But it was convenient, wasn't it?' said Sarah grimly, as he got back to his feet. He handed the phone to her and she slid the batteries back into what was left of the casing.

'You're right. It was convenient. I do want to stay here, and so yes this will obviously help me. And yes, I'm sorry it had to happen like it has, Sarah, but I want our arrangement to be as amicable as we can make it.'

'Amicable? How can it be amicable, Woody? You're buying me.'

He stared at her, his expression hardening, his eyes glassy. 'You had a choice.'

'What choice would that have been?' she said. 'You know as well as I do that I had no choice. There was no other way out that I could see. So it was a case of take you up on your offer or see Ryan killed and me beaten up or worse – and still owe those thugs the money? I didn't have any kind of choice and you know it. You're forcing me into this.'

'Force is such an ugly word, Sarah,' Woody said in a calm even voice, as if he was the reasonable one. 'And this is not just about me; there is Ryan to consider too.'

Sarah stared at him.

'It's him who made the decision. Him who borrowed the money. Without you he would probably be dead by now.' Woody smiled. 'I'm part of the solution not the problem. You need to see it for what it is. It is purely a business arrangement, a solution that is mutually beneficial to all parties. Perhaps it might be easier if I spoke to Josh. What do you think? After all we don't want him messing things up or getting tangled up with Farouk, or ending up in an alley like Ryan, do we?'

Sarah couldn't take her eyes off him. 'Is that a threat?'

He smiled but there was no warmth in his expression. 'No, I'm just saying that if you think about it, it's better if Josh knows nothing about our arrangement, that way he can't say anything that would screw things up, and he can't get himself into any trouble. Farouk isn't someone to mess with.'

'What does Josh have to do with Farouk?'

'Well obviously I had to explain to him how our deal was going to work out.'

'You told Farouk about me and Josh?' said Sarah.

Woody nodded. 'He wanted to know exactly how Ryan was going to get the cash. What the deal was. He wanted to be certain that he would get what was owed to him, and that we weren't trying to scam him.'

Sarah bit her lip. 'I need to explain to Josh.'

'I've already told you, you can't explain. Would you like me to do it for you? Just have a word.'

'And tell him what? You just said yourself that you can't explain – so what are you going to tell him? That you're marrying his girlfriend? That you're buying her to ensure her brother doesn't get his head kicked in? I love him, Woody. I have to talk to him. I want to explain what's going on. How's it going to look if you do it? The fact I can't or won't talk to him will only make things worse not better. He's worried about me. He's not going to give up. I'm not saying that he'll be happy about it but he deserves to know what's going on. Please.'

Woody hesitated, and then he nodded. 'You're right. It would be better coming from you. But you can't tell him about us getting married; you understand that, don't you? If anyone finds out that this is a sham marriage we will be arrested. And if that happens then you'll be left with your little brother's loan to pay off and those thugs on your doorstep.' He smiled, leaning back against the table. 'You should be grateful that I'm helping you out.'

'Grateful?'

He nodded.

Sarah stared at him, surely he couldn't be serious? Apparently he was. He held his ground, facing her down.

'What do I tell Josh then?' she said.

They were standing face-to-face, practically toe-to-toe. Sarah felt anything but grateful. She felt driven into a corner and angry and hurt, and more than all of those things she felt powerless to change any of it. 'If it's just a business arrangement, and you've already told Farouk, then why shouldn't I tell Josh?'

'Because I said so. Farouk won't be telling anyone, but if you tell Josh, then how do you think he's going to react? And who will he decide to tell about it? And if you tell him then who else will you think needs to know? It has to be a secret, Sarah. You can't say anything. Is that clear?'

'So what can I tell him? *What*?' Her voice was rising. 'How can he and I carry on our relationship if I'm getting married to you? I love him, he loves me. He was going to move in with me. How can we do that now? *How*?' she demanded, voice full of tears. She knew that the truth was that they couldn't, not without telling Josh the truth, not without some sort of an explanation, and Woody had made it clear that that wasn't on the cards.

He shrugged. The wrecked phone rang in Sarah's hand. She turned it over. 'It's Josh,' she said, holding the phone out towards him.

'Then you'd better answer it then, hadn't you?' said Woody.

Sarah stared at him. 'I thought you just said I wasn't to talk to him?'

Woody nodded. 'I did, but you're right, you need to tell him yourself or he'll just keep ringing and coming round, causing trouble.'

'He's not causing trouble. He wants to talk to me.'

Woody smiled. 'So there we are – you've got your wish. Talk to Josh.' He pressed the button to speaker phone and set the handset down on the table.

'Hello?' said Josh.

'Hello,' said Sarah nervously, sitting down at the table.

'Sarah?' She could hear the relief in his voice. 'Is that you? I'm glad I've finally managed to get through to you. I've been really worried. Are you all right?'

'Yes, I'm fine. Thank you.'

'Are you sure, you sound a bit odd.'

Sarah's eyes met Woody's.

'No, I'm fine. Really. Just—'

'Just what? What's the matter? It's been hell not knowing how you are and what's going on. Is Ryan okay now? Has he got any idea who did it? I was just on my way round. What happened?'

So many words, so many thoughts.

Sarah didn't know where to start. Woody raised his eyebrows, a gesture of encouragement, an admonishment to get on with it, she couldn't decide which.

She took a breath. The truth was that there was only really one option if she wanted to go through with this and keep the two men she loved most in the world safe.

'I'm so sorry, Josh. I didn't know how to tell you. I can't see you again,' she said softly, so softly that she could hear the sound of her heart breaking over the top of the words.

'What?' Josh gasped as if she had punched him. 'What do you mean? I don't understand. Let me come round – let's talk.'

'I can't,' she said thickly.

'What do you mean you *can't*? What's happened? What's the matter?'

'I just can't,' she repeated. She looked up at Woody. His expression was neutral but there was something in his eyes, something dark and triumphant that made her shiver. 'I didn't know how to tell you. I'm not ready,' she said, not taking her eyes off Woody. 'It was a mistake. I think it would be better if we didn't see each other again.'

'Sarah. Wait. We don't have to rush this, we can take our—'

'Please, I've got to go now,' she said, before Josh could finish. She knew what he was going to say. 'I'm so sorry, really, really sorry.'

Woody nodded.

And with that Sarah hung up and closed her eyes tight shut, trying to hold back the tears.

'There, that wasn't so hard, now was it?' he said.

The sob bubbled up from low in her belly, a tidal wave of sorrow and grief. 'How can you possible say that?' she sobbed. 'I love him.'

'I didn't ask you to finish with him. Did I?'

Sarah swung round, to face Woody, the frustration and fury bubbling through her. 'What else could I have done – what else? Tell me? I hate this – do you understand. Between you and Ryan you have destroyed my life.' The truth was she didn't see any other way out, and she loved him too much to get him mixed up in whatever it was that Woody or Farouk had planned. And she had sensed the threat.

The phone rang again. This time Woody took out the batteries and set them and the phone alongside her.

'You need to pull yourself together,' he said. He held out his hand. 'Why don't you let me keep your mobile for you, then he can't hassle you.'

She shook her head. 'I'm not giving you my phone. For god's sake, Woody. Why would I want to do that? All my numbers are in it and I need it for work. No, haven't you had enough?' She replaced the batteries.

He shrugged. 'Please yourself.'

As he spoke her mobile began to ring again.

'I was just trying to make things easier for you. This will soon all be over. We've got a wedding to arrange.'

She took a breath but before she could speak, Woody continued. 'I don't want anyone to have any doubt that this wedding is the real thing. You understand, don't you? You have to look like you mean it.'

'Or what?' she snapped, backhanding the tears away.

'Let me explain how things are, Sarah,' he said leaning in so close that she could feel his breath on her face. 'I've given Farouk's friends a little sweetener to keep them off Ryan's back until after the wedding. It'll hold them off till then, but it won't hold them forever. I've told them they can have the rest as soon as we're married. You understand? So it needs to work. If it falls through then we'll both be in big, big trouble. You understand me?'

'How do you know that will work?'

He grinned, a long lazy unsettling grin. 'I know Farouk,' he said. 'I know how he thinks. I know how he works. I know what he wants. Trust me it will be just fine. He'll wait, just not for long.'

Cambridge Evening Times
Unidentified body found in barn by school children

Police are seeking information from the public after the badly decomposed body of an adult male was found by school children in a derelict field barn near Soham, Cambridgeshire while they were searching for a lost dog.

A police spokesperson told reporters that they were awaiting forensic reports to help establish the identity of the man. The body had been there some time and attempts to identify the body had been hindered both by the passage of time and by a failed attempt to burn down the field barn at some stage, though the police were unable to confirm that these two incidents are related.

Police are currently working on the theory that the man may be in the country illegally, possibly as an agricultural worker. Recent raids on local farms have uncovered large groups of men working illegally, and kept like virtual prisoners in a number of isolated locations throughout East Anglia.

Any members of the public who have any information should contact ...

Sarah

'And then Woody told me the reason he was home was that he had made an appointment for us to go and see the registrar and that the sooner we went the better.'

'And you agreed to that?'

'It felt like the ground was slipping away from under my feet. It didn't feel like I had any choice. He said they would want to ask me questions to make sure it wasn't a sham marriage. I laughed.'

'And how did he react?'

'He didn't think that it was funny. He said he was paying me a lot of money to keep my mouth shut and bail Ryan out and that I needed to understand what was at stake, and that if they found out that we were lying, if he got into any kind of trouble, *then the law would be the least of my problems, he didn't like to think what would happen if he didn't pay Farouk.'*

'They?'

'The authorities. The immigration people. He said I needed to get my head around the idea that this had to work and work well. "Be happy, smile" he said. "You're going to get married. You'll need to learn these questions and answers before we go to the Register Office".'

And how did that make you feel?'

'Sick.'

Chapter Eleven

'So how did you and Mustapha meet?' the Registrar was asking. She was smiling, her voice had a warm upward lilt; she had a pen poised over a pad, and although it might seem like any other conversation, these were the questions Sarah needed to get right for the wedding to go ahead. She tried to remember to smile, after all this was meant to be a happy occasion.

The woman tucked a stray tendril of hair back behind her ears. She reminded Sarah of her mother; she had a kind tired face that good make-up and an expensive haircut couldn't hide, and for the briefest of moments Sarah wondered if it wouldn't be better if she just told the truth, and stopped all this before it went any further. She wanted to be with Josh; she wanted her life back to how it was, not this charade.

The woman lifted her eyebrows in an, *"I'm waiting"* expression.

'Through my brother. Ryan brought Woody home,' Sarah said with a smile. See that wasn't so hard, now was it?

'Woody?' said the woman, tipping her head to one side.

'Mustapha. Everyone calls him Woody,' Sarah said quickly, broadening out the smile, wondering then if it had been too quick. She wondered if the woman would think she was too glib, too slick, could she guess that Sarah was bending the truth? Could she see that Sarah was lying?

The woman nodded and wrote something and then glanced down at the paperwork in front of her. 'And it says here that you are currently living together?'

Sarah nodded.

'And how long have you been cohabiting?'

Sarah glanced upwards; Woody had been coaching her all week. 'Don't just recite it,' he'd said. 'Like you've learned it by rote – be normal, be natural. Hesitate, reflect, consider.'

She didn't feel either normal or natural. 'Almost a year; about ten months now I think.'

The woman was still smiling, apparently moving her attention away from her checklist. 'Okay. And will any of Mustapha's family be coming to the wedding?'

Sarah smiled back; she knew this one: 'No unfortunately not, his dad is quite elderly and infirm, and his mum doesn't want to travel on her own. It's a real shame but you can understand it, and Woody has said we'll go over there as soon as we can. I think they're hoping there will be another ceremony once we get there. Certainly a big family party. So no, but lots of his college friends will be there, and mine, obviously.'

The woman raised her eyebrows. 'So will you be converting?'

Sarah hesitated. 'I'm not sure...' she began, no longer on safe ground, no longer on script. Was the woman even allowed to ask that? Sarah wondered if she should say something or refuse to answer, but how would being that defensive look? 'I don't think so. To be honest I'm not really religious,' she said.

'But if you're thinking of having a ceremony in Quetta...'

'I know, Woody and I keep talking about it. I'm hoping that maybe we can just get away with a big family party. I'm not sure how it works over there.'

The woman nodded and wrote something down on her pad. 'Is Mustapha religious?' Her tone was casual.

Sarah shook her head. 'No, not really.'

'But I can see he might want to please his family. I believe there is the equivalent of a civil marriage; maybe they have the equivalent of a blessing. It might be worth trying to finding out? I can give you details of who you will need to contact.'

Sarah nodded. 'Thank you,' she said, attempting a smile. 'You know what men are like with arrangements.' Don't try too hard.

'And what about brothers and sisters, other family?'

'My brother, Ryan, will be coming. He's going to be giving me away. But Woody is an only child. He has cousins though and we've invited them. I'm really hoping they'll be able to make it. It would be so good to have some of his family there.'

Sarah had no idea if this was true or not but it was what Woody had told her to say. 'Family and photos, that's what we need,' he'd said.

The woman was still smiling and nodding. Sarah, back on safe ground, made the effort not to sigh.

'So there we are, we're more or less there,' the woman said, glancing down at her list. 'Have you thought about what you want for the wedding? For the ceremony?'

'I haven't thought about much else,' said Sarah, glancing up to see Woody waiting for her out in the foyer. He was looking at her, smiling. He had already had his question and answer session. Sarah made the effort to smile back.

'We obviously need to talk to you both about flowers and guest numbers and what music you'll be having. And the readings – if you'd like readings? We have a booklet if you need some inspiration. I know it can sometimes be a bit daunting.'

Sarah nodded.

'And have you chosen your dress?'

The woman seemed genuinely interested. Sarah

122

felt herself redden. 'Not yet – I wanted to make sure we had got a date. You know, so I could plan. But I've been looking,' she added hastily.

The woman nodded. 'Very sensible, you need to be sure that you've got the right one. Anyway now you can start sorting things out, can't you? Full steam ahead.'

'Yes,' said Sarah.

'Excited?' asked the registrar.

'Not exactly,' said Sarah.

The woman raised an eyebrow.

Sarah managed to laugh. 'I'm a bit nervous,' she said.

The woman nodded sympathetically. 'You're not alone in that but I'm sure you'll be just fine,' she said. 'And try not to fret too much. We'll make sure you and Mustapha have a lovely day. You're in safe hands, trust me.'

If only that were true, Sarah thought, as the woman got to her feet, indicating that the interview was over.

Sarah

'I couldn't sleep. I lay awake at nights thinking about everything that had happened, playing it over and over, and thinking about what I was doing. I wanted to talk to Josh face to face but after that day, when Ryan came home and I talked to Josh on the phone, everywhere I went Woody or Ryan came with me. I felt like a prisoner.'

'They followed you?'

'They took me or came with me, or waited for me to come out. Everywhere.'

'But hadn't they both told you that it was just a piece of paper?'

'I know that that is what they said, but that

123

wasn't how it felt. It felt like a sticky trap; like I was stuck. It felt like a dream half the time, I kept expecting to wake up. The worst part about it was I kept thinking that I hadn't done anything to find myself in that position. The thing with Ryan and the money and Woody and the visa. None of that was anything to do with me except that I was the answer. The answer to all their problems. And I couldn't see any way out – then one evening when I was about to go off to work Woody asked me if I wanted to invite the people from work to the wedding.'

'From the nursery?'

'And from the restaurant. They were talking about it in the kitchen, the two of them, Ryan and Woody, drinking beer, saying it would look much better if people came, and then Ryan said that maybe we could have the reception at the restaurant, and wondered if they could get a discount on the catering. Laughing like it was some big joke.'

'Had you talked to Ryan about what was going on?'

'He wouldn't talk to me about it. Not directly. I kept trying to get him on his own, tried to make him see sense and see what he had done, but he just said that it would be fine. Fine. There was nothing fine about it. He didn't even say he was sorry anymore. And then Woody said that he would organise the food, and that I needed a dress – you know, like a proper wedding dress.'

'And how did you feel?'

'Like a piece of meat.'

'And did you talk to Ryan about that?'

'I tried to but something had changed between us after that day when he came home from hospital. It's like he was blocking me out. Like he wasn't on

124

my side anymore. It was him and Woody. He kept telling me to lighten up, like it was nothing, that it would be over and done in no time, and then we could all get on with our lives. And I could see that for him it was true. By marrying Woody I had bought off Farouk; Ryan was home scot-free. They were talking about what they'd do, once things were settled.'

'Who were?'

'Woody and Ryan.'

'Okay and what did you think they meant by settled, Sarah?'

'Married, I suppose, with his right to remain. Woody kept saying that he could make some real money then. He and Ryan were always in the kitchen talking about what they would do next, how they planned to set up in business now they were going to be family. Next of kin.

Ryan kept on about how he had always wanted a brother. It was so crazy. It was like he pushed me to the outside edge. I wanted to shake him and try and make him understand. It felt like I'd sold my soul to save him, but he didn't see it that way at all. Once the bruises had faded he didn't seem to have any sense of what he'd done or what he'd done to me, and he was still swanning around in the van he'd bought like nothing had happened. Nothing. It felt like things were slipping away from me. Ryan wasn't paying anything towards the bills because with his fingers being broken he couldn't really work, and Woody said he was paying enough already – I practically had to beg the two of them for money to keep going.'

'And you were still working?'

'Yes, all hours that god sent, although it wasn't easy. The two of them didn't want me out of their sight. I think they were both afraid I might change

125

*my mind or make a run for it or something. And
they wanted me to tell everyone about the wedding.'*

Chapter Twelve

'Oh my god, you're getting married?' whooped Anessa, throwing her arms around Sarah and hugging her tight up against her chest. 'That is just brilliant. I'm so pleased for you. You are such a dark horse, Sarah. I didn't realise you and Josh were—'

'No, not Josh,' Sarah said hastily, stepping away and stopping Anessa dead in her tracks.

It was her first day back at work and she had been mulling over when to say something. Time, Woody said, was pressing. They hadn't got long. The wedding was just a matter of weeks away.

Sarah and Anessa had been busy restocking the plant tables out in the retail poly tunnels, trying to get everything sorted before the weekend rush. The air was heavy with the scent of loam and water, and the sweet high notes of the jasmine that they had been arranging on one of the displays.

Anessa pulled a face. 'What do you mean *not* Josh? But I thought...' She grinned. 'You're pulling my leg, aren't you?'

Sarah could feel her colour rising. 'No, no I'm not. I've been seeing someone else for a while, on and off before I started seeing Josh. I don't think either of us realised that it was serious, and then I met Josh and...' She paused. She had been rehearsing the lie, trying to make it sound plausible so that it would fend people off but now, said aloud, it sounded crazy.

Anessa was waiting, hanging on her every word.

'It's complicated,' Sarah fudged, waving Anessa's curiosity away. 'I think seeing me with someone else made him realise that he wanted to settle down. Wanted to make a commitment. ' She paused, not quite able to meet Anessa's eye. 'And me too, and so he asked me to marry him and I said yes.'

'So who is it then?' pressed Anessa.

'Woody,' Sarah began.

'Oh my god, not your lodger?' Anessa squealed. 'Oh wow. That is just so bad. You are such a naughty, naughty girl.' She wagged her finger at Sarah. 'I thought you said he was a bit of a nerd. Mind you they do say it's the quiet ones you have to watch. I'd never have guessed.' Anessa was giggling now. 'I never had any idea. Wow, that is just amazing. Bloody hell.'

Sarah realised that Anessa was totally taken in.

'So when is it, then? I am getting an invite, aren't I? Is it a church do?' She paused. 'He's Muslim presumably?'

Sarah hesitated. 'We're having a register office wedding. Saves all the hassle. Neither of us is really religious.'

Anessa nodded. 'God, that sounds so sensible. I wish someone would tell that to my mum and dad. So what are you going to wear? Have you got your dress yet? I saw this most amazing dress the other day. It would look fabulous on you. Maybe we could nip into town sometime and I could show it to you?'

Sarah nodded. Within no time at all the blue touch paper on the rumour mill caught light. By the end of the day everyone at the nursery, including half the customers knew that Sarah was getting married.

*

'Sarah, Sarah. Wait! Please.'

Sarah swung round at the sound of her name to see Josh running across the car park towards her. It had just started to rain, big fat droplets of rain that exploded onto the dry dusty tarmac. She was heading home. It was a few minutes after six and the nursery had closed for the day. Josh had pulled his jacket up to his ears; he was dressed for work in jeans and a tee shirt. His expression was somewhere between a smile and something more serious.

He had to have been waiting for her to come out. The sight of Josh made Sarah's heart ache. She hesitated for a split second, wondering if there was some way she could explain to him what was going on, something she could say that would make it right, but hadn't Woody already impressed on her she couldn't say anything, not a word? And that implied threat that if she didn't keep quiet that Josh would be in as much danger as Ryan. She turned and, putting her head down, hurried away from him.

'Please, wait,' Josh said, as he caught up to her, breathing hard. 'What on earth is going on? Can't we just talk, Sarah? Just stop for a minute, will you? What's happened? Have I done something?'

Sarah shook her head.

'No, no it's not you,' she said, trying hard not to catch his eye in case he could somehow see the truth. 'I'm really sorry, Josh. I can't stop. I've got someone waiting for me,' she said.

'I don't understand.'

Sarah glanced without focusing across the car park to where she knew Woody was parked up by the fence. Since she had gone back to work he had been dropping her off at the beginning of her shift and picking her up when she was done, and had told her that he thought it was a good idea if he gave her a lift until the wedding, maybe even longer, just in case she got any ideas. That's what he said, *any ideas*. He'd been laughing when he said, but she knew he meant it; he didn't trust her. She guessed he was worried that maybe she would change her mind about the wedding – as if she could. It felt as if she was on a very short leash. While at home Woody barely spoke to her but when she was out he had made it clear he would be watching her like a hawk.

So, even though Sarah couldn't see his face she knew Woody would be watching her now.

'Surely you can spare a couple of minutes, Sarah. Please,' Josh said.

She shook her head. 'I'm sorry. I really can't.' She pulled her coat tight around her and was about to walk off again when Josh caught hold of her arm.

'Look, will you just stop and talk to me? For god's sake, Sarah, what'll it take? I just don't understand what happened. Are you okay? I'm worried about you.' She could hear the frustration in his voice along with his concern, distress and confusion. 'I'm not going to hurt you or be angry, Sarah, I love you. I thought you loved me. I don't understand what's going on here. I'd just like some sort of explanation. Is it too much to ask?'

Of course it wasn't. Sarah made the mistake of looking up, and heard the breath catch in his throat when he saw her face. She didn't know what it was Josh saw there, but when he spoke again his tone was more anxious, softer, worried. 'What the hell is going on, Sarah. Are you ill? Is that what this is about? Let me help – let me in – I want to help you.'

She shook her head. 'You can't,' she said, 'I'm fine. I just need to get home.'

'You don't look fine.'

'Really, I am, but I have to go.'

'When can I see you?' he said, as she pulled herself clear of him. 'We could meet up for a coffee or something. Or lunch? Whatever it is, whatever the problem is, at least let's talk about it. Let me help you.'

'You can't, Josh. Please. I can't see you again,' Sarah said, trying hard to keep the emotion out of her voice. 'Please just leave me alone.'

'What do you mean, *can't*?'

'I mean I don't want to,' she said, more carefully.

'I don't believe you. What the hell is going on here, Sarah?'

'Nothing. Please go now, Josh, *please*. I don't want to see you again. Do you understand?'

'I understand what you're saying, but I don't believe you.'

'I have to go now,' said Sarah.

And with that she pulled away from him, her heart pounding as she hurried across to the car. When she got to the passenger side Woody leaned over and opened the door for her. 'Get in,' he said, tone neutral.

Sarah nodded and did as she was told, keeping her chin tucked down onto her chest.

Josh stood watching the car as it pulled away. As they drove out of the car park, Sarah could see him in the wing mirror, Josh finally turning and slowly walking back to his truck.

'So what did he say to you?' Woody asked, pulling out into the early evening traffic.

'Nothing much,' Sarah dropped her bag into the foot-well and made a show of arranging her coat so that she didn't have to look Woody in the eyes. She didn't want him to see the pain and the welling glassy tears. She didn't want to give him the pleasure.

'I'm not stupid, Sarah. I saw him talking to you. What did he say to you?' he pressed.

'He just wanted to talk.'

'And?'

'And nothing. I told him it was over. That's all.'

'So, did you arrange to meet him? To talk to him later maybe?' Woody's tone was reasonable, almost conversational, as if the main thrust of his attention was elsewhere, but Sarah wasn't fooled. It felt like he was trying to lull her into a false sense of security, to catch her out, to make her trip and fall.

'No, of course not. What can I say to him?' she said, deliberately keeping her tone light to match his.

'So why was he here? Did you ring him? Arrange for him to meet you after work?'

'No. He just turned up. And I told him I didn't want to see him again. He wants to know why. It's not unreasonable.'

Woody nodded as if there was some possibility that he might agree. They joined the rush hour queue; Woody with his eyes firmly fixed on the road, said, 'Maybe I should ask Farouk to have a little word with him.'

Sarah turned and stared at him. 'What?'

'Maybe. I mean what does it take to make this guy back off? He's rung the house, left god knows how many messages on the answer machine, and now pitched up here. How many hints does the guy need? Seems to me that if he can't take no for an answer, maybe Farouk can help him with that.'

Sarah swallowed hard, tempering her voice. 'Why would you want to do that? What has Josh ever done to you?'

'Turning up here after you told him it was over, ringing. Maybe he needs the situation explaining to him a little more clearly.'

'I'm already doing what you ask, Woody, leave Josh alone.' She tried to make it sound like a command and not as if she was begging.

Woody turned round and grinned, then threw back his head and laughed. 'Had you worried there, didn't I? You should see your face. What sort of person do you take me for?'

Speechless, Sarah stared at him; wasn't that the problem? She had no idea what sort of person Woody was.

'Just make sure you leave him alone, don't contact him, don't answer any calls. And if he turns up here

132

again, or at the house, I want you to tell me, is that clear?'

'You're going to know anyway – you pick me up, you drop me off.'

He dropped his hand on her thigh. 'Only because I care about you, Sarah. I don't want you getting any funny ideas, and I don't want Farouk getting any either, if you get my drift. There is too much at stake.'

'You think Farouk will come after me?' said Sarah, appalled. The idea hadn't crossed her mind. She certainly hadn't considered Woody might be picking her up to protect her from Farouk. 'I thought you said we were safe, that you'd sorted it?'

'I have. But it always pays to be careful where Farouk is concerned,' Woody said. 'When are you at the nursery next?'

'Friday.'

'Okay, I want you to take the invitations in with you. We haven't got that long to get everything sorted out.'

'The invitations?'

He nodded. 'Yes, the wedding invitations; I printed them out this morning. Like I said before, the more people we have there the better.'

Sarah wanted to win at something; to feel some sense of control. 'Have you told your parents yet?' she asked.

'No.'

'Why not? You could email them. Or Skype them. Surely you should say something.'

'No,' he snapped angrily. 'And I don't want to talk about them. And I don't want you to talk about them. Is that clear?'

'Why not? Won't they want to know why you're staying in the UK, why you're not going home? Won't they want to know you're getting married?'

'No, just leave it alone.'

'But—'

The look he gave her dried the words in her throat.

Sarah

'So, you didn't have any contact with his parents before the wedding?'

'No, Woody was adamant. I wondered if he had fallen out with them about something else, maybe they didn't want him to stay – I don't know, but he was really uncomfortable about discussing his family.'

'How did the wedding go?'

'I was in a bit of a daze the whole day. It didn't feel real. Quite a few people came to the registry office. Although I didn't know half of them they seemed to know me. Some of them were friends of Woody's, quite a lot of Ryan's friends, and some people from work, some from the nursery, a couple from the restaurant. My boss couldn't come so he arranged for the flowers for the registry office.

'It was like a bad dream. I kept thinking I'd wake up. And I kept thinking – hoping – that Josh might turn up and save me. You know, like they do in films. I wanted to look over and see him there.'

'As a guest?'

'No, god no, not as a guest, standing there beside me instead of Woody.'

'And did you think that Josh might show up?'

'I didn't honestly know. I wondered if someone at the nursery might have said something to him. Told him about the wedding. I suppose I was grasping at straws.'

'So did he?'

'Turn up? No, and he didn't come to rescue me either.'

'And did Josh ring you before the wedding?'

'He might have – but... '

'But what, Sarah?'

'I don't really know if he called or not. I lost my phone. About a fortnight before the wedding it just vanished. I'd got no idea where I'd lost it, I was going through my handbag and just realised that it wasn't there.'

'You lost your phone?'

'That's what I assumed. I looked everywhere for it.'

'Was it on a contract?'

'No, pay-as-you-go. I rang to see if I could get my number back but then Ryan said he'd got an old phone that I could use. I needed one for work so I borrowed that one.'

'And you didn't see your phone again?'

'Not then, but later.'

Chapter Thirteen

'You look absolutely amazing, Sarah, you know that? And I just love your dress. Is it vintage?' Amy asked, topping up her wine glass as she did so. She worked at the nursery; she was in her twenties, blonde and plump. While Sarah and Anessa usually worked together on whatever needed doing, Amy worked on the tills and was good to work with if you didn't mind doing most of the work yourself.

Amy's hands were unsteady; the wine splashed onto the table, looking for all the world like a puddle of blood as it soaked into the white cloth. 'Whoops,' she giggled, making no attempt to clear it up, instead she steadied herself against the table and waggled the bottle in Sarah's direction, in invitation. 'You fancy a little top up?'

Sarah shook her head and pulled a roll of black plastic bags out of the kitchen drawer. 'No thanks. I've got one on the go somewhere,' she lied.

Amy sighed theatrically and then, grinning, poured the remainder of the wine into her own glass – not that she needed any more, she was already drunk. 'And you've lost so much weight,' she said, taking a handful of peanuts from a bowl tucked in amongst the debris on the table. 'Me and Anessa were saying you must be what? An eight now? Did you go on some sort of diet plan, or was it just nerves. What do they call it? The wedding day diet?'

She patted her own rounded belly. 'I'm living in hope that it'll work for me some day. Been a long time since I could get this lot into any thing close to a size eight. Not that I'd really want to, you know? I think I really want a man who likes me for what I am.' She fielded a wet belch with the back of her hand. 'They do say you're never as skinny as on your wedding day, don't they.' She took a slug from her glass and peered past Sarah. 'Ooh that's nice. You know Anessa is in there chatting up your husband, don't you?'

Sarah smiled indulgently. 'She's welcome.'

'Oh come on, you don't mean that. He's quite cute, your Woody. Not my type but I can see the attraction. Quiet. Strong. Anessa said he comes from the same place as her mum and dad do, wherever that is.'

Sarah nodded. 'Quetta. It's in Pakistan.'

Amy laughed. 'If you say so. I've got no idea, me. I'm lost as soon I'm out of Cambridge. Suppose you'll be going over there on holidays now? Bit different from a week in Spain.'

The kitchen table, along with every surface and worktop in the kitchen was littered with empty glasses, bottles, trays, dishes and discarded paper plates. Through the open door into the hall and from the sitting room beyond came the chatter of voices and laughter and the bass beat of dance music.

Amy picked up the bowl and tipped the last handful of nuts into her open mouth. 'You're not going to lose any more weight though, are you?' she said, with her mouth full. 'Only you're beginning to look a bit drawn round the eyes and a bit tired. Mind you I suppose planning this lot is enough to make anyone tired.'

Sarah, glancing out of the kitchen and through into the sitting room, realising that she hadn't been listening, pulled a face. 'What?'

'Weight. You're not going to lose any more, are you? That dress looks totally amazing on you but you can be too thin. I mean not that you are, not at the moment. But I don't think most blokes want to sleep with a skeleton. They like a bit of flesh on your bones. Don't you reckon?'

Sarah nodded but didn't reply; instead she began collecting up some of the debris, scooping it straight into the rubbish bag. While she'd come out of the sitting room on the pretext of checking up on the food and drink, in reality she just wanted to be on her own and get away from Woody and Ryan. Amy had caught her on her way out into the garden. Clearing up in the kitchen was a half-way house solution.

She took another look into the sitting room; Woody and Anessa were standing over by the sofa deep in conversation. Maybe Amy was right, maybe he was chatting her up. Sarah watched for a moment or two longer. Woody was laughing at something Anessa said and leaning in close as if he didn't want to miss a word.

'You can't do that,' Amy protested, breaking into Sarah's train of thought, as Sarah, with most of her attention fixed on the events in the other room, slid another pile of dirty paper plates into the rubbish bag.

'Sorry? Do what?' she said, bemused.

'Be in here clearing up. Not today. It's your wedding day; you shouldn't be clearing up other peoples' mess. Come here, let me help you. You go back and grab a dance with Woody and I'll do that. Save him from Anessa.'

Unsteady on crazily high heels Amy started to gather up some of the empty packets and pushed them into the sack, plastic cutlery and oddments of food scattering across the floor. She giggled. 'Maybe it would be better if we left it tonight, me and Anessa could come back and help you tomorrow if you wanted. We don't mind. You're not going away, are you?'

Sarah smiled grimly. 'It's fine. We'll manage.'

Amy leaned in close to Sarah, her breath sour

with the smell of white wine. 'You're a real dark horse, Sarah, you took us all by surprise, you know. Fancy you bagging yourself two decent fellas. Mind you, they do say it's always the quiet ones you've got to watch, don't they? I'm impressed.'

Sarah stared at her without speaking.

Amy tapped the side of her nose. 'But don't you worry, I won't let on about Josh.'

Sarah felt her colour rising. 'What's that supposed to mean?'

'Bit of fling before you settled down, was it, eh? And who can blame you. He's very easy on the eye.'

Sarah wondered if Amy was expecting some kind of a reply. 'Woody knows,' she began.

'What, about your romantic weekend away? Anessa told me that it was going out with him made Woody see what he was missing. But then again it must be nice to have two blokes fighting over you. Get it while you can that's my motto,' Amy slurred. 'Seems a real pity though. Josh seemed much more your type. Mind you, I won't say anything if you don't, and who wouldn't? That Josh is really fit.'

'Another one for the album?' said Ryan, popping his head around the open kitchen door, making Sarah jump. He peered out from behind the camera he had been carrying around all day. His eyes were bright, his face red, and he was grinning like a loon. It didn't take a genius to work out he was also pretty much wasted.

'Come on, come on, get in a bit closer. That's it – and a bit more. More. Say cheese.'

Amy leaned in even closer to Sarah, and putting her arm around her shoulder, held up her glass and mugged a huge smile, while Ryan snapped away.

'Lovely, I just want one more,' Ryan said.

'He was round the yard again yesterday morning looking for you,' Amy said, sotto voce. 'Josh.' And then to Ryan said, 'I'm thinking of getting a refill, d'you want one, Sweetie?'

'Just hang on there, won't be a minute. Don't go anywhere.'

Ryan was fiddling with something on the back of the camera, while peering myopically at the image on the screen.

'Drink?' Amy pressed.

'In a minute,' he said, attention elsewhere.

'What did you tell Josh?' said Sarah to Amy, dry mouthed.

'I've got it now. Can you just get back how you were,' Ryan said, waving them closer together. 'And smile; it's a wedding not a wake,' he giggled.

For him maybe.

'So what did you say,' Sarah pressed.

Amy was still grinning at Ryan and saluting him with her wine glass. 'Nothing much, we didn't really get a chance to talk. He came in and asked if you were there and then when he found out you weren't in he went. Why, what would you like me to tell him?' Her tone was mischievous. 'I mean Josh is a bit of a catch – presumably I'm right in thinking he's out of the frame now? Now you're married.' She laughed and raised her eyebrows.

'There we go. Come on. Let's just have one more. And smile,' said Ryan, still snapping away. Amy's smile was barracuda wide.

Sarah stared back at Ryan, willing him to go back to the party, but he didn't move.

'Are you going to come back in with everyone else, and have a dance?' he asked Sarah. 'Woody asked me to look for you. He's being pestered by some mate of yours.'

'He didn't look like he was being pestered to me.' Amy grinned. 'See I told you. Anessa. It's always the quiet ones you've got to watch.'

Ryan, oblivious, pressed on. 'He wanted to know where you were. I said I'd come and find you.'

'Can you tell him I'll be there in just a minute,' said Sarah, wanting to do no such thing. 'I just need a breath of air. I've got a bit of a headache.'

Ryan nodded. 'Okay, but don't be too long. He's getting a bit – you know – you know how he gets. You should be in there. With him.' And then to Amy said, 'I didn't catch your name. Are you having a good time? It's a great party, isn't it?'

Amy nodded.

Sarah stared at him wondering if he had any idea what he had just said. He lifted his camera to take another shot of the two of them. Amy pouted and giggled. 'Looking good there,' Ryan purred.

'So are you going to stop and have a drink with me then?' asked Amy, indicating the cans of beers stacked up on the counter top. 'Or are you too busy?'

'Don't mind if I do,' said Ryan. 'I just need to make sure we get lots of photos.' He turned his attention back to Sarah. 'You really ought to go back in there in with everyone else. Woody is getting worried.'

Woody had already coached Sarah on how important the wedding photos would be. *'You have to look like you mean it,'* he'd said that morning, standing at her bedroom door. That morning and every morning for the past week. *'Look like you want to be there. It's the only way it's going to work. It'll soon be over. I promise,'* he had said.

Sarah had been struggling to get into the wedding dress that she'd bought on Ebay. Not that it was too tight, far from it, instead it looked like she had borrowed it from a big sister. Sarah tried it on when it first arrived, and it had been fine then. She hadn't been able to bring herself to try it on in front of the mirror – after all, it only needed to fit – except that

141

now it didn't. It gaped under her arms, and around the neckline, and hung like a sack over her waist and hips. There were some safety pins in the dressing table drawer and a wide gold belt that she'd taken off another dress that she hoped, fastened around her waist, might bring it in a bit.

'Do you mind,' she'd snapped. Woody had knocked and then immediately opened the door. He looked her up and down, his expression neutral.

Everyone at work had asked about the dress, the dress, the damned dress, as if it was the only thing that mattered.

'Sorry. I thought you'd be ready by now. I just came to see how you were getting on. We need to be leaving in a few minutes. We're going to get married, remember?' he had said, with a lazy grin.

As if she could forget. She said nothing. What was there to say?

'It's meant to be a joke. You know, me opening the door and just walking in. It's what married people do.'

'I don't care what married people do,' she said. 'And you know full well that this isn't about being married, it's about *getting* married. Now can you get out of my bedroom and let me get ready?' Although she was wearing a slip underneath it, Sarah held the dress tight up against her body. Cream silk armour.

'Is that what you're wearing?' he asked.

'Yes, why?'

He pursed his lips. 'Nothing, I was just asking.'

'It fitted when I bought it,' she said defensively.

Woody looked her up and down and nodded. 'I'm sure it will look better when it's fastened. Do you want me to help you do it up? Or are you worried it might be bad luck for the groom to see the bride?'

'How much worse can it get?' she said grimly. 'This really isn't how I ever imagined my wedding

142

day being. I'm not sure I can do this, Woody.'

His tone softened. 'Of course you can, Sarah. It won't be long. Let's see what we can do with the dress, get the day over, and then we can get on with the rest of it.'

She looked up at him, until now his attitude had been cold, crisp, business-like, angry even. 'The rest of it?' she repeated.

He nodded. 'The rest of our lives. Just for today,' he said, 'Imagine that this is what you want, that this is what you've been dreaming about. That this is your moment – because in so many ways it is.'

Sarah stared at him, and felt her eyes fill up with tears. 'How can you say that?' she muttered. 'How can you possibly for one moment think that any of that is true?'

'I know you don't want to do this. I understand. Okay? Let's just put on a good show, make it work. Please,' he said, 'just for today. 'After all we're helping each other out. And because of what you're doing, you've saved Ryan and you've saved me.'

Sarah couldn't help wondering if he truly meant what he was saying, and then from behind his back he produced a bunch of red roses. 'I know they're not much, but I picked them for you, from the garden,' he said. 'I didn't think you'd have thought about a bouquet.'

He held them out towards her. They were wrapped around with cream tissue paper and raffia that had been in the kitchen drawer.

'Hang on; let me help you sort the dress out first.' He set the bouquet down on the dressing table. 'Do you want to put it on inside out and I can pin up the spare material. You've lost a lot of weight.'

'Worry,' she said grimly, pulling the dress on over her head.

He smiled. 'Haven't I already told you. There's

nothing for you to worry about now. It's all sorted,' he said. As he spoke he pulled a little tub of pills out of his suit jacket pocket and glanced at the label. 'Do you want one of these? They'll help calm your nerves. Just settle you. You look tired. I took them when I was doing my exams last year. They'll take the edge off.' He held them out towards her.

Sarah shook her head. 'No, thanks.'

'You're sure? Just one? They're not addictive.'

She nodded. After a moment or two he dropped them back into his pocket and picked up the box of safety pins.

'Turn around,' he said.

She found it disconcerting to have Woody standing so close to her, his fingers resting lightly in the small of her back as he zipped the dress up. She could feel his breath on her skin, smell his aftershave, pick out a thread of stubble across his jaw that had been overlooked. He worked methodically around the dress, getting her to put her hands on her head, and turning her around while he pinned the fabric where it gaped.

He was gentle, solicitous, standing back a couple of time to gauge the effect, reassuring her that it would all be just fine, and for a moment Sarah wondered if she had misjudged him. Maybe he really was helping them out after all, maybe he had just been clumsy in the way he had gone about it. Maybe.

Finally with the makeshift alterations made she put the dress back on, right sides out.

'There you are,' Woody said, turning her gently so she could look into the mirror. The improvement to the dress was immediately obvious. Sarah was thinner, paler, with dark rings under her eyes but the dress looked just fine now.

'That's better, isn't it? Let me just fix the belt for you. There we are. You look lovely.'

144

'Thank you,' she said, unsettled and completely wrong-footed by his kindness.

As if he could read her thoughts Woody said, 'I want this to work, Sarah. And I don't want to rush you but we really need to be going soon. I reckon another ten, fifteen minutes at the most, will that be enough for you to finish your make up or do you want longer?'

'That will be fine,' she said. It would be long enough to put some concealer on to try and hide the dark circles, long enough to apply lipstick and draw on some eyeliner, but not long enough to make any of this right.

Woody picked up the bouquet and held it out towards her.

'There we are, the final touch,' he said. He smiled. As she took the roses from him, Sarah felt the bite of a thorn, and wincing, stared down at her thumb. A bead of blood, the deepest darkest claret blossomed on the pad.

'Oh god, I'm sorry. Here, here, quickly,' said Woody, grabbing a tissue from the dressing table. 'You don't want to get blood on your dress. I'm sorry I thought I'd cut all the thorns off. Let me look.'

He reached out as if to take her hand but she held it tight. 'It's fine,' she said, putting her thumb in her mouth, although even as she was saying it Sarah knew that wasn't true; as she took it out and nipped the tissue tight to stop the bleeding she knew that there was something left in the wound, the tip of a thorn that hurt as she applied pressure.

There was a moment of awkward silence and then Woody had smiled and turned away. 'Okay. Don't be long, will you?' he said.

She had shaken her head and sat back at the dressing table, nipping her thumb and clutching it to her breast.

145

Sarah could still feel the thorn now, as she stood in the kitchen, watching Ryan and Amy flirting. She pressed her finger and thumb tight together so she could register the pain, just to let her know that none of this was a dream, however much she wanted it to be.

Ryan meanwhile had put the camera down and was cracking open another can. He glanced round the doorway as if there was chance he might be caught or told off. 'Did you see Mrs Howard from next door?' he said.

Sarah nodded. 'A little while ago. Why?'

'She said she wanted some copies of the photos. I was thinking it would be nice if I took one with you together. Woody was giving her the full charm offensive when I saw her. She must be eighty if she's a day. She was telling me that she thinks he's a real catch.'

'Does she?' said Sarah.

Ryan nodded and lapped up the suds where they bubbled out of the can. 'I better get going. Are you going back in? Maybe we can find her.'

'Or maybe Woody's hoping you'll rescue him?' suggested Amy. 'Go on, go and rescue your man.'

Sarah hesitated. 'Can you tell him I'm just talking to Amy in the kitchen?'

'I thought it was me talking to Amy in the kitchen,' said Ryan.

'That's right,' Amy slurred. 'And don't let him boss you about, start as you mean to go on, that's what I say. Show him who is boss.' She hiccupped and then she giggled and waved Ryan away with a little flap of her hands, and a salacious wink. 'I'll catch up with you later,' she said.

Ryan's grin widened. 'I'll hold you to that,' he said, heading back into the hallway.

The moment he was gone, Amy swung round. 'Okay so you can tell me now he's gone. I've been dying to ask – any man who pipped Josh to the post has got to be something special. So what's he like, this new husband of yours, aye? We thought you might be – well, you know.' She glanced fleetingly as Sarah's washboard flat stomach. 'Given you were getting married so quickly. I mean I know these days you don't have to get married, but you strike me as an old fashioned sort of a girl. Doing the right thing. Although to be honest I really thought you and Josh were the real deal—' Amy stopped mid-sentence. 'Sorry, not very tactful, under the circumstances.'

Ryan stuck his head back round the door. 'Woody said will you come in now. He's planning to do a first dance thing and I'm supposed to be videoing it. For the family album.'

Ryan winked as he said it.

Sarah pressed the thorn in her thumb; the pain was exquisite.

Chapter Fourteen

It was well after midnight before the last of the guests finally left. The house was a mess from top to bottom. There were bottles and cans, glasses and plates in every downstairs room, with odd ones left on the stairs and landing, and more on the tables out in the garden. Someone had been sick in the downstairs toilet and by the door there were upturned bottles wedged into the hedge, which glittered in the glow from fairy lights as they moved on the wind.

In the hallway on a table was a pile of wedding presents. There was a discarded plate in amongst them, along with half a can of beer.

'Thanks for coming,' Woody called after a gaggle of girls – the last of the guests to leave; they'd arrived late and brought vodka, and Sarah hadn't recognised them. The girls giggled and wobbled down the path towards the gate on impossibly high heels, holding each other up, doing a little fingertip wave as they headed off into the night. Sarah had no idea who they were, but they knew Woody and had been happy to pose for one of the endless wedding photos. Woody's precious wedding photos – between them Ryan and Woody must have taken hundreds.

Sarah was exhausted. Her head ached. She wanted her home back, but more than that she wanted her life back.

Ryan was drunk and some time during the evening had changed out of his suit and tie into a tee shirt and chinos. He had something red smeared across his front and there was a greasy stain on his trousers.

Sarah had taken off the wedding dress the minute they got back from the register office and, rolling it up into a ball, had stuffed it into a rubbish bag in her bedroom. As soon as she was alone she planned to dump it in the bin or better still burn it in the garden. If she never saw it again it would be too soon.

Woody was the only one still in his wedding outfit, his only concession to the late hour and the long day was that he had loosened his tie. As the front door finally closed Sarah felt the tension easing out of her shoulders. She headed into the sitting room, switched off the music and opened the windows, and opened curtains wide to let out the smells of the people, of beer and wine and hot dancing bodies and then she went into the kitchen and slumped down at the table.

No longer on show she twisted and wriggled the wedding ring off her finger, and when it wouldn't come off, put her finger in her mouth to get it wet to help ease it off. She hadn't realised that Ryan was watching her from the doorway.

'I just thought I'd come in and say good night,' he said. He was still holding a can of beer. 'It was a good do, wasn't it? It went well.' He looked round. 'Where's Woody got to?'

Sarah shrugged. 'I've got no idea,' she said.

He grinned. 'I thought that maybe I'd better make myself scarce. You know, leave the happy couple alone.' His tone was jokey and intimate. 'Wedding night and all that.'

Finally the ring started to move on Sarah's finger.

'What are you doing?' he asked.

'What does it look like?' Sarah said, finally easing the ring off. She got to her feet and, flipping open the pedal bin, dropped the ring into it, where it vanished in amongst the discarded wrappers and packets, the waste food, the cans, paper plates and cups.

Ryan's eyes widened. 'What the hell did you do that for? That isn't Mum's wedding ring, is it?'

Sarah stared at him. 'Seriously, Ryan? You think I'd wear Mum's ring for this?' She held up her hands to encompass the day, the wedding – the whole damned mess. 'Of course it isn't her ring, Ryan. I bought in on the market along with a scabby little engagement ring.' She rocked the second ring backwards and forwards and then, when it gave up the ghost, dropped it into the bin to join its mate.

Ryan frowned. 'I don't think you should have done that, I think you ought to wear them,' he said. 'At least for a little while. So that people can see that you're married. You know just in case.'

Her expression hardened. 'Oh really? That's your advice, is it? So that they can see that I'm married? Well, let me give you some advice, Ryan. I'm *not* married, do you understand? Not in any real sense of the word. And it wasn't a *good do,* it was a farce, and there is no way I want to be alone with Woody. Ever. Do you understand? Is this how you imagined I wanted to get married? Is it? The only reason I'm doing this is so that you don't end up dead, Ryan.'

He opened his mouth to speak but Sarah cut him short.

'I've been trying to keep the peace for weeks, trying to get through it, trying to make everything sweet. Well, now I have. It's all done and I'm finished with it. And I'm finished with you. Do you understand? That's it. I can't understand how you could get yourself into this in the first place but worse, you got me into it too. Never ask me to do another thing for you. *Ever.* If you ever borrow any money again you can sort it out yourself. And if your share of the bills isn't here every week on the nail then I'm not picking up the slack. Do you understand me? That's it. No more, Ryan, no more. You have no idea what you've done, have you? Not a bloody clue. And I'm going to arrange for the basement to be billed separately for electricity, gas and council tax.'

He stared at her. 'Oh for fuck's sake, Sarah. We talked about this.'

Sarah stared him down. 'For fuck's sake, what?' Her anger finally bubbling up like hot lava after weeks of keeping a lid on it, weeks of Ryan healing, weeks of fear and shock and feeling like she had no choice and now this, this horrible parody of a wedding day.

'I've bailed you out for the last time, is that clear? You're on your own now. I'm counting down the days to when we can sell up and go our separate ways, Ryan. I've had enough.'

His jaw dropped. 'Sarah,' he started. 'You can't mean that. We're family – we're—'

'We're what? Family? Don't you dare talk to me about family. You sold me off to pay your debts off – that isn't my idea of family,' she snapped.

'It wasn't like that,' he began.

'No? Well that's what it feels like from where I'm standing. All the weeks of keeping quiet, of not saying anything, of having you and that bastard Woody following me around like I'm a dog on a leash, making plans for the future when between you, you killed my future. I love Josh, Ryan, do you understand? I wanted to be with him. I thought he was it – the one – if I was going to marry anyone it was going to be him. Well I'm done now. I'm married, you'll have your fucking debt paid off, and Woody will get his leave to remain. Me? I've lost the man I loved and any self-respect I ever had. That's it. Now get out of here.'

By the time she had finished speaking Ryan was ashen. For a moment she thought he was going to protest or argue, or tell her that she was wrong, but instead he headed out towards the back door and the basement flat.

'I'm sorry,' he said, as he was about to step outside.

She shook her head. 'I told you before; sorry doesn't cover it, Ryan.'

And with that he was gone.

'You shouldn't be so hard on him.'

Sarah swung round.

Woody was standing by the kitchen door leaning casually against the frame, tie off now, waistcoat unbuttoned. 'And he's right, you really should wear the rings for a little longer. Just for a few weeks. Just to keep up appearances. We have to keep this up for a while yet.'

'How long have you been listening?'

'Long enough. Ryan's not like you. He's weak. You see what needs to be done and then you do it. I admire you for that. He isn't capable of behaving in that way. As far as Ryan is concerned nothing is ever his fault, nothing is ever his responsibility or his to deal with. He needs you, Sarah.'

Sarah looked up at him, her tone icy cold. 'My relationship with my brother is none of your business, Woody. And I'd appreciate it if you kept your thoughts and your pop psychology to yourself where Ryan is concerned.'

He nodded in a gesture that Sarah hoped meant that he conceded the point, but she could see that he wasn't done.

'And what about you?' she asked. 'Do you need me too?'

He smiled. 'At the moment, yes, but not for long. I promise you that it will soon be all over and done with. There are a few things I need to sort out. Don't worry, I want to be free of this as much as you do.'

Sarah very much doubted that.

'It is just a means to an end,' he said.

'For you, maybe.'

152

Woody grunted. 'For you too.'

Sarah had no intention of continuing the conversation with him and said nothing.

Apparently making the effort to change the subject Woody glanced round the room. 'I thought we could leave the cleaning up till the morning.'

Sarah pushed herself to her feet. 'There's no *we* about it, Woody. There is just me and Ryan.'

Woody grinned. 'I think you'll find you're wrong, Sarah, we're all one happy family now; at least that's what everyone else has to believe. And if they don't, and I find out that it's you? Let's just say Farouk owes me one for getting him his money back.'

If Woody was hoping she was going to respond to the threat he was disappointed. The day had already numbed any fear she had. She sat very still, her eyes not leaving his, the bile rising in the back of her throat, until finally it was Woody who looked away first and left the room, closing the door quietly behind him.

When she was sure that he was gone, Sarah ran across the kitchen and threw up into the sink, tears streaming down her face as she sobbed, all the stress, all the panic and fury finally unleashed, making her head hurt and her throat raw.

When she was done, Sarah rinsed out the sink, washed her face and then took a roll of black plastic sacks out from the kitchen cupboard and started to clear away the remains of the party. Over the next few hours she gathered up all the rubbish, along with the glasses and plates, packed the dishwasher, opened the remaining windows, wiped the surfaces down, plumped the cushions, straightened the curtains, cleaned the bathrooms, swept and washed the kitchen floor, and finally hoovered all the way through the downstairs rooms, claiming the house back, struggling to claim herself back along with it.

It was daylight by the time she climbed the stairs and headed for bed. For a moment Sarah paused on the landing and looked up towards Woody's room on the next floor. There was light coming under the door and she was sure she could hear him moving around. The floor creaked, the old boards moving under his weight and she wondered fleetingly if he was going to open the door.

She paused for a beat, feeling the hairs on the back of her neck rising – and then she hurried into her bedroom, turning the key in the lock and sliding a chair up under the handle.

Sarah

'Tell me about the photos, Sarah.'

'Photos?'

The ones that Ryan and Woody took of the wedding. Do you know why he wanted so many?'

'He told me that he wanted as much evidence as he could get to support his application to stay in the UK; wedding photos, party photos, all sorts of proof that we were a real couple. He said it would help his case. The morning after the wedding he brought some down that he had printed off, and then he put them in frames around the place. To be honest they made me feel sick.'

'But you didn't stop him?'

'No, I thought that if someone from Immigration came round they would help his case, and the sooner he got his leave to remain sorted out the sooner he would be out of my life.'

'There are a lot of photos here, Sarah. There must be two or three hundred in one box alone.'

'I know, every time we were home together Woody would get the camera out and get Ryan to take photos of the two of us.'

'The happy couple?'

'I think that was what he had in mind. It was like he was trying to prove a point. And then there were all sorts of business plans for the future. Empire building. He and Ryan were thick as thieves working on those together, and then Woody said we had to provide details of savings accounts, financial details, birth certificates, all that sort of thing. For the interviews.'

'Interviews?'

'With the Immigration Office.'

'Okay. And how did those go, Sarah? Did you go with Woody?'

'No. I thought that I'd have to – I mean I assumed they would want to see both of us and interview me about his application. I've seen it on TV, but Woody said that I didn't have to go unless they specifically asked to see me.'

'Not once?'

'No, he never asked me to go, and as far as I know they never asked to see me. I never had any correspondence about his application. Nothing. I assumed I would have some contact. I thought they might ring me. Or call round. I'd thought it would be really complicated with lots of red tape.'

'Didn't that strike you as odd, Sarah? After all, surely your being his wife and being British was the back bone of his application?'

'I know. I mean it wasn't the only odd thing – but yes, I did wonder whether I needed to contact them, but I was afraid that if I did it might jeopardise his claim – let sleeping dogs lie and all that. I did try to talk to Woody about it but he said it was all in hand, that he had filled in all the forms, and now we just had to wait and that if they wanted to see me then they'd let him know. I've never had any dealings with Immigration before so I wasn't sure exactly *how it worked and he seemed so sure of what he was doing. But yes, it did seem a bit odd. I had thought that we would have to go there as a couple to see people – you know, in Immigration – and lie. I was really worried about that.'*

'It made you uncomfortable?'

'Yes of course, I'm not a liar, but like with the wedding I didn't see that I'd got much choice. He kept telling me that if anyone found out about what I'd done I would go to prison, him too – and that he had told Farouk that if he got deported or arrested that they would come after me and Ryan.'

'So you're saying that he threatened you? That the threats continued even after you got married?'

'Yes, yes they did. But you have to try and understand that they weren't direct. It was more like this steady pressure – a long, long threat – like he was pressing down on me all the time.'

'Okay, and what about the loan? Ryan's loan?'

'Once we were married Woody started to go out a lot more. He was out most evenings, and during the day, the occasional night. When I asked him about the money for Ryan he said he had squared it away.'

'And you took it to mean what?'

'That he had repaid it. That Farouk would leave us alone.'

'Okay, and did Woody seem all right with that?'

'He told me that he saw it as an investment in his future.'

'An investment?'

'Yes.'

'And what do you think he meant by that?'

'I suppose I took it to mean that he'd got what he wanted, the chance to stay in the UK and make a life for himself here.'

'So as far as you were concerned as soon as he

had his right to remain he planned to – what? Leave you and begin his new life?'

'Something like that.'

'Not stay and make a life with you and Ryan?'

'No.'

Ryan and Woody

'I'm serious, Ryan. I can handle the money side of things and sort the finances out. And I reckon that you can do a lot of the building work and you've got the contacts for the stuff you can't manage yourself.' Woody's voice was calm and matter of fact. 'What do you reckon? It could be the beginning of a family empire. And it'll get your sister off your back. Not to mention mine.'

Woody grinned and took a long pull on his pint. They'd put away quite a few since they'd got down to the pub. Ryan hadn't got any money so he wasn't buying, which meant he wasn't counting, but he was more or less certain that it was more than he'd usually have mid-week.

'I reckon we could make maybe ten grand each after costs. Easy – maybe more. Come on drink up, slacker.'

'I'm all right, thanks, mate,' Ryan said; his glass was more than half full. He nodded towards the gents. 'I won't be a minute.'

Woody acknowledged the gesture. He seemed to have developed a real taste for booze since that first time when they'd met at the bookies, and he was holding it better. Over the last few months the balance of power had shifted. Whereas once upon a time it had been Ryan showing Woody the ropes, now Woody was in the driving seat, and he was driving hard and fast. Ryan, standing at the urinal, smiled at his own joke, *hard and fast,* nice analogy or was it a metaphor? The money thing; the twenty grand that had been the real kicker. Ryan tried not to think about it too much if he could. He just let it sit there in the back of his head in a box. A box that he preferred to keep tightly shut. It made his whole body ache if he spent too long dwelling on what had had happened and the consequences.

When he got back, Woody was chatting to the barman. Ryan slid back onto his stool, and glanced down at the bar, unsure why he still had a full pint.

'So what do you think?' Woody said.

'About what?'

Woody laughed. 'Come on, keep up. Doing up this flat. It's there for the taking. I've seen the place; it looks to me like the renovations are mostly cosmetic. It just really needs sprucing up, but there's plenty of room in the budget; new kitchen, maybe tiles and stuff in the bathroom, lick of paint. If I was you, in your position, I'd be jumping at the chance. This place is a real gem, and I know the owner. I'm certain we can get it for a good price before it even goes on the market – private sale, no commission. Get in there, tart it up, get it back on the market in no time at all. What do you say?'

'Sounds good but I can't put any money in, you know that,' said Ryan.

Woody waved the words away. 'Of course I know that. I'm not asking you to put any money in, am I? I'm just saying that you should think about coming in with me. Ten grand, maybe fifteen, twenty each if we're lucky. Home free. Just think about that.'

Big money had bad memories; the bruises might have faded but there was still something not right with his back, and whenever he walked home Ryan spent a lot of time looking behind him. And then there were the dreams. The chasing one had him waking up with his heart banging like a drum. He could still see the dream if he closed his eyes, the one where they caught him and dragged him into an alley, behind the bins where it stank of vomit and urine and in his mind's eye he watched them kicking him, kicking him over and over again until he was sure he would die. But the worst part of it was when he was on the floor and he felt himself slip back into his body, bleeding, hurting, and there was a man sitting on his chest, crushing the breath out of him as he pressed his thumbs deep into Ryan's eye sockets.

In the darkest parts of Ryan's dream the man just kept on pressing till Ryan could feel his thumbs pressing down, down in his brain, deep into the soft warmth of his skull.

If he closed his eyes Ryan could feel him now. Not that Ryan had told anyone, but in the night he could feel the man close by and hear his voice. The soft, soft sound of his voice, sing-song, in amongst the pain and the fear. He had started to sleep with the light on because he couldn't bear to wake up in the darkness. No amount of money could put that right.

'It sounds like a good thing. But I'm not sure; look what happened last time,' Ryan said, his tone rigidly even.

'Yes, but this isn't like the last time, is it? This isn't a loan, Ryan. This is a job, an opportunity, a sure thing. I want you in on this. I could really use your expertise.'

As he spoke, Woody nodded towards Ryan's glass.

Ryan shook his head. He had lost count of how many they had had so far. 'No, thanks,' he said. 'I told Sarah I'd be back early tonight.'

Woody glanced down at his watch. 'Too late for that, mate. For fuck's sake you'd think you were married to her not me. You need this job, you need something to get her off your back. This would do it, Ryan. Jesus, what will it fucking take to get you to

159

see? This is a dead cert.'

This wasn't the first time that Ryan had noticed that when he was away from the house Woody spoke quite differently; he was freer, his language more colourful, less considered, more streetwise.

Woody twisted the wedding ring round on his finger, unlike Sarah's this one was gold; a big chunk of gold. Woody waved the barman over. The man, pulling a pint for someone else, clocked them and nodded an acknowledgement that he'd seen them.

'This is a job and an investment. We do one flat up and sell it on, make ourselves a little money and use it to seed the next project. What do you say? I thought you'd be more enthusiastic. It's right up your street.'

Ryan hesitated. Although he hadn't said anything to Woody, since the wedding he was more and more worried about Sarah, not just what she might say about him being late, but how she was in herself. He had never seen her this low, not even when their mum died. She was so pale and so thin she looked like she might break, and he knew that it was his fault, although he tried not to look at it head on because it made him feel sick.

Once or twice he had tried to find the words to tell her how very sorry he was and how he would never let anything like it ever happen again, how he knew he had let her down and if there had been any other way out of the place that he'd found himself, that he would have jumped at it, but Ryan had said the same thing so many times in the past that he knew she wouldn't believe him; words were cheap.

Ryan knew that he had to do it for real this time, do something to prove that he really could turn things around. Ryan wanted Sarah back to how she was before all this, back to being jokey, and feisty and strong, laughing in the kitchen, talking to him,

160

telling him off, hugging him.

The truth was that he missed Sarah. The other Sarah, the one that didn't look like a whipped dog. She was making him feel bad. Several times he had wondered if there was any way he could find Josh and explain to him, tell him about what had happened, tell him about how Woody watched her like a hawk, taking her to work, picking her up, checking the phone bills, maybe he could find a way to put things right.

Ryan glanced up at Woody, and revised the thought, more importantly he wondered if there was any way that he could put things right without dropping either himself or Sarah right in the shit.

Woody was still talking. 'The flat is down by the river, second floor. As far I can see, it is close to perfect. Although obviously I'm no expert – and this is where I'm hoping you'll come and give it a look – but to me, it doesn't look like it would take much to tart it up and bang it back onto the market. It's quite a big place; there's a chance we could maybe even split it into two studio flats.'

Ryan bit his lip. 'I'd need to take a look at it, man. I mean, I've got people who I could ask if you really want to go ahead.'

Woody nodded.

'But I'm not sure. There's always a risk,' said Ryan warily. The beer seemed to be slipping down without him paying it much attention. It had been a little while since he'd been out for a session, but it was coming back to him.

Woody laughed. 'Oh, come on. There's a risk in everything but this is bricks and mortar, the market is on the up. You must have seen it in the news. It makes it the perfect time to buy, we can buy cheap and if we can't sell it then we can always rent it out. Plan B, but it'll work as long as the rent covers the mortgage, and let's face it people are always looking for a decent place to live round here. River views close to the city centre. What's not to like? Win, win, I reckon. Come on, knock that one back we've got time for another one if we don't hang about.'

Ryan hesitated; what the hell, he wasn't going to make an early night of it now. He gulped the beer down and set the glass alongside Woody's.

'It sounds good. But I'd need to look at the job and look at the figures, after all that shit with the money last time. If I'm completely honest I'd be worried about taking something like this on. On the books or even self-employed it is one thing. Don't get me wrong, it sounds like a good idea, but I just want to be able to show up at the end of the week with my share of the bills. I owe it to Sarah to get it together.'

Woody slapped him on the shoulder. 'Oh, come on, man, you've just lost your bottle that's all. This is a sure thing. Look, if you're worried about it, how about I just pay you a day rate? You can project manage it for me. What do you say? At least come along and take a look at it. See what you think.'

Still Ryan hesitated. 'I dunno. I mean, I can see where you're coming from, but I've already said I'd give my mate a hand with an extension he's doing over at Dry Drayton. If it comes off that's probably three, if not four, weeks' work. And then...'

Woody sighed and nodded. 'Okay, look, please yourself. I'm not going to twist your arm. I know what Sarah is like, that woman's got your balls in a bucket, you know. If you don't want a slice of it, that's okay with me. I'll find someone else.' His tone was matter of fact. 'I just wanted to give you first shot that's all. Keep it in the family.'

Ryan nodded to acknowledge the offer. As he spoke, the barman came over and Woody ordered them a couple of scotches along with two more beers, slipping the guy the money to pay for it.

Ryan chewed on his lip; maybe he had been too hasty, maybe this thing with Woody was just the chance he needed. Maybe this was it, the thing that would finally set things right. 'I told Sarah that I'd be back early, I said—'

Woody pulled a face. 'Oh, pack it in. You want to just hand your balls over now, mate? Get it over and done with. We can post them to her.'

Ryan took a long pull on his pint. There was silence for a few minutes.

'Okay. I suppose it wouldn't hurt to take a look at the flat.'

Woody grinned and slapped Ryan on the shoulder. 'Good man, good man, that's the spirit,' he said. 'There are just one or two things I need to set up before we can go and have a look.'

Ryan

Ryan unlocked the back door and stepped inside out of the rain, shucking off his damp fleece and hanging it up just inside the kitchen door before toeing off his wet *Cat* boots. Bloody weather. Usually he would head downstairs to his flat but he was hoping that Sarah was home. Midweek there was a good chance he would be able to catch her on her own without Woody being around. He needed to talk to her. Make his peace. Tell her about the scheme Woody had in mind, tell her that he planned to try and sort something out, make it right for them both.

The sky outside was dark with the promise of more rain. There was no way they'd get the concreting done in this, which was a bastard as they were being paid by the day and he'd barely made it through till lunch time before getting rained off.

It was warm in the kitchen and smelt of home.

The door into the rest of the house was open and he could hear music or maybe the radio coming from the sitting room across the hall. Ryan owed her an apology, an explanation. He tracked the sound down.

The sitting room door was ajar. 'Sarah?' he called.

The room was empty, the TV burbling away in the corner. It wasn't like her to watch daytime TV, maybe she was sick. There was a pile of paperwork on the coffee table. He didn't plan to look. Although he made a show of ignoring it, Ryan knew all about the bills and the work on the house that needed doing. He took a cursory glance and stopped. This wasn't Sarah's paperwork, it was Woody's; there were a few bills, paperwork for his car, a loan agreement and something else. Something all together more interesting. Ryan reached over and picked it up. It was a lined A4 pad with signatures all over the first page and the second – Woody's signature. He had obviously been practising signing his name over and over again.

Ryan stared at it, trying to work out what it meant, when he heard someone up on the landing going into the bathroom. He could hear Woody upstairs, presumably talking into a phone.

Very carefully, with his eye firmly fixed on the door, Ryan tore out the second page, rolled it up and tucked it into his shirt and then, heart pounding, made his way back into the kitchen. He considered going straight back down to the flat but the mud and water on the kitchen floor would give him away if Woody had the wit to notice, so instead he slipped his jacket back on, opened the back door again and this time shut it hard and called out. 'Hello, Sarah? Hello. Anyone home?' And then he took his time taking his jacket off, hanging it up – making a show of arriving.

There was no reply so he called louder this time.

Seconds later there were the sounds of footfalls on the stairs and Woody stuck his head round the door.

'Hi,' said Ryan running his fingers through his damp hair. 'Sarah about, is she?'

Woody shook his head and hastily closed the hall door behind him, cutting Ryan off from the rest of the house. 'No, she had to go into work this morning. They rang to see if she could cover another shift.'

Ryan nodded. 'I thought you would be in college today.'

'I'm busy doing an assignment, papers all over the place.'

He was moving toward Ryan encouraging him back out of the house. Ryan grinned. 'Aren't you going to at least offer me a cup of tea? I'm soaked.'

'Sorry, mate it's not a good time, I'm up to my ears. Books, papers, notes all over.'

Ryan nodded. 'Okay, fair enough. Can you tell Sarah I dropped in?'

Woody nodded. 'Sure.'

Ryan crouched down to put his boots on. 'Don't forget your jacket,' said Woody.

Ryan nodded. 'I'll get it later. It'll dry better up here over the radiator than it will downstairs. Do you mind?'

Woody shrugged.

'I was thinking about the flat.'

Woody's eyes narrowed.

'You know,' said Ryan. 'The one you were thinking of doing up?'

He saw comprehension dawning on Woody's face. 'Oh yeah. I've put it on the back boiler a bit while I'm finishing my assignment off.'

'So is it off?'

'No, no, not at all. I'm still trying to sort a few things out. Why – are you interested now?'

Ryan pointed to the window. 'Yes, especially if the

165

weather carries on like this. Nice indoor job would suit me down to the ground.'

Woody nodded. 'Fair enough. Let me see what I can do,' he said.

Sarah

'So after the wedding. What was life like, Sarah?'

'It's so hard to describe; it felt like I was in limbo, waiting for whatever it was that was coming next to happen. I could feel it coming, like the change in pressure when a storm is on the way. Trying to get back to anything close to normal was impossible.'

'You were still working?'

'Yes.'

'And were you having a sexual relationship with Woody?'

'No, no it was never like that between us. I think that he despised me. Us.'

'You and Ryan?'

'Yes. I caught him looking at me sometimes like I was something dirty. And like I told you, he was out a lot of the time. But even when he wasn't there I could feel him in the house, like he was never really gone. And he would just turn up without warning, as if he was trying to catch me out, so it felt like I was living on edge all the time.'

'So the marriage was never consummated?'

'I hated him.'

'Woody?'

'I got to the stage where I couldn't bear it when he was there. I spent a lot of time in my room. Ryan told me that I was being melodramatic, but it felt like he had set us up. Used us to get what he wanted. And the house felt different.'

'In what way?'

'Tense, I couldn't relax. Like I said, it felt like we

were waiting for something else to happen.'

'You and Ryan?'

'Yes.'

'And what about Ryan? How did he seem?'

'Uneasy, unsettled, unhappy. He was working but he was drinking more. I felt like I was on the outside all on my own.'

'And what about friends? The people at the nursery? The restaurant?'

'Anessa tried to talk to me about Woody.'

'Talk about what?'

'At the wedding she had tried to talk to him about where his family came from in Quetta. Where they lived. She went over there a couple of years ago with her family for a wedding, but she said that Woody wouldn't talk to her about his home. When I went back to work after the wedding, she wanted to know what I knew about him.'

'And what did you tell her?'

'Nothing very much. What could I say to her? I only know what he told me, so I told her that. I think she thought he was just being rude.'

'And what did you think?'

'Honestly, I don't know.'

'And did you discuss the conversation between you and Anessa with Woody?'

'No, I was afraid he would make me give up my job at the nursery, and to be honest work was the only time I was away from the house. I had to watch what I said, but it was better than being stuck at home, and I was afraid of saying too much. And I was worried in case Josh came into work. I kept an eye out for his truck. I didn't feel safe.'

'With Josh?'

No, at home. I just got the feeling that there was something going on.'

'Can you explain?'

'Before the wedding Woody was very controlling, but he was even more so after we were married. He told me he didn't want me answering the phone, that I should let it go to voice mail, and that he would pick up the messages when he got home. And that I wasn't to answer the door – and he kept his room locked all the time. Before this thing with the money and Farouk, I'd gone up there and run the hoover round once a week, dusted. I know it sounds crazy. I mean it's not like I'm that paranoid or fragile but he made me feel as if anything could happen, anything at all and nothing good.'

'And you agreed to the new rules?'

'It wasn't about agreeing; he made it clear that it wasn't in my best interests to break them.'

'What does that mean, Sarah?'

'He made me feel uneasy, vulnerable.'

'Woody threatened you?'

'Not directly, but he told me that if I didn't do what I was told, things could get difficult for all of us.'

'Difficult? What did you take that to mean?'

'I don't know really. I kept thinking that maybe Farouk might come back but I don't really know. I just kept wondering how long we could keep it up, living like that.'

'And did Woody give you any idea how long you'd have to keep up the pretence of being married?'

'He said that there were legal formalities that he needed to get sorted out, things that needed to be signed and witnessed, and then it would just be a matter of time before it was all over. And then he would move on.'

'He said that? Move on? We need you to say yes for the benefit of the tape rather than nod, please. Sarah.'

'Yes, he said he would sort things out with me, and then he would move on.'

'And he was out a lot?'

'More and more. Sometimes he was out all night. Although he would pop back at odd times. As I said before it felt like he was trying to catch me out. I thought he was at college or staying over with friends. He was studying for his finals.'

'For his MBA?'

'Yes. That's what he had told me at the beginning when he came to rent the room. Anyway, I got back from work early one afternoon and I was in the kitchen, sorting out the recycling, and the rubbish. There was a bag in there, in the bin we keep for things we needed to burn; when I looked inside I realised the stuff wasn't mine, and that they were all addressed to Woody. To Mustapha. I think he had probably planned to burn them. He was always outside in the garden burning things. And I found some letters.'

'Letters.'

'I kept them in the biscuit tin. The one on the table over there.'

'But they're photo copies.'

'I know, I was worried what he would do if he knew I'd seen them, so I copied them.'

'Onto your computer?'

'No, I've got a printer that you can use as a copier.'

'Okay, and had you got any idea what was in them?'

'No, not at the time, some were official, but lots of them were hand written – what looked like personal letters. I couldn't understand them but they looked personal. And...'

'And?'

'I suppose I was like Anessa. I wanted to know

more about him. I wanted to try and understand what was going on. I thought if I knew more then I could find a way to get rid of him. So I steamed open the letters and copied them and then put them back in the rubbish so that he wouldn't know that I'd seen them.'

'Risky. What if he had come in?'

'I don't know. I did them one at a time. Took them out one at a time.'

'And what did you find out?'

'It took me a while but there were all kinds of other things, things I could read. First of all he hadn't been attending lectures. There was a note from someone asking if he was okay, asking when he was coming back, and reminding him to hand an essay in. And letters asking him to pay things, things he was in arrears with. And then there were the personal letters.'

'Do you read Urdu or Pashto?'

'No, I did think about asking Anessa if she could read then, but she had been odd with me since the wedding; a bit distant, so I asked one of the regulars at the restaurant if he would translate them for me. I mean, I paid him and I took off the address and things.'

'And he agreed?'

'Yes. I told him they were for a friend. I don't think he was convinced.'

'But he did translate them?'

'Yes, as a favour.'

'So what did they say, Sarah?'

'One was from Woody's father; he sounded really upset. He wanted to know why Woody hadn't called home or answered any of his letters or phone calls. It said that his mother was very upset that she hadn't heard from him, and when his father had rung the college to find out where he was, they'd told him that Woody hadn't attended any of the courses that semester.'

'Did what you found give any idea of how long this had been going on?'

'Since he moved in, roughly – I think – from what it said in the letters.'

'And this was all news to you?'

'Yes, completely. I mean, he left the house every day, and up until that point I had assumed he was going to college. The letter said that his father was very disappointed, and that if Woody didn't get in touch that they planned to stop his allowance.'

'Which would mean his income stream would be cut off?'

'Yes, I suppose so. Although he always had money.'

'And had you any idea why he stopped contacting his family?'

'None, or going to college for that matter. When he first took the room he said he was likely to get a distinction; the highest grade. I mean, why give that up? I didn't understand. And also it was obvious from the letters that Woody hadn't mentioned wanting to stay in the UK or told them what he was doing.'

'By doing, do you mean marrying you?'

'Yes. I also wondered if maybe he had told them and they were upset about him wanting to make his life over here, although his father didn't mention it in any of the letters. I had wondered why he wasn't in touch with them. He never rang them, never talked about them.'

'And did you ask him about it? About them?'

'Yes, after I found the letters. I asked him if he had told his parents about his plans. He was dismissive, as if he didn't want to talk about it. So I suggested that he should email them and put their

171

minds at rest. I didn't say I'd read the letters, just that I thought that if he was my son I'd like to know how he was and what he was doing. It was horrible; he was livid. He said his parents were his business. He said I might try those games on Ryan – he meant trying to control him – but it wouldn't work on him. And anyway—'

'And anyway what? Are you all right? Do you want to stop? We could have a break now if you'd like to, Sarah.'

'No, I'm fine. It was just horrible. He was angry and really nasty. He said they would never have let him marry someone like me, and then he said that he was engaged and they had arranged a marriage for him at home, that there would be a huge scandal. They would be disgraced if they knew he was already married. If anyone contacted me, anyone at all, asking for him then I wasn't to take the call or tell them anything.'

'Okay, I just want to look at my notes, Sarah. So, during this time had you seen Josh or heard from him?'

'No, I hadn't. One of the things Woody had done just before the wedding was to change phone companies and we'd lost our old number. And I'd already got a new mobile phone from Ryan when I lost my old one.'

'You let Woody change your phone number?'

'When I got in from work one day he just said that he had changed the phone company. I was annoyed about it, but it didn't occur to me that he wouldn't have asked to keep our number. By the time I realised we had lost our number it was a done deal.'

'Did he say why he changed phone companies?'

'At the time he said it would save money. Afterwards when I thought about it, I thought it was *probably deliberate so that we had a different number. At first it made me think it was about Josh, but then I wondered about Farouk or maybe Woody's parents. I thought maybe when he first moved he might have given them the house number. But certainly it felt like there was more to it than he was letting on.'*

'Okay. So then what happened?'

'I put the letters back in the rubbish where I'd found them, so that he didn't know that I'd seen them.'

'I mean did you talk to him about what was going on? Did his behaviour change? Did he seem at all worried about the things his father had said? The threat of losing his allowance? I presume he hadn't got any other source of income?'

'I don't know where Woody was getting his money from, but he didn't seem at all worried. I wondered if maybe he had rung his dad or talked to him about it since getting the letters. He didn't discuss his private life with me, and as I said when I asked him about his family he was really angry, so I'd got no way of knowing. He could have sorted it out and he just wanted to get rid of the letters.'

'Okay.'

Ryan

'We need to talk.' Ryan had caught up to Woody in the road.

Woody was locking up his Beamer and heading into the house. 'Yeah, what about?' he said, slipping on his leather jacket and dropping his keys into his pocket, as Ryan hurried after him.

'I've been following you,' he said. 'The last few days.'

Woody looked at him and laughed. 'What the fuck

173

is that supposed to mean?'

'You went to your old flat.'

'And? Some sort of law against it, is there?'

'What were you doing there?'

Woody shook his head. 'I was picking up some post and catching up with my old landlord, if you must know.'

Ryan pulled a face. Woody grinned and slapped him on the back. 'What the fuck is the matter with you, creeping round after me? Haven't you got anything better to do? Like work for a living? What brought this on?'

'Something's not right, man.'

'Don't talk bollocks, Ryan. The only thing that's not right is you. Get a grip. Actually, as it happens, it might've been a good thing me popping round there, me and the landlord got talking and there might be some work he could put our way.'

'What do you mean *our* way?'

'He owns a lot of houses and flats that he lets out, and he was telling me today that he is looking for someone to help him maintain them. You know, lick of paint here, maybe a bit of basic plumbing, sorting stuff out for tenants and clearing up between lets, that sort of thing. He's not getting any younger. Maybe you're the man for the job? If we set up this building business maybe maintenance is something we should think about taking on.'

Ryan didn't bite.

Woody stared at him and then shook his head. 'What? What's niggling you?'

'You go there a lot,' Ryan said flatly.

'Yeah?'

'Yeah,' said Ryan.

'What's it got to do with you where I go? I play chess with the old man, okay? He likes it. Me and him we always got on well.'

174

'And what about Farouk?'

'What about him?'

'I thought you were frightened of him.'

Woody shrugged. 'Things change.'

Ryan nodded. 'You're right, they do. You see the thing is, Woody, I'm beginning to think that there's something else going on here.'

Woody raised his eyebrows. 'You serious?'

'You have to understand where I'm coming from. I'm trying to find a way to make it right for Sarah. I've been thinking about this a lot. I want you to leave us alone. To go. Leave. Move out.'

Woody laughed. 'What are you on about?' he said, sounding incredulous.

Ryan wasn't laughing. 'I think you set me up.'

Woody snorted. 'What? How do you work that one out? I forced you to be a piss-head and borrow twenty grand? I don't think so, mate. Now get out of my way, will you. I've got things to do.'

But Ryan didn't move. 'I'm asking nicely,' he said. 'I just want you to leave me and Sarah alone. Go, you got what you wanted, and if anyone shows up from immigration we'll lie through our eyeteeth for you, and I swear as soon as the house is sold you'll get the money back. Every last penny. On my life.'

'Oh you swear, do you?' snorted Woody. 'That's rich coming from you.'

Ryan sighed. 'You're up to something.'

'I don't know what you're on about. You're sure you've not had too much wacky baccy?'

Ryan slipped his hand inside his jacket and pulled out a sheet of paper. 'So what's this all about then?'

Woody pulled a face. 'What is it?' he said as he took it from Ryan.

It was a photocopy of the page Ryan had taken from the notebook on the coffee table. He had played safe, got it copied at work, and hidden the original.

There were two columns of Woody's signature, one down each side of the page. It was his trump card.

If he was shocked or wrong-footed Woody certainly didn't show it. 'So?' he said, handing it back. 'What does this prove? I like to sign my name. There's no law against it.'

Ryan held his ground. 'I don't know what it proves or what it means, but I think you're up to something dodgy, and I'm going to go to the police with what I know.'

'What you know? *What you know*?' Woody laughed. 'Are you fucking crazy? They'll arrest us all, including your precious sister. Do you want that? Sarah in prison and all thanks to you. She despises you now, how's she going to feel if you get her locked up? Dragged through the court? In the papers? How do you think that's going to go down? And those guys who beat the living shit out of you last time? Well, they might not be so lenient next time, you hear what I'm saying? They said you'd got it coming.'

Ryan held his hands up. 'Look, I don't want a fight, all I want is you gone, Woody. Away from Sarah, away from me. Gone. And if I go to the law I'll tell them that you coerced Sarah and threatened me, but I don't want to do that, mate, I really don't. I just want you out of the house.'

'So this is what I get for helping you out, is it?' Woody said sadly. 'Putting myself on the line for you?'

Ryan sighed. 'Don't think I'm not grateful, man. I am. I'm just saying it's time to move on. Please. Leave us alone. You've got what you want.'

'What makes you think that?' Woody said, making his way up the path into the house, and then he turned and slapped Ryan on the shoulder. 'Come on, lighten up. I thought you and I were friends, Ry. Tell you what. How about we have a drink and talk about it. I'm sure we can work something out, and I really do have a job in mind for you. I've finally been down to have a look at that flat by the river that I was telling you about? I mean, that with some property maintenance – now that would be a sweet little earner.'

Ryan stared at him. 'You're not listening to me are you? What about that?' he said, waving at the piece of paper with the signatures on it that Woody still had in his hand.

'What about it?' said Woody as he unlocked the front door and crumpled the sheet into a ball.

Josh

'Would you identify yourself for the tape?'

'Sure, my name is Josh Durrant.'

'And you were in a relationship with Sarah Reynolds during the spring and summer of last year?'

'Yes, that's right.'

'And would you say, Mr Durrant, that your relationship was serious?'

'Yes. Yes, it was or at least I thought so. We'd talked about moving in together. Talked about a future together. Getting married. I thought Sarah was it.'

'It?'

'Yes, you know. *The one.* I thought that we would spend the rest of our lives together and I thought – I believed, I suppose I still believe – that she felt the same.'

'And when did you find out that Sarah was married?'

'She wasn't, at least not when we first started seeing each other and then she was. I know that sounds crazy. It seemed crazy. I didn't really understand what was going on. We had had this great weekend away, and then she just stopped taking my phone calls and texts. In the end I was getting this recorded message saying that the phone was switched off, but to begin with it just went to voice mail.'

'Frustrating?'

'Yes and no. I knew she had been through a rough time losing her dad and then her mum. And then her brother got beaten up. I mean, it wasn't easy for her to just let go and have some time and space for herself. That's what I loved about her. And then I thought that maybe I was pushing her too hard, that she was getting cold feet, or that it was maybe too soon, although up until that point she had seemed as keen as I was.'

'About what?'

'About me moving in. About us being together. We had talked about it a lot. My lease was about to run out and it seemed like a natural progression. We even talked about buying a place together after she and Ryan had sold the house. Me and Sarah together, our new start.'

'And so what happened, Josh? Do you mind if I call you Josh?'

'No, not at all. It just stopped. Just like that.'

'Stopped? You mean Sarah finished the relationship?'

'No, it wasn't like that. It was more like someone turned a tap off mid flow. She suddenly just stopped answering my calls and texts. I went round to the house several times, but there didn't seem to be anyone there, and then when someone did answer the door it was either Ryan or Woody. I think they told me she was out, but then Woody said that I couldn't see Sarah and that she didn't want to see me anymore.'

'And you believed him?'

'Not at first. To be honest I didn't know what to believe. It just seemed so weird. I didn't know what to think.'

'And did Sarah's behaviour strike you as odd?'

'Odd? It was bizarre. I mean, I've been dumped before but never like this – and the fact that this guy Woody wouldn't let me speak to her was weird. He was the lodger. He kept saying it would be better for everyone if I just left her alone and didn't come back. First of all I was really worried and upset and then...'

'And then what, Josh?'

'I got angry. I couldn't help wondering if this was her thing. Some sort of game. I mean, you don't know, do you? I wondered if she maybe got off on leading guys on then dumping them. There are some real loonies out there.'

'You thought Sarah might be mad?'

'God no, quite the reverse. We've all fallen foul of crazy birds, but Sarah never seemed like that, which made it so hard to work out what was going on.'

'So can you tell me what happened next?'

'I was driving into the city when I saw Sarah. In the street. It took me a minute to realise that it was her, and I was driving so I didn't stop. She looked really awful.'

'When you say awful?'

'Pale, thin, dark circles under her eyes. It occurred to me that maybe she was ill.'

'Did you know about Ryan being beaten up?'

'Only after I went round to the nursery to see if I could see her there. They told me that she had taken some time off to be with him, so I thought I'd ring again to see if she was all right, maybe go round to see if there was anything I could do to help.'

'And what happened?'

'I left a message on the house phone and then a

179

little while later she rang me back and told me it was over. Just like that. No letting me down gently, no, *this is not about you it's me* thing. Just it was over.'

'And how did that make you feel, Josh?'

'You sound like a counsellor.'

'Sorry, you want to tell me anyway?'

'I was hurt, angry I suppose, and I was confused. It had been going so well with us. The other thing is the phone call just didn't feel right, but I didn't really know what to do about it. I suppose I wanted an explanation and not getting one was the hardest part – but she had made it perfectly clear to me that it was over.'

'And so you moved on?'

'No, not exactly.'

'What happened?'

'I went into a bit of a spin. You know what it's like, I renewed my lease, got drunk, worked like a dog, all the usual things men do when they get dumped, and then I got a phone call. It must have been a couple of months later.'

'So who called you. Sarah?'

'No. No. It was Ryan.'

'You're certain that it was Ryan, Josh?'

'Absolutely. I recognised his voice.'

'And what did he have to say for himself?'

'It sounded like he was in a pub. He was drunk. It was really noisy. I had to keep asking him to repeat what he said.'

Ryan

'Josh? Is that you, Josh?'

'Yes, who is this?'

'It's me. Ryan. Sarah's brother. You remember.'

'Of course I remember. Are you okay? What's up? Is Sarah okay?'

'Sorry, the signal's not very good here. I've just come outside for a cigarette and I need to be quick.' With the phone clamped to his ear Ryan looked left and right, keeping a weather eye out for Woody. 'Have you got a pen handy?'

It had been a long evening. Despite his reservations, Ryan had finally agreed to go and look at the flat, from the outside, just to humour Woody, and get him off his back. Woody, despite Ryan pressing him about his trips to the old flat and the signatures, behaved as if nothing had happened, which had wrong-footed Ryan totally. He had expected Woody to come clean, or be annoyed or do something, but in fact he had carried on as if nothing had happened.

Ryan had assumed that they would go straight to the flat but Woody had other ideas. So now the plan was one more drink in the Raven, which fronted the river, and then they'd take a stroll down the river bank, along the tow path to the property – nothing too obvious as Woody had warned him that there were a couple of other developers sniffing around. So the plan was to just cast an eye over the place from the outside.

The flat sounded too good to be true, but even if it was rougher than he was saying, if Woody was going to shell out for a day rate, cash in hand, he'd be a fool not to at least take a look. He'd had a bit of a dry spell workwise since the thing with Farouk. There had been the odd couple of weeks here and there, and this week he would have a couple of days, but nothing solid or regular. In reality he couldn't afford to turn down a few weeks regular money, not at the moment, and as Woody didn't know the first thing about building, then maybe – finally – Ryan could get a bit of pay back, a bit of cream on the cake after all the crap that life had been handing him out for the last few months.

'Are you pissed?' Josh snapped at the other end of the phone.

'No,' said Ryan. 'I mean yeah, okay I've had a bit. A couple of pints or so, you know.'

'Yeah, I know. Look, whatever this is about—' Josh began, everything about his tone suggesting he was planning to cut their conversation short.

'No, wait,' said Ryan, hastily. 'Please. Don't hang up. It's about Sarah.'

Whatever Josh was going to say Ryan heard the words jam up in his throat. 'How did you get this number?' he said grimly.

'Sarah had it on a pad in the kitchen. And it's not how you think, Josh. You know, with Sarah.'

'What the hell is that supposed you mean?' Josh asked. 'She dumped me, Ryan. And I'm not in a great place just now so if you just want to tell me what this is about and then get the fuck off my phone. End of story. Game over.'

'Have you got a pen?'

'You just asked me that...'

'She loves you.'

At the far end of the line Josh made a choking sound that might have been a laugh or maybe it was just disgust. 'Really? Well she's got a funny way of showing it,' he said. 'Not wanting to see me. Not taking my calls. Changing her phone number.'

'He changed it so no one could ring her.'

'He?'

'Look just take this fucking number down, will you?' Ryan hissed, glancing left and right, certain now that he was being watched. 'He'll be coming back in a minute or two and he'll kill her if he knows I've given you her new number.'

'Who wi—'

182

'You got a pen?'

'Yes.'

A second or two later Woody appeared in the doorway of the smoking area. Quick as a flash, Ryan made a point of lolling nonchalantly against the wall and saying, 'I'll ring you later, yeah. I reckon two days should cover it. There's not a lot of work in it, is there? I'll nip round later in the week and give you a price.'

'What the fuck are you talking about now?' said Josh at the far end of the line.

'You got that number?' said Ryan pointedly.

'Yes, but...'

'Ah, there you are,' said Woody, making his way through the press of people, as Ryan killed the phone and slid it into his jacket pocket. 'I wondered where you'd got to; I thought you might have headed off without me.'

'No, I just got a call from someone about a job. Starting in a couple of weeks.'

Woody nodded. 'You might not need it if the flat job comes off. Here we are; I thought you might like a little night cap.' He handed Ryan a shot glass.

'You've got to be joking. What the fuck is this?' Ryan said, trying to give it back to him. 'Trying to get me drunk are you?'

Woody laughed and slapped him on the back. 'No, they were giving them out in the bar. Some kind of promotional thing, probably tastes like shit. Anyway I'm not that kind of a guy, and you're not my type.'

This time they both laughed. Woody lifted the glass in salute. Ryan lifted the glass to his lips to take a sip.

'Come on,' said Woody, 'get it down you, then we can take a look at that flat, it's not far from here.'

Ryan narrowed his eyes. 'Are you sure you want to go now? I mean I'm happy to go and have a look

183

round with you, but what are we going to be able to see in the dark? How about we go round after I come in from work tomorrow when it's light? To be honest, Woody, all I was thinking about doing was getting myself home and into my pit. I've got a day's work tomorrow, and I really need the money. It's going to be hard enough getting up as it is.'

At least that's what he meant to say; the words that came out weren't quite as clear as he intended.

Ryan had been meaning to, trying to, cut back on the booze since the thing with Farouk and the money. Okay, so Sarah's wedding had been an exception and there had been a few nights out when Woody had insisted on him coming along to keep him company, but Ryan was trying to sort himself out. At least that was what he kept telling himself. The trouble was once he started drinking he found it hard to stop. Sarah was right about him when she said he hadn't got an off switch. And yes, Ryan knew that tonight he was drinking more than he had planned to, more than was good for him, although in his defence, he told himself – and planned to tell Sarah if she asked him – he wasn't paying, and he was trying to find out what Woody was up to. And it helped him sleep if he had one or two. It stopped the dream about the man with his thumbs in his eye sockets. And Woody *was* paying, even when he gave Ryan the cash to go up to the bar for him.

Over the course of the evening, when he gave it some thought, Ryan had concluded that Woody taking him out in the evenings and paying for the drinks was most probably because Woody felt bad about the loan, and Farouk's mates reneging on their deal, and the good hiding he'd had, and that Woody was trying to make it up to him, prove that he was a good guy and that even though he looked as if he was up to something, truth was that he wasn't. That, and the thing with Sarah.

Ryan couldn't bring himself to say the word *married* or think too long about the fact that his sister was now Woody's wife. Thanks to him. *Thanks to him...* And he was still no closer to knowing what the signatures were about or why – after saying he was afraid of Farouk – Woody was going back to his old flat. His thoughts were jumbled, he swung between thinking Woody was as sound as he had always been and the growing sensation that all was not well. The booze didn't help clear his head but instead just added another layer of confusion.

Out in the street and outside the confines of the pub and the shelter of the little smoking area, the night air held the first promise of autumn. Ryan shivered and pulled his jacket tighter round him. He could have sworn it had been a lot warmer earlier, late summer warm, sitting outside warm, but now he was chilled right through to the marrow. His instinct was to turn and head for home but Woody was in the lead and was already making his way down towards the river and the towpath alongside it.

The bars and restaurants along their side of the Cam were mid-week busy. It was getting late. A few people were sitting out at tables but the chill on the edge of the wind was shepherding most of them back inside. Music trickled out into the growing darkness along with the sounds of laughter and voices.

There was a row of punts moored along the river's edge, they moved to and fro in the breeze, tapping and touching, lulled by the current. The reflections from lights on the pathway were chopped and fractured by the little waves so that they looked like shards of broken black glass. Here and there the first fallen leaves skittered across the pathway. No doubt about it – autumn was on its way.

Ryan pulled his tobacco and papers out of his

pocket, planning to stop and roll himself a cigarette, but Woody had stuck his hands in his pockets, tucked his head down, and was forging ahead.

'Hang on, wait up,' said Ryan, tucking his baccy away and hurrying after him. It was a job to keep up with him. The alcohol wasn't helping. Ryan's legs felt like a distant rumour. After a few hundred yards the two of them left the last of the midweek drinkers and a straggle of tourists behind them. Ryan was finding it hard to keep up and catch his breath, and was relieved when Woody finally slowed the pace. They had already gone a lot further along the path than Ryan expected.

'Fancy a little puff?' said Woody, pulling a joint out of his inside pocket as they headed further down the towpath.

Ryan stared at him and laughed. 'You're kidding me, right?' he said. 'All this time I've known you and I never had you pegged as a smoker.'

Woody shrugged. 'There're a lot of things you don't know about me, man. So, you want some or not?' he said, as he held it out towards him.

'Yeah, why not,' said Ryan. 'So, what else is it you're keeping to yourself then?' He wondered if this was maybe the moment to press Woody a little harder about the signatures.

Woody grinned. 'That would be telling now, wouldn't it? You've got a light, right?'

Two things struck Ryan as he took the joint, the first was that it wasn't lit and second was that Woody was wearing leather gloves. He couldn't remember seeing them when they were in the pub, or come to that ever seeing Woody wearing gloves before. It was cold but not that cold.

'Is it much further?' Ryan asked, glancing ahead. The path was lit by lamps that created great pools of yellow light between parentheses of shadow.

Woody shook his head. 'No, it's not too much further now.'

Ryan sparked up and took a long toke on the joint. He grinned as the smoke filled his lungs and he felt the sensation curl out from a warm soft centre of his chest. 'Wow. That's some good stuff. Been keeping this to yourself.' He took another pull. 'Nice.'

'I only like the best,' Woody said, as they finally fell into step. Ryan offered him the joint back. Wood shook his head. 'No, you're all right. I'll have some in a minute,' he said, all the while tapping his pockets as if he was looking for something.

Besides the gloves he was also wearing a backpack that Ryan hadn't noticed earlier either. 'Where did you get that?' he asked.

'Wake up, mate,' Woody laughed. 'It was under the stool. Come on, get with the programme. The weed's not that strong.' His hands were still working over his body.

'What do you need, man?' Ryan asked, as Woody's searching became more animated. 'Lost something?'

Woody sighed. 'I reckon I must have left my phone in the pub.'

'Bummer.'

'Or maybe I've dropped it. I'm going to have to go back and have a look for it.'

'What, you're going to go now?' asked Ryan, glancing over his shoulder, thinking about the long walk back.

'Yeah too right, top of the range, 4G,' said Woody, still searching his pockets.

'Maybe someone will hand it in,' suggested Ryan.

Woody snorted. 'Yeah and maybe the tooth fairy will pop round later and drop it off at the house. Can I just borrow your phone? I'll call mine. Maybe, if I dropped it we'll be able to hear it ringing.'

187

Ryan nodded and handed Woody his phone. Woody keyed in a number and waited. Ryan was about to speak when Woody held up a hand to silence him. They both listened, but there was nothing but night sounds and the distant rumble of the traffic. Before the call went to voice mail Woody hung up.

'Bollocks. Worth a shot,' he said, as Ryan tucked his phone back into his jacket.

They were a lot further along the towpath than Ryan had been in a long time; in fact he wasn't all together sure where they were. Last time he'd come anywhere near this far was with a girl he'd been seeing, an exchange student – French, big brown eyes, naughty mouth. He grinned and took another pull on the joint; dirty little thing she was and the two of them way too horny with nowhere to go. That had been before his mum got really ill, before he had the flat, long before any of this with Sarah and Woody and the money. He tried to remember the French girl's name. Although her name eluded him he remembered that they had walked down the towpath hand in hand, hands all over each other, looking for a quiet place, any place, maybe under the trees, maybe under the willows.

It was getting muddier now, slippery under foot, the verges on the side of the path less manicured and a couple of the lights were out.

'Are you sure that this place is down here?' Ryan asked, glancing round. 'Maybe we should just go back and just see if we can find your phone? Come back in the daylight? I'm mean it's pitch fucking black down here.'

The combination of booze and blow was making his head spin.

'Stop whining, man,' said Woody. 'We're more or less there now. I just need to get my bearings and work out which one it is.' He was glancing up at one of the buildings that ran along side where they were walking. It was a little ahead of them in the darkness, behind a fence and patch of grass. Woody was peering up into the gloom.

'I think it's that one just there, look,' he said, pointing. 'You can see the back of it from here. Third floor, left hand corner – the one with the lights on and the blinds. Although it could be the next one up. It gives you an idea of what the view is like.'

'Are you sure?' said Ryan, craning his neck to see what Woody was looking at. 'It's a joke. I can't see bugger all.'

'Yes, I'm sure that this is it,' said Woody and with that he looked up and stepped back, and Ryan – on the outside of the path – followed his lead, and as he did so he felt his foot slipping backwards, not a lot, but just enough to throw him off balance. Ryan laughed nervously and swore under his breath. He hadn't realised quite how close he was to the edge.

At the sound of his voice Woody looked back over his shoulder in Ryan's direction, and as Ryan tried to regain his balance Woody swung round and reached out towards him.

But he realised Woody wasn't planning on grabbing hold of him. Instead Woody pushed him in the chest, hard, flat handed, palms level with Ryan's heart, toppling him over backwards, sending him into the river.

Hitting the surface was an icy cold wakeup call.

'What the fuck,' Ryan thought in the split second before he plunged beneath the surface. The water eagerly poured into his open mouth, the words – and new words – and a welter of thoughts lost in the deluge, all tasting of mud and something oily and dark. The water was bone-chillingly cold, and shocked the breath out of his lungs. Sober, Ryan could have probably clambered out. But drunk, stoned and totally disorientated the water grabbed at him with eager hands, and held on tight, soaking his jeans, his boots, the heavy plaid jacket he was wearing, filling him up, holding him down, pulling him under.

It was crazy; all he had to do was find his footing. Ryan knew it wasn't that deep and he could swim, for fuck's sake. His head was full of thoughts, razor sharp and all begging for attention and at the same time they felt as if they were a long way away, so very, very far away that he couldn't quite catch them. If this was Woody's idea of a joke it was lost on him, but he knew that soon Woody would grab hold of him, help him out, pull him to the shore. He would do it in a moment or two, he would, Ryan was certain of that. They were friends, mates. And then they'd laugh about this, laugh for months, years – fucking Woody, what a joker, trying to frigging drown him, the dipstick.

He tried not to panic, tried not to freeze up, and tried instead to bottom out. If he could just find the bottom he could push himself up to the surface and Woody would grab his jacket and pull him out on the bank. He'd probably hock his lungs up, ditch the booze all over the grass, and they'd laugh about it some more as Woody tried to avoid getting sick all over his fancy running shoes.

Ryan tried to stand up. He seemed to be going down a long way. Shit, he had seen people punt on the Cam day in, day out. It couldn't be that deep. He tried to strike out for the bank – it wasn't that far, but the water grabbed hold of his clothes, the water sucking him down and holding him tight. It felt as if it wanted him for itself.

Ryan tried to call out before he realised that he was still under the surface, and as the cold water filled him, he stopped fighting, and all thoughts seemed to slip away, bright like sparklers, and float downstream. He could see them glittering in the lights – all those thoughts, all his ideas, all of his future. He felt tired, sleepy almost, and then it occurred to him that maybe this wasn't happening at all, maybe he was dreaming or maybe Woody hadn't just put mary-jane in the joint, maybe it was something stronger, weirder – shit it was some sort of a hit if it was – and as the last thought bubbled up through his mind he started to laugh and as he did his lungs filled with water and this time he couldn't taste it.

Under the water it was dark as night but Ryan could see the lights above him and reached up one last time, instinct now rather than reason forcing himself to fight the pull, surfacing briefly, too shocked now to call out, too full with the river and the cold and the certainty that he was going to die, to do anything other than let the water take him. In that moment he could see Woody standing there on the bank watching him, making no effort to rescue him, his face no more than a white oval in the gloom. Then he was gone and there was darkness and the sound of Ryan's heart as it struggled to keep him alive, and then even that was too far off, too distant to disturb the peace he had found.

Woody stood still and quiet there by the water's edge, waiting until he was absolutely certain that Ryan wasn't going to resurface. When he was sure, he calmly continued down the towpath till he got to a pathway where he could cut through the buildings and get back to the road. As he did, it started to rain; Woody smiled to himself. He had chosen this route carefully, and carried on walking so that his footprints wouldn't appear to double back at the point where Ryan had gone in, but hopefully now the rain would wash away any last remaining traces of his having been there at all.

He walked briskly, purposely, but not so fast as to attract attention. A street or two from the river he slipped off the backpack he had been carrying, and paused for a moment to ease off his trainers. Taking out the shoes he had brought with him, he put them on. Gloves still on, Woody glanced left and right before dropping the trainers into a carrier bag, along with two firelighters and a pile of crumpled newspapers. Pulling out a few of the scrunched pages he held them in his hand.

Mid-week, the street he had chosen to walk back along was lined with wheelie bins. Glancing round to make sure no one was watching him he picked a bin at random and lifted the lid. It was half full with plastic bags and fast food cartons and smelt of pizza and the sweet fetid scent of decay. Smiling, Woody dropped the carrier bag in alongside all the others. He added a hefty squirt of lighter fluid, a flick of his lighter to ignite the newspaper, and a stick he had left in the hedge earlier to prop the bin open – before carefully peeling off his gloves and adding them to the pyre in the bin. It took less than a minute for the fire to take hold, though Woody waited until he was certain the bin was well and truly alight before turning and heading for town. Now even if the police found the shoeprints down on the towpath there would be no trainers to match them with.

Woody was back in the pub before closing time, in time to retrieve his phone from where he had hidden it in a planter, close to where he and Ryan had been standing earlier. If the police tracked his phone they would be able to see where he was when Ryan slipped into the Cam, and it wouldn't be there with him.

After a few minutes watching the comings and goings, Woody got up, slipped off his wedding ring and tucked it into his inside pocket, all the while apparently concentrating on checking his phone, but just in time to collide with a big blonde girl who was navigating her way between the tables carrying a tray of drinks. She looked a little tipsy, her hair a little awry. He didn't hit her hard, the collision wasn't overly dramatic nor did it cause much damage but it was just enough to be memorable.

The girl squealed; the tray slipped sideways out of her hands, the contents clattering to the floor in an explosion of glass, orange juice and booze.

'Oh excuse me, I'm so sorry,' said Woody, catching hold of her arm so that she didn't slip.

'You wanna watch where you're going,' the girl snapped right back at him in perfect estuary English, as she made a show of tidying herself, and he stooped down to pick up the tray.

Woody smiled up at her. 'Will you forgive me?' He raised his eyebrows, part question, but heavy on the flirtation. She reddened and giggled.

'Depends on what you're planning to do next,' she said.

People around them grumbled and stepped around the mess, a man picked up the one bottle of mixer that hadn't been smashed, and on a raft of Chinese whispers word spread across to the bar staff to get over to them with a brush and dust pan and a mop and bucket.

Woody meanwhile had taken his wallet out, and was guiding the woman back towards the bar. 'Let me replace your drinks for a start. What can I get you and your friends?' he purred, while his hand settled into the small of her back. 'Haven't I seen you somewhere before? Do you work at the university?'

She smiled and shook her head. 'No, I work in

Boots.'

'Really? Maybe that's where it was then. So what do you want?' he said, as they eased their way to the front of the press of customers.

'I've got a list,' she said, slyly.

Woody grinned. 'Really?' he said. 'I like a woman who knows what she wants. Best we work our way through it then, aye?'

The girl giggled. 'Cheeky.'

'So, what's your name then?' he asked.

'Carol. Carol Mullings.'

Woody held out his hand. 'Pleased to meet you, Carol. I'm Woody,' he said.

'Really?' she looked at him quizzically and pulled a face. 'I thought – well you know – that it would be something much more exotic.'

He laughed. 'It is, but Woody is what my friends call me.'

'So what is it really?'

'You don't want to know,' he said. 'Maybe I'll tell you later.'

She nodded. 'Later? That sounds like a nice idea. So, Woody, did you bump into me on purpose?'

He pulled an innocent face. 'What, and spill good booze? No, I don't think so. Would I do a thing like that just to meet a gorgeous woman?' he continued in a voice that implied that that was exactly what he had done. 'Me and my friend are just out for a quiet drink.'

The girl glanced round. 'So where's your friend now then?'

Woody grinned. 'Gone. He said he had to go home. Lightweight. Didn't want to be out too late on a school night.'

The girl peered at him for a minute or two, considering what he had just said and then finally she said. 'What is he like a teacher or something?' At

194

which point the barman glanced in their direction.

'What can I do you for?' asked the man.

Woody nodded towards the blonde. 'Tell the man what it is you want, Honey.'

Carol giggled. 'Where to begin,' she said, winking at Woody.

The barman laughed. 'Now, now, Miss, keep it clean,' he joked.

Carol moved in so close that their bodies touched, as they waited for the barman to sort out their order.

'Shouldn't you be getting back to your friends?' he asked. 'I can bring the drinks over if you like; make sure they all get there in once piece.'

'They can wait a bit longer,' she said. 'You live round here, do you?'

He smiled. 'No, how about you?'

She took the drink that he offered her. 'Not far.'

'Really? In that case maybe I ought to walk you home, make sure you don't get into any more trouble.'

Carol held his gaze, eyes bright with mischief. 'Not backwards in coming forwards, are you, Woody?'

He raised his eyebrows. 'Who me?' he said.

She laughed, closing carmine lips round the straw in her cocktail and sucking gently. 'Yes you,' she said, as she pulled away, her tongue working on the end of the straw.

He grinned; the suggestion clear as day.

Sarah

Two women out jogging found Ryan the next morning. In the reeds. On a bend in the river. They thought it was a black polythene bag at first. Till they saw his hands. Floating. It was dark when the police came to the house. I don't know why it took

195

them all day to find out where he lived. I didn't ask.

'I couldn't work out what the noise was to begin with. I'd been reading and fallen asleep on the sofa in the sitting room. The noise woke me up. There were voices and the sounds of banging and hammering. I suppose it was maybe half past eight, maybe nine. I'm not altogether sure now. I'd been sound asleep, and then I realised it was someone knocking at the door. Hard. And then I was hard awake. First of all I thought that it might be the men who had come before. The ones who had beaten Ryan up. And then I heard Woody talking to them, and heard them say they were police. And then I thought that maybe they had found out about me and Woody and they had come to arrest us both. But whatever the reason was that they were there, I knew that it wasn't to bring us anything good.'

Chapter Fifteen

'You'd better come in,' said Woody, as he opened the front door. 'I'm not sure exactly where my wife is. Come on through. Sorry it's so dark in here. I was upstairs. I hadn't realised how late it was. I'll just get the lights.'

From the sitting room Sarah could hear the low rumble of voices. She didn't know whether to feel relieved or anxious that Woody had answered the door. Standing up she straightened her clothes and ran her fingers back through her hair, trying to tidy herself up. She had fallen asleep on the sofa when she got in from work, and between then and now it had got dark, and cold too. Still feeling slightly disorientated Sarah opened the door into the hallway, making a concerted effort to wake up, blinking in the glare of lights that Woody was busy switching on.

'Sorry,' he was saying, talking over his shoulder as he moved around switching the lamps on. 'I was studying upstairs. Ah, there you are, Sarah. Are you okay?'

Sarah turned. There were two police officers standing in the hallway, both very still, both very young, both composed with sombre expressions.

She said nothing, waiting for one of them to speak. Her body might be still but her mind was working overtime. What did they know? Would they put her in handcuffs? Would they let her get changed out of her work clothes before they took her to the police station? And more to the point, how had the police found out about the sham marriage? She hadn't said a word to anyone, not a word, and couldn't imagine Woody would have said anything –

which left Ryan; maybe Ryan had said something.

It didn't take a great leap of the imagination to guess that it had to be him. Drunk maybe. Stoned. Bragging. Sarah closed her eyes, wondering what the hell he had said and to whom. Would they take her straight to prison? On remand. Sarah waited, her pulse banging like a drum.

Woody caught her eye and said, somewhat unnecessarily, 'It's the police.' As if she couldn't see for herself, and then he said, quickly, as if she had asked. 'It's about Ryan.'

'What about Ryan? What's happened now?'

'We need to talk.' He spoke gently, holding out a hand towards her. 'Why don't you come through into the kitchen so we can all sit down?' He spoke to her as if she was a child or possibly ill, in a voice so tender and so contrived that she almost laughed.

'She's not been sleeping well,' he said, as an aside to the police officers. 'She probably had a bit of a nap, took a sleeping tablet. Leaves her a bit groggy.' He smiled at her. 'She worries me sometimes. Always rushing about, looking after everyone else, anyone but herself.'

Sarah stared at him, wondering why he was lying, and if that was what a husband might say, a real one, someone who genuinely truly loved her. 'I didn't take a sleeping tablet,' she said.

He nodded. 'Oh well – that's good,' he said gently, as if it was a cause for congratulation.

Woody was so clever; and then her attention shifted to the other thing that he had said.

'What about Ryan? Where is he? What's happened now?' she asked, torn between relief at not being immediately arrested, and a great rush of panic. 'Where is he?' she said. 'Is he all right?'

'Just take it steady,' Woody said calmly, beckoning her closer.

'You told me he would be safe,' she said, as she crossed the hall. 'You promised me that you take care of it. You said...'

Woody turned towards the officers. 'Ryan got himself into a bit of trouble a few months ago. He was beaten up pretty badly. It was really nasty. I said that I'd keep an eye on him. Keep him out of trouble. He's always been a bit of a handful. Great guy but always – well you know.' Woody smiled. 'Bit of a lad.'

One of the officers, the male one, nodded. 'We'll need some details, Sir, if you don't mind.'

Woody nodded too. 'Yes, of course, although Ryan was a bit sketchy about exactly what happened to him. Your lot seemed to think it was a case of being in the wrong place at the wrong time. Didn't they, Sarah?' he said, turning to her for confirmation.

The officer made a little noise of acknowledgement. 'I'm afraid it sometimes happens, Sir.'

'So what's happened to him this time?' Sarah pressed. She didn't like the way they were talking to each other and not to her. The way they were talking over her head. 'Where is he now? Is he okay?' She sounded shriller than she intended.

No one quite met her eye, and then Woody said, 'Why, don't we go into the kitchen and I'll put the kettle on.'

Before anyone had chance to move, Sarah snorted. 'Don't do this to me, Woody. He's my brother. I don't want to go into the kitchen; I want to know what's happened to Ryan. Tell me. Where is he? What's happened to him?'

She saw the look that passed between the three of them and felt icy fingers track down her spine.

The female officer cleared her throat. 'I'm terribly sorry, Mrs Ahmed. There's no easy way to say this. His body was recovered from the Cam first thing this morning. He was found by two women while they were out running.' She spoke in a low, even voice. 'I'm so very sorry.'

Sarah stared at her, ignoring what she heard. 'So is he in hospital?' she asked. Sarah saw the look again. The one that passed between them and excluded her, as if she was mad or fragile, or a child.

'I'm afraid that your brother is dead, Mrs Ahmed.' the woman said.

The officer had been right; there was no easy way to soften the blow, no words that would make it easier or untrue. The breath caught in Sarah's throat, and when she finally opened her mouth to speak a noise spilled out, a soft, long, low keening sound, that rolled up from deep down in her belly and seemed to fill her whole head.

'No,' she whispered, 'No, no, *no*. That can't be right. It can't be.' Woody caught hold of her arm as her legs folded under her and as he pulled her close she could smell perfume on his clothes – perfume and cigarette smoke.

Her eyes widened.

'I'm so sorry,' he said. 'So very sorry.'

Sarah rounded on him. 'How can he be dead? How? You said you'd take care of him. You were with him last night. How could this happen? You went for a drink, you said that he'd be safe,' she said, accusingly, the words tumbling out of her mouth unchecked. 'You said. You promised me.'

'I know, I know,' Woody soothed. 'And he was fine when I was in the pub with him, Sarah, absolutely fine.' She knew from his tone that he was saying it not just for her benefit but also for the two officers. 'We were at the Raven. He left before I did. He told me that he was coming straight home, said he'd promised you that he'd be home early. He said he'd got to get up for work. I stayed for a bit longer. I got talking to some people.'

'Some people?' Sarah stared at him. 'Who?' she said, before she could stop herself. 'Who were you with?'

Woody's gaze didn't waiver. 'Just some people,' he repeated. He glanced at the police officers. 'I can give you their names if it'll help.'

Sarah hesitated. The policewoman was already eyeing her up like Sarah was some kind of crazy. 'So where was Ryan when you were talking to these people?' she pressed.

'I don't know,' said Woody. 'He'd had a bit to drink, but he seemed fine to me. He said he was coming home. And then a bit later he rang me but hung up before I could take the call. I assumed I'd see him today so I didn't bother ringing back. I thought if it was something important he'd leave a message or text me.'

'How do you know it was Ryan?' Sarah asked, swinging round to confront the two officers.

The female officer said, 'Your brother appears to have had his wallet and all his personal possessions on him. He had money on him, his phone.'

Sarah was too stunned to cry. Woody looked away.

'So you're sure?' Sarah pressed. 'How can you be sure?'

The woman nodded. 'I'm sorry. We found a wallet with credit cards and a driving license which was pretty conclusive, and which rather rules out robbery. We will need someone to come down and formally identify the body.'

'I'd be happy to do that,' said Woody. 'My wife is obviously very upset.'

Sarah stared at them. 'Now?' she said.

'No, not now, tomorrow morning will be fine. We can send a car for you if you would prefer?'

Woody waved the words away. 'No, no, it'll be fine. I'll come in first thing tomorrow. Where do I need to go?'

'No, I don't want you to go. I want to see him,' said Sarah.

'Are you sure?' Woody asked. 'I mean, we don't know what sort of state he's in.' He turned towards the policeman for some kind of confirmation. 'Was he beaten up? Are you looking for someone else, you know, for whoever who did this?'

The officer shook his head. 'It would appear at the moment that it was an accident, Sir, although we're obviously not ruling anything out. And I'm afraid there will have to be a post mortem.'

'Ah,' said Woody. 'I see. Well—'

'He's my brother,' Sarah said. '*My* brother.'

Woody patted her shoulder. She stared at him. 'I know, Sweetie. Everyone understands how you must be feeling.' And then, turning his attention to the officers, Woody continued. 'I can be in tomorrow first thing. And if there is anything we can do, anything at all, then we will. Obviously.'

Both police officers nodded.

Woody caught her look. 'And I'll bring Sarah in. Of course. Obviously. She is Ryan's sister, next of kin.'

'What happened to him?' she asked. 'I don't understand? He was only going out for a drink. What was he doing down by the river?'

'We're not altogether sure at the moment exactly what happened or why your brother was on the riverbank. We've appealed for any witnesses to come forward. First indications are that he appears to have fallen in from the towpath, although I'm afraid we don't have any other details at the moment, but I promise you we'll do out best to find out. I'm sorry to bring you such bad news.' As the officer spoke he took a card out of his pocket and wrote something down on the back of it. 'This is where you'll need to go tomorrow, and if you've got any questions, anything at all, you can always contact me on the number on the other side. I was wondering if we can perhaps just ask you a few questions while we're here?'

Sarah stared at him. He was smiling at her. It felt as if she had walked into someone else's life. Woody was nodding, all loving husband and good citizen. 'Yes, of course, no trouble, shall we go through?' he said, opening the kitchen door. They followed him inside. Sarah watched them go. Woody came back for her, solicitous, gentle, taking her arm, leading her inside, sitting her down at the table as if she was an invalid.

'We can always come back, if you'd prefer,' said the officer, eyes firmly fixed on Sarah.

Woody waved the words away. 'No, we'd rather do it now, wouldn't we, Sarah? I doubt either if us will be able to settle now, will we, Honey? Not until we know what happened.' He switched on the kettle as he spoke, fumbling with the teapot, looking for the teabags. 'I'm not sure that there is much more we can tell you.'

'Here, let me do that, my colleague has just got a few questions,' said the male officer.

While the policeman made tea, the policewoman sat down at the table with Sarah and took out a notebook. Her voice was low and even, solicitous – kind. Was Sarah up to this? Would she mind talking about Ryan, answering a few questions about him? Did Ryan have any money worries? Was he depressed? Did he have a history of drug or alcohol abuse? Sarah shook her head.

'He liked a drink, but no more than anyone else. And no, he wasn't very good with money – but I

203

think things were okay at the moment, not good but he wasn't in any trouble about money.' She felt herself glancing up at Woody for confirmation. Woody nodded. Even as she was doing it Sarah wondered if the policewoman noticed because she wrote something down in her notebook. 'And what about drugs?' she asked.

Sarah felt tears trickling down her face. 'How can he be dead?' she whimpered. 'How?'

The woman nodded and turned to Woody, who sighed. 'I'm not sure what I can tell you really. I think he occasionally smoked the odd joint, you know, recreational stuff, but nothing harder as far as I know.'

'And was this a regular thing?'

Woody shrugged. 'I really don't know. I don't think so.'

His hand dropped down over Sarah's. She stared at him; her first instinct to pull it away, but how would that look? She hated the weight of it and the heat of it. As if reading her mind Woody's fingers tightened around hers, something that from anyone else, and anyone watching, might be interpreted as a gesture of comfort but Sarah knew without doubt was a warning.

'You said you and Ryan had been out for a drink yesterday, Mr Ahmed?' the policewoman said. 'Can you tell me how Ryan seemed to you?'

Woody bit his lip and took a breath, apparently considering his reply. 'He seemed fine to me. We'd both had a bit to drink. Nothing particularly heavy. It was a week night and he told me several times that he couldn't be late because he had work today. When he left I assumed he'd gone home and gone to bed.'

'Do you know what time that was?'

Woody pulled a face. 'Not really, not that late. Half past ten, maybe a bit after? I can check my phone if you like?'

The woman nodded and made a note. 'So, you didn't go with him?' she asked.

Woody shook his head. 'No.'

'And what about emotionally? How would you say he was?'

'He's *my* brother,' Sarah interrupted.

They all looked at her. 'We know, Sweetie,' he said. Sarah felt Woody's fingers tighten around hers, and then he continued. 'He seemed okay. He said he'd got a bit of work on at the moment. He and I had been talking about maybe finding somewhere to do up. A project we could both get involved in.'

'So you're a builder too, are you, Sir?'

'No, no not at all, but I've got some business expertise. And we were keen to work together.'

The woman nodded. 'And how would you describe your relationship with Ryan?'

'He's my friend. Actually I knew him before I knew Sarah. In fact that was how we first met. Ryan introduced us, didn't he?' Woody managed a smile, which turned into a choking sob that caught in his throat. 'Oh god, I'm so sorry, this is terrible. I can't believe he's dead. He's such a nice guy. Are you sure it's him?'

The woman made the slightest of gestures with her head. It might be tiny but it was unequivocal. They hadn't made a mistake; they were in no doubt, Ryan was dead.

'God,' said Woody. 'I can't believe it. I was only with him a few hours ago. We'd been talking about the idea of working together – big plans – big plans.' His voice crackled and finally broke.

Sarah watched Woody; it was a masterly performance. It felt as if she had been written out of the picture, side-lined by his obvious grief. They were talking now about Ryan getting beaten up, about how

205

Woody thought there was more to it than Ryan had been telling people. Sarah listened, wondering how the hell he had the front to spin them a tale like that when he knew exactly why those men had been after Ryan and who they were. He could probably give the police their names and addresses.

The policeman was nodding. They drank the tea. The male officer joined them at the table.

Woody was getting into his stride now.

'So you're saying that Ryan had enemies?'

'No, not enemies, just that he had more going on than he was telling us.' He glanced at Sarah apparently for corroboration.

'Us?' said Sarah, unable to keep quiet any longer.

The policeman glanced across at her, but it was Woody who spoke. 'What I mean is that I think he probably knew who those men were and kept quiet about it. He didn't talk about it very much. In case it made things worse. I think he was afraid of the consequences of splitting on them; at least that was the impression I got.'

He was watching Sarah as he spoke. She caught the message loud and clear; it wouldn't do for her to tell them whatever it was she thought she knew, not now, not ever.

The policeman was looking down at his notepad. 'So, he didn't mention any names?'

Sarah shook her head. 'No, but he seemed okay recently. He was working. Helping out.'

'Helping out?'

'Yes, paying his way,' said Woody, snatching the conversation back from her. 'Ryan was always a bit casual about money and we had to remind him that this wasn't a hotel, and that we aren't a charity, didn't we, Sarah? He could take all that kind of thing for granted, bills, helping out round the place, you know, unless we reminded him.'

'So he lives here with you?' said the policeman, glancing round the kitchen.

'Yes and no. He lives downstairs. In a self contained flat,' said Woody.

'Would you mind if we took a look at it?'

'No, not at all, would we, Sarah?'

'No,' she said, getting to her feet, which finally gave her the chance to pull her hand out from under Woody's.

'Where are you going?' he said in surprise. Sarah wondered if he thought she meant *No, they couldn't look,* and was surprised how good it felt to wrong foot him.

'I have to go upstairs and get the spare key.' She looked at the policewoman. 'I won't be a minute.'

The woman nodded.

Sarah took the stairs two at a time. They had to be wrong about Ryan. Surely she would know if he was dead. She would feel it. A few more minutes and they would all be on the basement steps, unlocking the flat and he would be shouting, 'What the hell are you doing. Can't you knock? I'm asleep in here. What do you want?'

She hoped that when he saw the police he had the good sense not to panic and to keep his mouth shut till they had chance to explain what this was about, not blurt anything out. Alone in her bedroom Sarah opened the dressing table drawer and rummaged through the debris, trying to remember exactly where she had put the spare keys. They had to be there somewhere; she pushed aside a tangle of earrings and cheap jewellery; maybe they should just go downstairs and knock. She emptied the drawer out onto the bed. There was no sign of the keys.

After the thing with Anna, it had struck her just how crazy it was to have the spare keys to the whole house hanging on a row of hooks just inside the kitchen door, and so she had brought them upstairs and dropped them into a tin. She'd put it into one of the drawers in her dressing table. But which drawer?

The middle one wouldn't open; something was catching on the lip. She tried to tease it free with her fingertips. Once upon a time it had been her mother's dressing table and Sarah had never really cleared it out, not properly, so there was an overlap of possessions. Carefully, Sarah pressed down the thing that was causing the drawer to stick, teasing it backwards and forwards, until finally the drawer gave up and opened. Sarah smiled; it was a little jewellery box that had belonged to her mum. It had been a while since she had seen it and without thinking Sarah lifted the lid.

Once upon a time the whole thing had been covered in tiny glittering tiles and little white shells all of which had long since loosened and dropped off so that now the pattern was picked out in glue and dust, but the inside of the box was pristine. As the lid opened a tiny ballerina in a pink tutu stood up and began to turn *en pointe* to the theme tune from Doctor Zhivago, rotating on a stage of deep buttoned dark pink velvet, her dance reflected in a small mirror set into the lid.

The sound of the music stopped Sarah dead in her tracks. A memory appeared fully formed into her head like a snippet of film; a time when they used to dance round the bedroom to the music box, Sarah with long hair, caught up in bunches, dancing with a redheaded doll, while Ryan, just a little boy, a toddler with a mop of curls, danced, standing on his mother's feet, holding onto her hands. Their mum would spin him around and around, until they got dizzy and they would all laugh so much, so very, very much, and fall over onto the bed, giggling like crazy, while over by the window their dad would sit in an armchair, a blanket tucked up round him, watching and smiling, the skin on his face yellow and thin as parchment and drawn tight over his skull.

The music slowed and faded, and the image died; Sarah felt a pain in her chest, in her heart, a pain so fierce and so hot that she thought for a moment that she might be having a heart attack.

Ryan couldn't be dead. There was no way. No way. He couldn't be dead. He was too precious, too special. Ryan was all she had. Her lips began to tremble; her hands joined it, the tremor spread until it felt as if her whole body was going to shake itself apart. She had to do something – she just couldn't remember what it was – and then Sarah saw the pile of things on the bed and remembered the key.

Feeling as if she was coming unravelled, Sarah threw things out of the drawers, onto the dressing table top, onto the floor, onto the bed until she found the tin box and inside it the spare keys for the basement flat, for the house, for the car, for their whole life. And then she set the box down on the bed where she could see it, and with butterfingers dragged a brush through her hair, so that she looked at least a little presentable. On the dressing table the dancer watched her in silence. Sarah picked up the key, and oblivious to the chaos she had left behind, closed the bedroom door, and hurried downstairs.

It felt like she had been gone hours, and it surprised her that the three of them were still there sitting in the kitchen waiting for her. They looked up as she opened the door. Sarah couldn't help but wonder what they had been talking about in her absence, and knew that it must have been about her.

'I found the key,' she said, holding it out in her open palm.

The policeman nodded. 'Good. We're all set then. And you're okay to do this?'

She looked at him, feeling her lips start to quiver again. 'If I don't think too much,' she muttered. 'I don't want to believe it.'

He nodded, and she could see the compassion in his eyes. 'I know. We can wait until tomorrow if you'd rather.'

Sarah shook her head. 'I need to do it now. I want him to be in there. In the flat. For him be to cross that we've disturbed him.' Her voice sound crackly and uneven, like a bad recording on an old gramophone record.

The policeman took the keys from her. 'You're sure?'

She nodded.

'I'm happy for me and your husband to go down and have a look if you'd prefer?'

Sarah shook her head. 'No, I want to go.'

And so she led them out of the kitchen and down the steps to the basement flat. There were still bin bags and other rubbish stacked up in the light well; Sarah reminded herself that she would really have to have a word with Ryan when she saw him, when this nonsense was all over, when he turned up and they cleared up this misunderstanding. He needed to get a grip, be tidier, get his act together.

The security light snapped on above the door. Sarah knocked. No one answered. Sarah lifted the letterbox and called into the darkness 'Ryan? Ryan, are you in there? We need to come in.'

It occurred to her that maybe he had had a couple of beers after work, maybe he was tired, maybe too tired to hear them. Maybe he was asleep, grabbing a nap on the bed. The policeman knocked harder; she had a sense that he was humouring her.

After a moment or two and with a growing sense of urgency Sarah slid the key into the lock and turned it. For an instant the door resisted, which gave her even more hope, chances were that he had dropped the latch on the inside when he'd come in, maybe even remembered to put the chain on – but then it swung open, catching on the mat and the pile of magazines and papers stacked behind the door.

The flat still smelt of frying, old sweat, and stale water. The security light went out, plunging them into darkness; Sarah reached inside to find the light switch. There was a flicker as the fluorescent tube sparked and then the room was flooded with cold unforgiving light. The kitchen table was strewn with dirty dishes. There was a newspaper folded and propped up against a fruit juice carton, as if waiting for its reader to come back.

'Ryan?' Sarah called again, although she couldn't help notice the look that passed between the police officers as they followed her. The kitchen floor was sticky under foot. 'Ryan?' Her voice was louder this time. Stronger.

She pushed open the hall doorway and beyond that the one into the bedroom, turning lights on as she went. 'Ryan, are you in there?'

He wasn't. The bedroom curtains were closed and looked as if they had been that way for a long time. Sarah flicked on the light. The bed was empty, the duvet rolled back to reveal a rucked nest of sheets. The bedside table was covered with mugs and glasses, the TV remote, magazines and book. A scrum of pillows had been scrunched up against the headboard. There was a book open face down on the bedcovers, saving the page, as if Ryan had just slipped out to grab a mug of tea or a shower.

Sarah looked into each room in turn: the tiny sitting room, stacked with clutter, the second bedroom, the bathroom, calling his name as she went. She didn't care that they were watching her. She didn't care what they thought. She needed to be

211

sure. And then, when even she had to concede that he wasn't at home, Sarah left the police officers to look round and went back upstairs.

She could see that Woody was torn between staying with them and coming with her. She could see his gaze working over the place – the table, the bookshelves, the bedside table. She wondered if he was afraid that there was something in the flat that might betray them. Was he afraid that Ryan had kept a diary or maybe made a note about their wedding or the loan, or the men who had loaned him the money, which would somehow lead back to Woody – or was there something else?

Holding his ground and making no effort to leave, Woody caught her eye as if to let her know that he was aware that she was watching him. 'I won't be minute,' he said.

The policeman, seeing his hesitation said, 'It's all right, Sir, we won't be long. We'll bring the key up when we're done. You can go with your wife if you like.'

'Shouldn't someone stay down here with you?' asked Woody.

'Well, you can if you want, Sir. But it'll just be a quick look around. We won't be long and we won't touch anything or take anything. We just need to take a quick look to see if there is anything obviously amiss.'

Still Woody hesitated.

In the end Sarah left them to it and went back upstairs. She felt cold. In fact by the time she got into the kitchen Sarah was shivering so much that she couldn't think and could barely undo the door. Eager to try and get warm she grabbed one of the jackets from the row of hooks just inside the door and wrapped it around her shoulders, trying to hold off the chill while she put the kettle back on to boil. It took her a second or two to realise that the coat she'd taken was Ryan's work fleece; the good one he took with him on cold days. He must have left it there. It smelt of him, of sweat and aftershave and tobacco smoke. The smell of him made her whimper, and wrap it all the tighter round her.

How could Ryan possibly be dead? He wouldn't leave her on her own. He wouldn't, however bad things got, however much they fought she knew that deep down he would never have abandoned her.

Tears ran unbidden and unhindered down her face. Without Ryan what would she do? He was the only other person who knew who she really was and who she had been, all the things they had shared were gone forever now. She started to sob. He was also the only one who knew about the sham marriage. The only other person in the world – however leery and unreliable – who was totally on her side. The only person who, against the odds, might be able to save her.

She backhanded the tears away with the sleeve and as she did something crackled in an inside pocket. Without really thinking about it Sarah reached inside and pulled out a folded sheet of lined A4 paper. Unfolding it carefully, at first glance she thought it might be a list and then she looked closer; the whole of one side was covered in signatures – Woody's signature. Sarah stared at it, her stomach doing a back flip. It didn't look like Ryan's handwriting but then again it wasn't meant to. Why was Ryan trying to copy Woody's signature? There was no good reason she could think of that led her thoughts to anything legal. If he was doing this what was it he was trying to sign? Cheques were the most obvious answer. She'd never seen Woody with a chequebook, but with Ryan anything was possible. Sarah could feel the colour rising in her face.

She took another look at the sheet of paper; not wanting to process the implications, not now, not this minute, not when she wanted to think the best of Ryan, and remember the brother that she loved, so instead Sarah refolded the paper and was about to slip it back into the jacket pocket when she notice that there were notes scribbled on the reverse side of the page; phone numbers and websites and some other bits and pieces, and those definitely weren't in Ryan's hand writing, they were in Woody's, which made even less sense. Very carefully, with her mind churning, Sarah slipped the sheet of paper back into the pocket where she had found it.

When she looked up Woody was standing just inside the kitchen door. 'What are you doing?' he asked in an undertone.

Sarah shook her head, wondering how much he had seen. 'Nothing. I'm cold. I was going to make more tea.'

He smiled. 'Good idea. I'm really so sorry about Ryan. Such a shock.'

Sarah glanced at him. Something rang false in his tone. Woody's smile widened. 'So, there we are, there's just you and me now,' he said.

Sarah didn't like the way that sounded.

Josh

'I read about Ryan's accident in the Cambridge Evening Times. I was stunned; really shocked. Ryan could be a pain in the arse sometimes but he was a good guy.'

'And he was also Sarah's brother?'

'Yes, I know. He drove her mad but I know how much she loved him. I wanted to do something; I wanted to say how sorry I was. See if there was anything I could do. She had always looked out for

214

him. Losing him – well I can't imagine how she was feeling.'

'And did any of our lot come and see you?'

'The police? Yes, a couple of uniformed officers came round to where I was working a day or two after the accident, apparently my number was one of the last calls logged on Ryan's phone.'

'Okay, and what did you tell them?'

'I presume you've got my statement there somewhere.'

'Humour me if you would, Josh. I'm just trying to piece all this together.'

'Okay. Well, I told them that Ryan had rung to say that Sarah wasn't happy.'

'Was that what he actually said?'

'No, but it was what he inferred. I can't remember exactly what he said word for word now, but it made me think that things weren't right with her. I wasn't exactly sure what was going on, but I could tell that Ryan was really worried about her.'

'Anything else?'

'The way he said it made me think that Sarah was in some sort of trouble, and afraid.'

'And Ryan did sound drunk?'

'Yes, yes he did.'

'Excessively so?'

'No, but I'd say he was pretty far from sober.'

'And did it sound to you like Ryan was in any kind of trouble or worried about anything else?'

'No, not at all, he sounded cautious as if he didn't want someone – whoever he was with maybe, to know that he was talking to me. But he sounded good.'

'And you told all this to the officers who contacted you?'

'Yes, although I don't know how much notice they took. I think they thought I was an ex-boyfriend with a grudge against Sarah's new man.'

'You didn't know then that she was married?'

'No, no I found that out later.'

'And are you telling me that the officers didn't take your concerns seriously?'

'To be honest I don't know what they thought. I found it hard to explain to them what my concern was. I told them that Sarah had finished with me just when I thought things were getting serious. I think they were sympathetic rather than anything else. They were more concerned about how drunk had Ryan sounded and his state of mind. And if I thought he was saying his last goodbyes.'

'I'm not with you.'

'They wanted to know if he had said anything about being depressed or wanting to take his own life. If he was suicidal.'

'And you told them what?'

'Far from it. He sounded fine to me. Yes, he sounded drunk and like he wanted to tell me something, but not depressed. It was like he wanted to put the record straight.'

'About Sarah?'

'Yes.'

'So what did you do then, Josh?'

'When, after the police came round?'

'No, after Ryan rang?'

'I called Sarah on the number Ryan had given me. Not that night as it was getting late, but the next day.'

'He gave you a number?'

'Yes, he told me it's Sarah's new phone.'

'And what happened when you rang?'

'It was switched off. I tried again later and it went to voice mail. I realised later, after I saw the story in the paper, that it probably hadn't been a good time.'

Sarah

'I didn't expect to be able to sleep that night after the police came to tell me about Ryan. I remember lying awake, staring up at the ceiling wondering if it was just a bad dream, and then it seemed like it was.

'I must have fallen asleep because it was really dark and I was running along the side of the river bank. I could see Ryan up ahead of me in the distance. He was turning to look back over his shoulder, to see if I was coming.

'I could see him waving, calling my name, pointing to something behind me on the towpath. And then I heard the sound of a voice, and before I had realised that it was Woody he grabbed me, putting his hand over my mouth, and then he was on top of me, forcing me down onto the path, into the mud. I could feel the weight of him on top of me, holding me down – holding me down...'

'Do you want to take a break, Sarah. We can stop—'

'No, no I want to tell you. It felt like I couldn't breathe. I couldn't get up. I kept trying to push him off but he was too strong.'

'In the dream?'

'In the dream, and then I realised that I wasn't dreaming.'

'He was in your room?'

He was in my bed. On my bed. Holding me down, with his hand over my mouth.'

'Woody?'

'Yes, yes. I was muddled to begin with – as if it was a dream – and then I was awake, and I knew that it wasn't. He leaned over and turned on the bedside light, like he wanted me to see that it was him. All he had on was a pair of boxer shorts. He pulled back the bedclothes, and grabbed the neck of my nightie and ripped it open.'

'Did you try to stop him?'

'To begin with no, I think I froze – although I was more shocked than scared, and I was angry too. And then some sort of instinct, a real fury kicked in and I tried to fight him off, push him away. I tried, I tried – I bit him, I tried to scratch his face. I tried, but I couldn't get him off me. I couldn't stop him. I couldn't. And in the end I just lay there like I was dead. Just lay there while he did that to me – why did I do that?'

'It's all right, Sarah. It's all right. Just take it steady. Do you want a drink or some water? We can stop—'

'No.'

'And you're certain it was Woody?'

'Yes.'

'And what happened next?'

'He raped me. You understand? He raped me, that's what happened next. Ryan was dead and Woody raped me, because he could, because there was just me and him, no one to help me, no one to save me from him.'

'Here, just have a drink. Take it slow. Like I said, we can take a break if you want to.'

'No, I don't want to. I want to go on. I need you to understand what it was like. When he was done, Woody just climbed off me without saying a word, not a word. Nothing. Then, when he got to the doorway he turned and looked at me. It was like I was trash, like I was nothing, beneath contempt. And then he shut the door behind him and was gone.'

Chapter Sixteen

Sarah lay full length in the bath, submerged beneath the surface, letting the water hold her, letting it press down on her. She had her eyes open, and moved her hands to create up a flurry of current, not much, just enough so she could feel the water moving over her skin.

Was this how Ryan had felt? Was this what drowning felt like?

The drip, drip, drip from the tap echoed the sound of her heart as the droplets hit the water. It felt as if it might be easy to just let go now, just let the dark, clinging, black grief and horror take her in and carry her away. She could feel the pressure in her lungs, on her chest, the water pressing down on the bruises Woody had left on her arms and wrists, on her thighs and deep, deep inside her. All she had to do was breathe in. Breathe in. How hard could it be?

Her ribs were sore, not that she could remember how that had happened. There had been a moment, a long moment when he had been fucking her when it felt as if she had been watching herself from the far corner of the bedroom, a long way off, up on the ceiling. And from up there, from the safety of her corner and the memory, she could see how hard she had fought, how he had held her, how much he had hurt her. She could see him biting into her shoulder, pinning her down, making her cry out in pain and fear.

But she wouldn't let him win; she had beat him by taking herself away, by denying him any power, by ignoring the triumph she had seen on his face, by blocking him out.

Sarah closed her eyes, embracing the dark, surrendering to the finality and tried to take a breath, letting the water into her mouth and nose, but immediately even before she had chance to think about it, Sarah found herself sitting upright, gasping, gagging, coughing and snorting the water out of her nose, struggling for air, feeling as if the water had burnt the soft tissue.

How was it she couldn't just damn well die? What was there to live for? What was it that made her fight? Some spark, some instinctive stubborn flame that wasn't ready to be snuffed out? How could it hang on when she wanted it otherwise? What was it that she had got to look forward to? She had lost Josh and Ryan – her whole life, and here she was, tied to Woody, the man who had trapped her and raped her. All she wanted now was to sleep and not wake up. Maybe there was some message in not being able to die.

Finally, slowly, painfully, Sarah hauled her torn battered body out of the bath. It felt as if her limbs were made of lead.

The water had long since gone cold. Not that Sarah cared. It felt like the world had broken. She was shivering and her skin was raw red from where she had scrubbed at it, scrubbed and scrubbed at every place that Woody had touched her; what she couldn't wash away was the memory of the look on his face. The contempt in his eyes, the disgust. There had been nothing at all about sex or desire in what he had done to her; she knew that it was all about the power. His power. He had reinforced her sense of fragility, her loss, her being trapped there with him. Locked together for as long as it suited him, and for the first time Sarah wondered if she would ever be free of him.

Now there was no one left to stand between them, no one to save her, no Josh, no Ryan. Sarah picked up a towel from the chair beside the bath and wiped her face, took another and wrapped it round her body trying to still the chill that had finally taken hold. If she was to stand any chance against Woody she had to wake up, she had to find a way to take control, to shake this feeling of helplessness and find a way out. There had to be a way. There just had to be.

Once she was back in her room Sarah stripped the bed, bundled the bedclothes up, along with the remains of her nightdress, and stuffed them into a rubbish bag, remade it with clean linen, locked the bedroom door, wedged a chair up under the handle, then curled up and despite all the odds fell into a dark deep dreamless sleep, that sucked her in and held her tight.

Sarah was ripped awake by the sounds of someone knocking at her bedroom door. Knocking hard. There was a moment of stillness and then she remembered where she was and what had happened; Ryan was dead and Woody... She stopped the thought dead in its tracks. Glancing down she could see the bruises blooming on her wrists.

'We need to be going,' he snapped through the door. 'You've got ten minutes. I've got places I need to be today.' And then his voice dropped to something all together more sinister. 'Or would you like me to come in there and get you up?' He paused. 'Ten minutes.'

She climbed out of bed very carefully, as if there was a chance that she might tumble and break; that was certainly how it felt. She slipped on clean underwear, a pair of good jeans and a sweater and then – without looking in the mirror, afraid of what she might see, pulled a brush through her hair. Finally, Sarah pressed her ear to the door, afraid that Woody might be there waiting outside. After a moment or two longer she opened the door a fraction, just to check. The landing was empty. With her heart beating like a drum in her chest she headed to the bathroom to brush her teeth. She stood by the sink and stared at her reflection in the mirror above; it was strange that there was so little trace of the things that had changed her life forever.

The marks around her neck could be hidden with a scarf, the bruising on her arms with the sleeves of her sweater. She wondered fleetingly why she needed to hide it: shame, fear? And what would happen if she found she was pregnant. She had already done the maths; it was unlikely, but once Woody had gone she'd ring the doctor's and ask for a morning after pill, blame a failed condom, a mistake, just in case. The prospect of ending up with a child as a result of the night before made her feel physically sick.

But would she tell anyone? Would she report it? Sarah looked into her reflection's distant closed away eyes. Certainly not now, maybe never – the truth was that along with the hurt and the anger she was embarrassed and ashamed; how could she have put herself in a position like this, *how*? This wasn't who she was; she had done nothing to deserve this. All she had done was try to make things right. Right for Ryan, right for Woody, right for everyone except for herself and somehow those good intentions had brought her to this place.

Beneath these thoughts, the leviathan, the bigger knowledge swam in dark breathtakingly cold waters. Ryan. *Ryan*, even forming the shape of his name in her head made her want to cry. How could he possibly be dead? How? Part of her was still hoping that someone had made a mistake. Maybe someone in the pub had stolen his wallet. Maybe he was hung-over and staying somewhere, staying with friends, waiting to sober up a bit before he wandered home, afraid of what she might say, afraid of how she might be with him.

Sarah stared at her reflection, into the pale, tired face, part of her mind refusing to believe what she had been told. Busy working out what she should say to Ryan when he got home.

She would make it clear that this time she was relieved, happy, and that between them they would sort this mess out. She would tell him about Woody and the night before, and together they would make a plan to get away from him. Together.

The sound of banging on the door made her jump. 'Come on. We need to be going, I'll be in the car waiting,' Woody said. 'You hear me?'

How had he guessed she was in the bathroom? Had she left the door to her room open? Had he been listening downstairs for the sound of her moving about; her feet on the bare boards?

The thought made her flesh creep.

She gave him time to go downstairs and then went into her bedroom and picked up a scarf to cover the bruises on her neck, along with her house keys and her handbag. He was in the hall by the door.

'Let me look at you,' he said. 'Make sure you look presentable.'

'What is that supposed to mean? I'm going to identify the body of my brother. How am I supposed to look?'

He grinned. 'Fiery this morning. Don't get ahead of yourself here, Sarah. We need each other, remember? I don't want you forgetting that. We're in this together.'

She stared at him. 'No, we're not. There is no *we*. I don't want to go with you,' she said. 'I want to go on my own.'

Woody's expression hardened and he shook his head. 'Not an option. We told the police that we'd both be there and we will, and if you so much as—'

'So much as what?' snapped Sarah. 'What will you do that you haven't already done? What's left? Tell me?'

He looked at her and laughed. 'Stop being so fucking melodramatic.'

She didn't look at Woody as she got into the car. She hoped he would think that he had won, that maybe she was cowed and beaten. What she didn't want him to see was the hate or the rebellion in her eyes; something had to change.

They said nothing during the drive. Sarah tried to make herself as distant and absent as possible so that no part of her touched him, not even her thoughts.

Sarah

'I know it's upsetting, Sarah, but I don't understand why, once you'd lost Ryan, that you just didn't ask Woody to leave?'

'It seems so straightforward and easy to you, doesn't it? But it wasn't like that – I thought – he kept telling me that we would be arrested if anyone found out about the wedding.'

'But you weren't planning on telling anyone?'

'I know, but he said the people from Immigration would come round eventually. We needed to keep up the pretence. We needed to be there together.'

'And you believed him.'

'I don't know now what I believed, but there was the money.'

'The money? I thought that the deal was if you married Woody the debt would be written off.'

'That was their deal, not mine. I hated Woody for what he had done to me. I was in shock. I hurt. But I intended to pay him off. Buy him off. I thought once he had got his money he would go. We'd be all square. There was no way I could clear it until I sold

224

the house. Although at that point I didn't understand the relationship Woody had with Farouk, and I wondered...'

'What?'

'That if I didn't do what Woody asked, he might send Farouk after me. After all Farouk had gone after Ryan to make sure he paid up.'

'But presumably you were in a position, once Ryan was dead, to sell the house.'

'That wasn't the first thing that crossed my mind.'

'I'm sorry, Sarah. I didn't mean to be insensitive.'

'But, yes you're right. I just didn't want to think about it then, not so soon after Ryan drowned. I know it's irrational but the house is all I have of my entire family. I didn't want to be forced into selling it straight away.'

'But you would have sold it?'

'Yes. I knew it was the only way to be rid of him. I wanted Woody gone. Paid off. Out of my life. And when I was more rational I realised it was the only way out. But first of all there was Ryan.'

*

There was a little bowl of white silk flowers on the wooden side table outside the viewing room. Alongside the flowers was an electric tea-light flickering in a ceramic lamp. Some economy version of an eternal flame, presumably. There were blinds sandwiched between the panes in the double glazed windows so that whatever was inside could be cut off from the comings and goings, the hustle and bustle, of the rest of the building. The blinds were closed tight shut, like white unseeing eyes.

Sarah took a deep breath to still her nerves. She already knew in her heart that Ryan wasn't sleeping it off somewhere. He wasn't staying over with friends or nursing a hangover. He was in the tiny, cold, featureless room deep in the bowels of the hospital.

The female police officer who had come to the house was there, along with a woman from the hospital who accompanied them down to the viewing room. She had the kindest eyes. 'Are you ready?' she asked.

Woody nodded. 'Yes, of course.' He made as if to step forward but Sarah was ahead of him. 'Would you like me to do it, Sarah? I'm happy to go in there if you want me to. 'He paused. 'I don't want you upset or frightened.'

Sarah stared at him, deliberately meeting his eye. She knew none of the conversation was for her benefit. The woman looked away graciously, giving them a little space; obviously this was an intimate moment.

Sarah shook her head. 'No, thank you. I want to do this on my own.'

'You're sure?' he pressed, and as she stepped away from him, he caught hold of her wrist and for a moment her sleeve rucked up to reveal livid purple bruising. It was only for a split second but Sarah knew the woman from the hospital had seen it. She saw her look, and then look away. Maybe now was the moment to say something, but she didn't.

'You're certain?' Woody said.

'Certain,' said Sarah. 'He is my brother.'

'Okay. Well, if you're sure that's what you want,' he said gently, but she could see the hardening in his expression, see the disapproval in his eyes, all at odds with his voice, but she didn't care, after all what could he do here?

Sarah glanced away from him and caught the woman's eye.

'Would you like to come with me,' said the

woman. Sarah gave the slightest of nods, and together they walked into the viewing room.

The body was in the centre of the room covered by a crisp white sheet. The room was cool inside. There was a very slight hum that cut into the silence.

The woman raised her eyebrows in question. 'Are you okay?'

Sarah nodded. 'Yes,' she whispered.

Her brother had never frightened her in life, she certainly wasn't afraid of him in death. With great tenderness the woman lifted the sheet and folded it back to reveal Ryan's face and a little of his neck. His skin was pale and blotchy, reddened here and there, the colour gone from his lips, and there was a graze across his forehead, but otherwise it looked as if he might be asleep, his features were in repose, his hair was tousled and still sun-bleached.

Sarah didn't mean to gasp, didn't mean to press a hand to her mouth to try and staunch the cry of despair. The woman's expression folded into something between a supportive smile and a look of concern. Sarah glanced at her; what a job to have. How many times had the woman stood here with people whose hearts were broken, whose lives were in tatters?

'Do you recognise this person?'

Sarah took a deep breath and nodded. 'Yes, it's my brother, Ryan.'

'Thank you,' the woman said, and then after a short dignified pause continued, 'Would you like a moment or two?'

Sarah hesitated before replying. It was odd, because although it was obviously Ryan's body lying there, he was absent. The real Ryan, her Ryan, was already gone. Just like in his flat the night before, it felt as if he had just stepped out. But she knew, too, that that was just wishful thinking.

'Thank you,' she murmured.

So Sarah was the one who told them that yes, it was Ryan and yes, she understood there would have to be a post-mortem and no, she didn't mind signing some papers, although none of it felt real.

On the drive to the hospital she had planned to touch him but now she was here she didn't want to feel Ryan cold. Instead, she talked to him. Told him how much she loved him, how she wished things could have been different between them at the end, how much she was going to miss him, how she missed him already – except that none of it was said aloud, the words were far too precious to share with anyone else, especially Woody who, now the formalities had been dealt with came in to be with her. Woody deserved nothing of this, no moment, no words.

'I want to go home,' she said after a moment or two more.

The woman nodded and covered Ryan's body. No one else spoke.

Josh

'I'd just got in from work. I picked up the paper while I was waiting for my supper to go ding. And there it was on the front page. *'Joggers find body while on morning run.'* I was skimming through it when I realised that it was Ryan; it took my breath away. I had to read it again to make sure I hadn't made a mistake. You never think it'll be anyone you know, do you? And then when I re-read the article I thought about him ringing me and I realised that he had to have rung me that night. With Sarah's phone number.'

'You had rung before then?'

'Yes, I just told you. I rang a couple of times after

Ryan had called me but when I hadn't heard anything and it was switched off, I wondered if I had made a mistake – maybe I'd misunderstood what Ryan meant. I mean, he was pissed. And I wasn't sure what good it would do. Sarah had made it obvious that it was over, it felt a bit like a picking a scab.'

'But you rang after you saw the newspaper?'

'Of course, whatever else had happened I cared about her. I couldn't imagine how it must feel. Given how things had been, I really hadn't expected Sarah to pick up the phone when I rang, so I was surprised when she answered first time.'

'She answered?'

'Yes'

'And what did she say?'

'To be honest it was me who did most of the talking. I told her how sorry I was to hear about Ryan. And said if there was anything I could do – you know, the usual things. They sounded kind of trite, but they're all I had.'

'You didn't talk about your relationship or Woody?'

'No, no I didn't. I was just so pleased to hear her voice but she sounded fragile and distant. I felt like if I didn't take it slowly – carefully – that I might frighten her away.'

'And did you offer to go round and see her, meet up?'

'No, not at that point, she sounded stunned and sort of out of it. I wondered if she had been taking something. I mean you see it in films and on TV don't you? People being sedated after a shock. I said I'd ring back at another time. She asked me how I'd got her number and I told her Ryan had rung me from the pub and she asked me when, and then she told me what I had already thought, that that was the night he died. She went quiet, and then I told her that whatever she needed I was there.'

'And did Sarah seem okay?'

'What sort of question is that? What's okay when you've lost someone like that? She was close to tears all the time. Like she was choking. I mean, you can't really blame her, can you?'

'Anything else?'

'Yes, just as I was about to hang up. She told me that she loved me.'

'And that was unexpected?'

'I thought that she had stopped loving me. I thought that's why she finished with me.'

'And what did you say, Josh?'

'That I loved her too. And then she said something like sometimes love isn't enough. I didn't really understand what she meant. She was upset. She told me that she didn't want me to get involved, that she didn't want me to getting hurt. And it might be better if I didn't contact her again.'

'What do you think she meant by getting hurt?'

'I'd been in pieces since we split up. Love or no love, I think she didn't want to offer me any false hope.'

'So, she was worried that if you stayed in contact that you might suffer emotional pain, there was not any threat of violence?'

'God no, at least I didn't read it like that. I thought she was trying to stop me getting mashed all over again.'

'But you felt you had renewed your connection with her?'

'Yes and no – like I said, it was hard to judge exactly what was going on. In some ways it felt better, but...'

'You were worried about her?'

'Yes, I've been worried about her since we split

up. The whole thing had just been so weird. I wanted to see her. Make it better. Isn't that what men are supposed to do?'

'So what did you do, Josh?'

'I suggested that we meet up, talk, no strings. Sort things out. And she just laughed and said that there was no such thing as no strings, that everything was all tangled up, all tied together and that she couldn't see me. That it was too dangerous.'

'Dangerous? She used that word?'

'I know. To be honest I wondered if Sarah might be having some kind of a breakdown. She didn't strike me as that kind of a woman but anyway, in the end I decided not to push it, and to go round to the nursery and see if I could talk to her there instead. You know, neutral ground where she felt safe. Maybe take her for lunch like we did when we first met.'

'And you told her that?'

'No, I decided that I'd just do it, just in case she said she couldn't or she made some sort of an excuse. I went early...'

Chapter Seventeen

The nursery had only just opened its doors when Josh drew into the car park and parked his truck up under the trees. The place was almost deserted. There were no customers in the main shop. Most of the poly tunnels and the big greenhouse were closed off to the public for cleaning and restocking. The only open tunnel was by the main entrance. It was packed with pansies, polyanthus and primroses, the path between the trays lined with cyclamen in every colour. Inside, a single, early-bird couple was wandering around picking out autumn bedding.

Josh made his way inside. He didn't recognise the girl on the till so instead he headed off through the shop into the plant court and towards the rest of the tunnels. As he turned the corner, he spotted a familiar figure in one of the closed tunnels, working at a potting bench. Josh picked his way round between the shrubs and trees in pots to the doorway and called out.

'Anessa?'

She looked up in surprise, and pushed back a strand of hair with the back of her gloved hand. 'Hi, Josh. You're about early this morning. How are you? Come on in. How can I help?' She glanced back over her shoulder to a trolley piled high with trays of new plants. 'Are you looking for winter bedding? We've just had some really nice heathers in.'

He smiled. 'I'm not after plants at the moment. I wondered if Sarah is around today?'

Anessa shook her head. 'I'm sorry, but she's not here at the moment. She's taken a few days off.' Anessa paused. 'You heard about Ryan?'

Josh nodded. 'It's one of the reasons I'm here, that and to see how she is. How's she doing? Is she okay?'

Anessa pulled a face. 'It depends what you mean by okay. We don't really talk much these days. I mean, we talk about work and things, but not like we used to. Not since she got married.'

Josh stopped mid-stride; it felt as if someone had punched him. 'Married? Are you kidding?'

Anessa reddened. 'Oh my god, I'm so sorry, Josh. Didn't you know? I thought you must have heard. She got married to that guy who was living there with them. The lodger. You know the one. I went to the wedding.'

'Not Woody?' said Josh in amazement.

Anessa nodded. 'It must have been a couple of months ago now, if not longer. I'm so sorry. I don't think Woody likes her working very much. He's always ringing her up, and he brings her here first thing and is here to meet her at the end of the day. Proper possessive I reckon. It would drive me crazy, but she won't hear a word against him.'

Josh shook his head. 'I don't know what to say. I kept away because Sarah was so upset last time.' His voice faded. 'I'd got no idea.'

Anessa sighed and peeled off her work gloves. 'Neither had we, it was a total bolt out of the blue. To be honest I thought...' she paused, as if measuring her words.

'What?'

'I thought that if Sarah was going to be marrying anyone it would have been you, Josh. Ever since I've known her she has always played her cards close to her chest. She's not one to open up much about her private life, but she was constantly dropping your name into the conversation; *Josh this, Josh that.*' Anessa smiled. 'She talked about you all the time and then, out of the blue, there was this thing with Woody. I tried to talk to her about it but she said there was nothing to talk about. I assumed you two had split up, and that she had maybe got together with him on the rebound. I mean it happens – you're feeling low and someone offers you a shoulder. But even so I was really surprised when she told me she was getting married to him. And so quickly too. But then she told me that she had been going out with him before but he wouldn't commit until he saw her with you – but I'm not convinced. I think she needed something to make it sound like it wasn't a spur of the moment thing.'

Josh nodded, trying to gather his thoughts. 'I don't know what to say. I spoke to her last night.'

'And she didn't tell you?' said Anessa.

'I didn't really give her much of a chance. I rang up when I heard about Ryan.'

Anessa shook her head. 'God, isn't that awful? I couldn't believe it. So sad. I mean, he was always a bit of a lad, but really nice, you know. He was such a flirt,' she said with a grin. 'And they were really close. I can't imagine how she must feel at the moment.'

Josh nodded. 'So have you seen her?'

Anessa shook her head. 'No, not since she rang in and told the boss about Ryan. I've tried ringing a couple of times but I can't get through. I was thinking of maybe sending a card but...' There was something else in her voice.

'But what?' pressed Josh.

Instead of replying Anessa shook her head again.

'I thought you might have been round there,' said Josh. 'Are you saying you haven't seen her at all since Ryan died?'

Anessa glanced over her shoulder as if there was some possibility that she might be overheard. 'I know it's not right, especially at the moment when she needs her friends, and if things were right between me and Sarah I'd be round there like a flash. I'd be

234

there now. Sarah and I have been friends for years, more or less since she started here. But it feels like Woody is always around, in your face, like he is afraid to leave her on her own. Something happened, something changed, and I don't know exactly what it was. It's like she just shut me out. I tried to talk to her before the wedding and afterwards, about Woody and what was going on, but she wasn't having any of it.'

'Sarah sort of pushed me away. She made it obvious that whatever I'd got to say she didn't want to hear it. I don't want to get into the middle of this, Josh, but I think there is something really odd going on there.'

'Odd? Like what?'

'I don't know what exactly, but at the wedding... ' Anessa hesitated.

'What?' pressed Josh. 'Please. I need to know.'

'Beforehand I said we ought to have a hen night but she told me that it wasn't her style – anyway I asked her why she was getting married so quickly and why him – I tried not to be heavy about it, but as her friend I was worried in case she was making a mistake. She more or less blanked me, and told me that basically it was none of my business, and that it was something she had to do. *Had to* is a funny way to describe getting married. I did wonder if she was pregnant. You know what Sarah's like, a bit old fashioned, and I could see that maybe that was why she felt she had to. So I asked her. And then she was *really* angry with me, and said of course not, so I asked her if she loved him, and she teared up and said that of course she did. But if I'm honest I didn't believe a word of it.'

'You were going to tell me about the wedding,' said Josh gently.

'Oh god yes, sorry. There were a couple of things

235

really that just didn't ring right. First of all at the reception back at their place Woody had had a bit to drink. It was quite late on, and they had only had like buffet food, crisps and snacks and things, most people had gone home. I was in the sitting room and he came in and started flirting with me. I mean, like really flirting, not jokey or anything.'

'This was Woody?'

Yes, I know – it was bizarre, and to begin with I thought maybe I might be reading it wrong, but the more I've thought about it since the more sure I am. He was definitely coming on to me. Anyway, Sarah came in and he stopped, obviously. Then during the conversation Sarah was telling Woody that my family come from the same region of Pakistan as his. My uncle – that's my dad's brother – has got an export business in Quetta. I've only been there once with my mum and dad when my cousin got married. We'd talked about it at work when I'd asked her about who Woody was. Anyway, I asked him if he knew any of my father's family. Just like conversation, nothing heavy – I know it was a long shot, but their business is quite well known in Quetta and my uncle is really well connected.'

'So what happened?'

'Oh god, Woody looked like a scalded cat. I think I wished him good luck in Pashto and his expression just froze, and he said that he didn't speak anything other than English in front of Sarah because he didn't want to exclude her. He was really short with me about it. Like *really* pissed off. I tried to make a joke of it, laugh it off, but he was deadly serious. And then he said that he didn't want to talk about Quetta, that that part of his life was over. His parents weren't coming to their wedding and them being so anti had left a sour taste in his mouth. They weren't very pleased about him marrying Sarah and as far as he was concerned he had cut all ties with them. This was his home now he said. The thing is, I can understand him feeling like that, but I didn't know about it and he was really abrupt and rude and he kept on about it. I mean, I didn't know how upset he was. Sarah was so embarrassed. So I backed off and changed the subject. But it was awkward, and...'

'And?'

'And I thought there was a lot more to it than that, but I couldn't put my finger on it.' Anessa hesitated and then waved the words away. 'Sorry, this is just me speculating. All I know is that I tried to talk to Sarah about Woody and the wedding a couple of days later. She'd already said that they wouldn't be going on a honeymoon. Reading between the lines I don't think they could afford it. Anyway she popped in to collect a present that the girls had bought her. Woody brought her in and was all smiles. She'd got cakes for everyone. She kept saying it was Woody's idea, and we all took photos.' Anessa stopped.

'The thing is, Josh, and it might just be my imagination but none of it felt right. It felt staged, like a show. And Sarah looked absolutely terrible. Woody kept joking about her having the hangover from hell, but I was there at the reception, she barely drank anything. I was worried about her.' She stopped. 'I still am worried about her, and more now that she hasn't got Ryan.'

Josh

'As soon as I got outside in the car park I rang Sarah. The call went straight to voice mail. I left a message to tell her that I was coming round to see her. I couldn't believe that she was married. It just seemed crazy. I loved her. I told her that I didn't care what she said or what excuses she had, I was on my way round, we needed to talk.'

'And what happened.'

'Nothing.'

'She didn't reply?'

'No, but like I said that wasn't going to stop me. I wanted to sort this out once and for all.'

Chapter Eighteen

Woody was in the kitchen when Sarah got downstairs. She was still in her dressing gown and pyjamas, and was surprised to find him still there. Over the last few days he had been gone by the time she got up. Instinctively Sarah pulled her dressing gown tighter around her, not that he noticed, instead he was hunched over the counter by the kettle. As Sarah stepped into the room he swung round, startled by the sound of her footsteps on the tiles; he had something in his hands. It took Sarah a moment or two to realise what it was.

'What are you doing?' she said. 'That's my handbag.'

'I thought we had already ascertained that what's yours is mine. Or would you like me to prove it to you again?'

She reddened, feeling her stomach flutter with a horrible mix of fury and fear, and looked away.

Woody laughed. 'I didn't think so,' he said, and then he tipped the contents of her bag out onto the kitchen table. 'Where is your phone?'

Sarah shook her head. 'Not in there. What do you want it for?'

'Mine's dead. Where is it?'

Sarah touched her dressing gown pocket; a reflex response. Woody grinned and held out his hand. 'Here, give it to me. I just need to borrow it for a little while.'

'But I need it with me in case anyone rings from the hospital. The woman said they would let me know when they were releasing Ryan's body.' Sarah's voice crackled as she spoke.

Woody nodded and took the phone out of her hand. 'I just need it for a day or two. You can have it

239

back.' He looked up, his gaze tracking round the kitchen.' And you need to sort this place out. Clean up. Clean yourself up. You're a mess. The house is a mess. What will people think?'

'What people?'

'We'll have to have a funeral, people will be coming back here.'

'What people?' she repeated. Who was there left? She thought fleetingly of Josh and wondered if he was already on his way. She glanced at the phone now in Woody's hand. It had taken all her will power to delete his message. There was no telling what Woody would do or say if he knew that Josh had her new number.

Instead of answering her question Woody thumbed through the menu on the phone. 'Did you clear the call log on this?' he asked.

Sarah looked at him; glassy eyed her expression in neutral. 'I don't even know what that means,' she said.

He glanced up, presumably to see if she was lying and then Woody nodded. 'Okay, well I'm keeping this for the moment,' he said. 'Look on it as a loan. You can have it back as soon as I've got mine sorted out.'

Sarah felt a flicker of panic. 'But what if the hospital calls?' she said. What if Josh called back?

'I'll let you know what they say.' He slipped the phone into his jacket pocket. 'And anyone else who rings up to give their condolences. You never know who might have got hold of your number. I'll field them for you, so you don't have to keep explaining what happened. I'll pass on what we know so you don't have to keep repeating it. Don't keep having to get upset.'

It was a lie, they both knew it. He didn't want her talking to anyone.

'Please,' Sarah said. 'Don't take it away. I need it.'

'I'll see you later.' He stopped as he reached the door. 'And we need to go shopping; there's nothing in the cupboards.'

Sarah stared at him. What was this, some show of domestic bliss for the benefit of the Immigration services? Or whoever it was he was expecting to come round to offer their condolences?

'I've been thinking,' he said. 'I think you should get yourself a new job?'

She stared at him.

'You need a fresh start,' he said.

Away from her friends, Sarah thought, but didn't say. Away from the people who knew Josh and Ryan and remembered how she was before she got married. A fresh start, which would make things easier for him, not her.

'That's not going to happen. I like my job,' Sarah said.

'Write a list of what we need,' he said as if Sarah hadn't spoken. She hated the way he had said *we,* there was no we, only her and him. Sarah couldn't remember a time when she had felt so alone.

'I have to go to the bank,' she said.

Woody grinned. 'No need. I've got money. We'll go when I get back. And get this place cleaned up. I'll be back in a little while, there's just something I need to sort out. And get dressed.'

When he got to the back door Woody paused and looked her up and down. 'You look tired. You're too thin. You need to take more care of yourself. I'm worried about you, Sarah. I don't want you to end up like Ryan.'

She stared at him, the words stopping her dead in her tracks. 'What is that supposed to mean?' she demanded.

'Oh come on, don't pretend you don't know what I'm talking about. I didn't want to say anything about it to the police, but I keep wondering about that night. At the pub? I know I told them that Ryan was okay but the truth was he had been depressed for weeks. We both know that. You know how he was. He couldn't keep a job down from one week to the next, never had any money, no prospects, totally unreliable and I know he was gutted that you had ended up having to bail him out.'

Woody paused, and then sighed. 'It doesn't take a mind-reader to see where his mind was going, Sarah. He was drinking more, pissing away any money he had got. He told me over and over again that he felt like he had let you down.'

Sarah shivered. 'Are you trying to tell me that Ryan killed himself?'

Woody lifted his hands in a gesture that implied anything was possible. 'You were the one who told him that he was on his own, Sarah. No more help, no more bailing him out, remember? He told me all about it. And I think there's a chance that he might have borrowed some more money. I just need to find out what the damage was. Ryan knew he'd let you down, Sarah. And he was depressed; a few drinks inside him and all he would talk about was how you'd be better off without him.'

'No,' Sarah hissed.' No, that's not true.' She slumped down onto one of the chairs by the kitchen table trying to process what Woody had said. He had to be lying. Surely Ryan wouldn't do anything so stupid. Surely. He must have known she would always be there for him whatever she said.

'I won't be long,' Woody said, closing the door behind him – not that she noticed.

Sarah sat at the kitchen table for a long time after he left, listening to the clock tick-tick-ticking away the morning and thinking about what he had said. If Woody was right about Ryan surely she would have noticed it; seen it. He had seemed a bit subdued before the wedding, but she had put that down to the situation with the money and the beating. Afterwards he hadn't maybe felt as close as before, but she had assumed it was because he felt guilty, not suicidal. He had been working on and off, and she thought he was okay.

She replayed the nights he had been in the kitchen planning jobs with Woody. He had seemed all right then. She couldn't bear to think that he thought she really had abandoned him. Sarah closed her eyes tight, trying to stop her mind slipping away into the great black well of grief and pain that threatened. She had to do something, anything to give her some sense of control.

Glancing round she knew that Woody was right, the house was a mess. The kitchen was littered with the debris from days of eating out of packets, from not washing up, from not being able to think about anything other than Ryan and what it must have felt like to drown, imagining the cold water soaking into his clothes and pulling him down, down. Sarah couldn't bear to think about it for longer than a few seconds but the thoughts crept up on her and came to her in her sleep. What would it be like not to have him in her life? Everything was falling to pieces.

Sarah glanced round the kitchen, seeing the place with fresh eyes. It was a mess. Josh had said he was coming round. She didn't want him to see her or the house like this. The sound of his voice on the voice mail had been like heaven. Clearing the call log had been something she had done when she had deleted the message; she had done it without thinking, clearing all trace of him. And thank god she had. She had planned to call him or text him back but perhaps her silence was even more compelling. She just prayed that he didn't try to ring again because then she knew Woody would want to know how he had got her number and if he had rung before, and she didn't trust herself to lie twice.

When Sarah heard the knock on the door a few minutes later she almost jumped out of her skin. Her first thought was that it had to be Josh, but when she looked round it was Mrs Howard, her next door neighbour, peering in, her hand cupped round her face as she looked in through the glass.

'Sarah?'

Sarah got to her feet and opened the door. 'Hello.'

Mrs Howard's eyes filled with tears and she bit her lip. 'Oh, Sarah. I just wanted to say very how sorry I am about Ryan. It must be terrible for you. I only saw it in the paper last night or I'd have been round sooner. Why didn't you come and tell me? You should have come round.' The old lady paused long enough to pull a handkerchief out of her sleeve and dab her eyes. 'Although I suppose you'd got other things on your mind.' As she spoke she pushed a card into Sarah's hand. 'I remember him when he was just a little boy,' the old lady began before tears cut her off.

Sarah felt her own lip begin to tremble, the tears pressing hard behind. 'Thank you,' she muttered. 'I'd invite you in for tea but I don't think that I've got any milk.'

'That's all right, dear. Do you want to borrow some?'

Sarah shook her head. 'No, I'm fine, thank you. I'm going shopping later.'

Mrs Howard peered round the untidy kitchen. 'It must be terrible for you. Your mum and dad and now Ryan. If there is anything I can do to help? Anything at all? Washing up – or a bit of ironing.' She paused. 'I really don't mind.'

'No, I'm fine. I'm just about to get dressed and

make a start, but thank you for the offer.'

The old lady nodded. 'If you're sure. Thank goodness you've got Woody.'

Sarah managed a thin smile. 'Thank you for coming round,' she said, moving towards the door.

The old lady took the hint. 'Well I won't stop. I can see you've got things to be getting on with. You will let me know when the funeral is, won't you?' Mrs Howard hesitated to leave. 'Actually, I was rather hoping to see Woody while I was here. Is he in? I just wondered how he got on. Did it help?'

'Sorry, I'm not with you?'

'He brought some things round for me to sign and witness the other day.'

Something about the way she said it piqued Sarah's interest. 'What sort of things?'

The old lady shifted her weight, obviously slightly uncomfortable. 'I'm not sure to be honest. I suppose I should have read them really. They say that, don't they? Read before you sign. But Woody said he was in a bit of a hurry and had to get them in, and he just needed me to sign and date them. You know, witness them.'

'Them?'

Mrs Howard nodded. 'There were quite a few. He said it was just a formality. I felt sorry for him; all those forms. And I didn't like to pry.'

'Can you remember what they were?' Sarah asked, making the effort to smile. 'Were they about his right to remain application?'

The old woman screwed her mouth up in an effort to concentrate. 'I'm not sure. I mean, I've signed quite a few things for him since he moved in, but I've always thumbed through them before.'

'And this time?'

'Well, it was obvious he was in a bit of a hurry, so I didn't bother. I think I had to witness one and sign some others.'

Sarah nodded, keeping the smile in place.

'He said it was really important that I saw him signing the papers. Keep it all legal and above board, he said. He said he didn't want there to be any problems over his signature. I mean you never know when it comes to legal things. Better safe than sorry.' She smiled. 'He is such a nice boy, you're so lucky to have found him, Sarah. It must be such a weight off your mind having him around dealing with all those kind of things.'

Something dark shifted in Sarah's head and she had a momentary flash of the sheet of paper she had found in Ryan's jacket pocket, the page of signatures, with Woody's name written over and over again. What if it wasn't Ryan who had been practising the signatures, but Woody.

Sarah stared at her. 'What kind of things were they?'

'Official papers, forms; to be honest I'm not a hundred percent sure. Silly really.'

Sarah forced a smile. 'Thank you for coming round, I'm really sorry but I need to be getting on, getting dressed.'

'Of course.'

Ryan's jacket was still upstairs in her bedroom where she had taken it off.

'And tell Woody that I hope it helped.'

'I will,' Sarah said, feigning gratitude, wanting the old lady gone.

Mrs Howard stepped outside into the porch 'Anyway, if there is anything you need. Any help, anything at all. All you have to do is ask. Have you got any idea when the funeral will be?'

Sarah shook her head. 'No, not yet. I'm waiting for the hospital to ring.'

'Oh yes, of course,' said the old lady. 'Well I better

be off, but you know where I am.'

Sarah nodded.

The moment Mrs Howard was out of sight Sarah locked the back door, slid the bolt across and hurried upstairs. Safe in her bedroom with the door locked she unfolded the sheet of paper from Ryan's pocket, carefully flattened it out and tried to work out exactly what it meant and what it told her. The signatures were written in black ink and were evenly spaced with a line or two between each attempt in two columns, one down each side of the page. It looked like the page had been torn from an A4 notepad. There were probably thirty attempts at Woody's signature, all very similar, all slight variations on a theme, but nevertheless each gaining in confidence.

Staring down at the paper Sarah wondered what it was that had needed signing and needed witnessing? And, assuming from the jottings on the back, that this paper originated from Woody and not Ryan, why would he need to practise his own signature?

She flipped the paper: on the back were some phone numbers and a website address just made up of a series of letters that meant nothing to her: www.inwol, but all of them were most definitely in Woody's handwriting, so where and why had Ryan got it?

What was it Woody had been signing that needed to be witnessed? What was going on? Sarah wanted to know. Maybe if she could find the pad that the page of signatures came from, and check out the website. She had no idea how long she had before Woody would be back. From experience it could be ten minutes or all day but if she was quick and careful. The idea hung in the air.

Quickly Sarah pulled the tin with the spare keys out of the dressing table drawer, tipped them onto the bed and began to scrabble through them. The spare keys for each of the bedrooms had a loop of ribbon through them. The one for the attic room was midnight blue.

Sarah snatched it up out of the pile and headed towards the attic, her heart thumping like a drum in her chest. She hesitated before sliding the key into the lock, pausing for a moment, every molecule of her body straining to pick up the sounds from the house. She had to be sure that Woody was out. Seconds passed but all she could hear was the steady ticking of a clock and the distant hum of traffic.

Sarah took a deep breath and with shaking hands slid the key home. Barely halfway in, it met resistance. For a moment Sarah thought she'd got the wrong key and tried again, but still it wouldn't go more than half way. Bending down to look Sarah could see there was something wedged in the keyhole. She pushed harder until whatever it was gave way, and then she unlocked the door and pushed it open.

Sarah wasn't quite sure what she had expected to find inside but this wasn't it. Sunlight flooded in through the dormer windows onto the rugs and the bare board floor. The sunlit attic was as tidy as a monk's cell, with not a thing out of place. Nothing stirred in the still morning air. The bed was made, the blinds were open and straight, the desk bare except for a jar of pens and pencils. Textbooks and novels were neatly arranged in the shelves, along with a row of box files and another of ring binders. There were no clothes, no shoes, nothing personal in sight. Leaving the door ajar Sarah wondered where to begin looking, a decision made all the harder by the fact she had no idea exactly what it was she was looking for.

She thumbed through the books. There seemed to

be nothing there that caught her eye, they were all mostly business text books, a little law, some on accountancy, a couple of dictionaries. The novels were mostly classic English literature. Should she take them out and shake them, search through every one, and how long would that take? The box files on the shelf below were numbered and contained collections of course work and cuttings. The course work pieces were all printed and bound. They were so beautifully presented it made her think again about why it was that Woody had decided to drop out when it was obvious he was a diligent and conscientious student. What had changed?

She thumbed her way through the next file. There were pages clipped together and filed from magazines and the financial pages of newspapers, all were business orientated. Sarah had just opened the second or third on the shelf when she heard a noise downstairs. For an instant she thought it might be someone knocking at the door, and remembered that Josh was meant to be coming round. Maybe he could help? It took her a second or two longer to realise that it was the sound of someone unlocking the front door.

She leapt to her feet. Working quickly Sarah slipped the bundle of papers back into the box file, slid it back in its place on the shelf and hurried across the attic, pulling the door closed behind her. Turning the key in the lock Sarah ran downstairs and across the landing to her bedroom. She had barely reached the bedroom door before Woody called up from the hallway.

'Sarah, where are you?'

'I'm up here,' she said; the duplicate bedroom key still in her hand.

'The back door was bolted,' he snapped.

'I know. I was worried that someone might come

in while I was upstairs,' she said, thinking on her feet, after all it was the truth. 'Those men.' She paused. 'Didn't you say you thought Ryan had borrowed more money?' Wondering for an instant as she said it if it was true and if that was a more credible and more terrifying reason for Ryan ending up in the river. 'I was afraid they might come back,' she said, with a genuine tremor in her voice. 'I was just going to have a bath and then get on with the cleaning.'

'Did you make a list?' he asked.

Sarah slipped the key surreptitiously into the pocket of her dressing gown. 'No, not yet. I was going to do that after I'd had a bath.'

'I have some business I need to take care of. I've just been down into Ryan's flat to start clearing it out. It stinks down there. The fridge is going to need sorting.'

Sarah felt her stomach do a back flip; while she had been searching his room Woody had been two floors below. 'I didn't realise you were down there,' she said unevenly.

'We're going to need to clean it out,' he said. 'The fridge, the freezer. The whole place.'

'Yes,' she said, although no part of her wanted to contemplate the idea.

'I'll make a start when I get back,' Woody said.

'Are you going out again?' she asked.

'Yes.' He smiled slyly. 'You can leave the back door bolted. I don't want you feeling nervous. I'll come in the front.'

Sarah nodded.

'I just came back to get my coat,' Woody said.

Sarah froze, as the realisation dawned that she hadn't put back whatever it was that Woody had so carefully pushed into the keyhole. The door had been locked from the outside. He had to have put the plug in place after he left the room; did that mean he was checking up on her or that he was just cautious by nature? And where was his coat? Sarah waited and watched as he strode across the hallway, wondering if he would turn to come up the stairs. Her pulse quickened.

When Woody got to the bottom of the stairs he took an overcoat that was hanging over the newel post. Sarah tried hard not to show her relief.

'Will you be long?' she asked casually.

He looked up. 'I don't know. Why?'

'I need to sort out the arrangements for Ryan.' She couldn't bring herself to say funeral.

He nodded and then he was gone, slipping on his coat, heading out the door.

As soon as he had closed it, Sarah spun round and hurried into her bedroom. She made a note of the web address and the phone number on the back of the piece of paper she had found then carefully refolded it and put it back into Ryan's jacket. Sarah needed to know more about what it was she was looking for before she went searching again.

Josh

'The traffic on the way to Sarah's was awful, there was an accident, a lorry shed its load on the Milton roundabout. The whole thing was snarled up and I got caught up in the tailback. It took me forever to get back into the city. Back to Sarah's.'

'And your plan was what?'

'I'm not sure I had much in the way of a plan. I just thought I'd go round there and talk. The previous conversation we had had on the phone, and the things that Anessa said had made me think that there was a chance that she might see me. To be honest I was getting pissed off with the whole mystery. I wanted some straight answers.'

'And so what happened when you got to Sarah's place?'

'That's just it; I didn't get there. I was coming through the traffic lights where you turn off towards her street when I saw Woody's car a little way along the road. He was parked facing towards me and pulled into the kerb. He was picking up a woman.'

'Sarah?'

'No, no it definitely wasn't Sarah. I got a real good look at her. As I turned the corner she was standing on the pavement. She was blonde, young, maybe late teens, early twenties, in a mini skirt, and when she climbed into the car he kissed her.'

'Haven't you ever greeted your friends with a peck on the cheek, Josh?'

'It wasn't a peck. He was all over her. Then the guy in the car behind him pipped, so after a moment or two Woody pulled away.'

'Driving towards you?'

'Yes.'

'Did he see you?'

'I don't think so.'

'And what did you do next, Josh?'

'I took the next left, turned round and followed him.'

'Rather than go and see Sarah?'

'I know it sounds crazy but you didn't have to be any kind of genius to see that there was something not right going on there. I had just discovered that Woody was married to my girlfriend, and there he is all over someone else? I wanted to see where they were going. What he was up to.'

'And?'

'I followed him to Kirby Road, a little way back. I wondered if he'd spot me. I mean, the truck isn't exactly inconspicuous, but I don't think he did. Kirby

Road's not that far away from Sarah's, but the street looked rougher. I don't know Cambridge that well, but it looked a bit more run down, lots of bedsits, lots of student shares by the looks of it.'

'And what happened?'

'Woody and the blonde got out of the car and went into one of the bigger houses. They were in a hurry. She couldn't keep her hands off him. Not that he seemed to mind.'

'So they went into the house? And what did you do?'

'I hung around for a few minutes and then I drove back to see Sarah. By the look of it I thought Woody was going to be busy for a while.'

Sarah

'My laptop was in the sitting room. I don't use it that often. I'm not much of a computer person, not really, although it was useful for things like advertising the rooms when I was trying to rent them. Ryan used to call me a dinosaur, but I can do basic things like email and buying online. Anyway I switched in on, and while I was waiting for it to boot up I'd planned to ring the phone numbers that were on the back of the piece of paper that I'd found in Ryan's jacket. The ones in Woody's handwriting.'

'Did you find out who the numbers belonged to?'

'Not then, no. There was no dial tone. At first I thought there might be a problem with the phone, so I tried hanging up a few times and then I tried the handset in the kitchen but that was dead too, so I traced the wire for the main handset back to the box on the wall. It's a behind a little table with the router for the Wi-Fi on top of it. I'd put the table there to protect the box and all the wires. When I pulled it away, the phone socket and the box behind had been

253

was smashed and pulled away from the wall.'

'You're suggesting that that was deliberate?'

'I don't know for certain but yes I think it probably was. I can see that it might have been an accident if something had fallen off the table onto it, but if that was the case why hadn't Woody or Ryan said something to me about it?'

'Did you think it was Woody?'

'Yes. Ryan was always using the Wi-Fi. He'd have said something.'

'Okay. Presumably this meant you couldn't get onto the internet?'

'That's right; the router was useless without a signal; I could have got onto the internet on my phone if I had had it but Woody had taken it with him.'

'So what did you do?'

'There was nothing I could do. I had no idea where the nearest phone box was. I was going to go back upstairs and finish getting washed and dressed. And then the doorbell rang and when I went to see who it was. And there was Josh.'

'You sound pleased, Sarah.'

'I don't think I have ever been so pleased to see anyone in my life, although I was nervous too, in case Woody came back. I know what he's like, coming back any time.'

'But you let Josh in?'

'Yes. Yes, I did.'

Josh

At first I couldn't believe Sarah was actually there at home and was prepared to let me in. I mean, it wasn't the first time I'd been round and tried to talk to her. And then what struck me was how thin Sarah looked, and tiny. So tiny. It made my heart ache. She just stood there in the doorway looking at me like she couldn't believe her eyes. She was in her dressing gown and this pair of pale blue pyjamas.

'You're smiling, Josh.'

'Sorry. It was just really good to see her, I'd missed her. I was going to hug her, kiss her – I'm not sure really, but as I stepped towards her she stepped away and said, "You can't be here. I don't know what Woody would do if he found you here". She sounded genuinely nervous. She told me that I ought to leave. And I told her that I thought he would be a while.

'"How can you know that?" she said. She told me that she never knew when he was coming back, and I wasn't sure what to tell her.'

'About the girl you had seen him with?'

'That's right. I mean, it would have been easy to say something but I wasn't sure how she would take it. I said it would be better if I came inside, but she was reluctant.'

'Okay, so did you force your way in, Josh?'

'No, of course not. No, but I wasn't going to talk to her on the doorstep.'

Chapter Nineteen

For a moment neither of them said a word, Josh just stood there in the doorway looking at her. It was Sarah who finally spoke, her voice thick with tears. 'I have missed you so much,' she murmured.

Josh swallowed hard.

'What the hell is going on, Sarah?' he said, though his voice was soft.

He held out his arms and she stepped into them. She felt like dry kindling, barely more than skin over bones. He was worried about hugging her too tight in case she broke.

When Sarah finally pulled away she had tears trickling down her face. 'You can't come in. And you can't stay here,' she said, looking past him into the road.' I don't know what Woody will do if he finds you here.'

Ignoring her, Josh pushed the door to behind him. 'It's all right. He won't be back for a while yet.'

'How can you know that? He could be back any minute,' Sarah whispered, peering out of the tiny window by the door. 'He does that. He comes back when I'm not expecting him.'

'I saw him a little while ago and I'm pretty certain he will be gone for a while.' He hesitated. 'I followed him back to a house in Kirby Road.'

Sarah stared at him. 'You followed him. Why?'

'Because,' Josh stopped, wondering how much to tell her. 'Because I wanted to know what's going on with you two. I wanted to talk to you and I wanted to make sure that he wasn't here so we could sort this out.'

Her gaze moved back over his shoulder towards the door. 'Kirby Road is not that far away.'

'I know.' Josh nodded. 'But it'll be okay. I

promise.'

'Kirby Road is where Woody used to live before he moved in here. I think he goes there sometimes to check for post and play chess with his old landlord. But you can't stay,' she said, getting increasingly upset. 'You really can't.'

'Stop it,' Josh said, holding tight onto the top of her arms. 'What are you afraid of? This is crazy, just tell me what is going on? There's nothing we can't sort out, Sarah. Nothing. I promise you. Do you understand? '

'I'm married,' she said.

Josh nodded. 'I know.'

Sarah's eyes widened.

'Anessa told me. I've been round to the nursery this morning. That's why I'm here.'

'It's not how it looks. I hadn't got any choice,' Sarah said. 'I wanted to tell you. You have to believe me.'

He frowned. 'I'm not with you. What do you mean, no choice?' Josh said.

Sarah bit her lip, evidently considering her reply and what to tell him and then she shook her head. 'I can't tell you,' she said. 'You have to trust me that this wasn't what I wanted.'

'What is that supposed to mean?'

Sarah hesitated. 'I can't tell you,' she said. Hadn't Woody impressed on her that she wasn't to tell anyone? Especially not Josh? She remembered the implied threat, subtle but there all the same. She stared up into his eyes. She loved him, and there was no way she wanted Josh hurt the way Ryan had been hurt. She couldn't save Ryan but she could save Josh. 'Please,' she said. 'You have to believe me.'

Sarah

'Did you think if you told Josh he would go to the police?'

'Maybe, I knew that he would try to do something about it and I was worried what might happen if he did.'

'You thought Woody might hurt him?'

'No, not Woody, Farouk. Woody had already told me that if we were picked up by the police Farouk would know it was me who had told someone. Woody wasn't going to say anything.'

'And you think that meant he would go after Josh?'

'I wasn't sure what he was capable of. Woody knew that I loved Josh. But there were other people too, even if Josh could look after himself, there's Anessa, Mrs Howard – I couldn't risk telling anyone.'

'So you were frightened of what might happen?'

'Terrified.'

Josh

'Sarah wouldn't tell me anything and was getting more and more upset, so in the end I didn't push it. I suppose I wanted to know where we went from there, but it wasn't the right time to ask and I'm not sure that she could have told me. I just felt relieved that I had finally seen her. I know we hadn't got anything straight but it felt like we had made a start. I wanted to help. Then she told me that Woody had taken her phone, and that the house phone was broken, so I gave her my mobile.'

'Wasn't that inconvenient?'

'No, not really. I've got two, one for work and one for personal calls. I just wanted her to know that she wasn't on her own and that she could contact me if she wanted to.'

'And then you left Sarah at the house?'

'You make it sound like it was easy. To be honest I didn't want to leave her at all. I tried to persuade her to come with me but she said that she couldn't leave. It was her home and there were things she needed to do. But she was walking on eggshells, looking out of the window, panicky that Woody might come back at any moment. I could hardly tell her he was more than likely in bed with a blonde barely out of high school, could I? But I thought if I left her the phone at least she could call me.'

'And so you were there, what, ten minutes?'

'If that. At the door she told me that she loved me, and I believed her.'

'Even though she was married to someone else?'

'Yes.'

Sarah

'As soon as Josh had left I called the numbers that were on the piece of paper I'd found in Ryan's pocket.'

'And?'

'They were both for firms of solicitors. They refused to tell me if Woody was a client of theirs. I wondered if maybe it was something to do with his right to remain application, but they wouldn't tell me. And then I went online on Josh's phone and looked for the website. It's a site called Willsonline where you can write your will and then download a printed version for people to sign and witness and then you scan it in and upload it to their site for safe keeping. Once I knew what it was I opened up my laptop. I couldn't get online on the laptop but I was able to get into the history and see if the site was on there too.'

'And was it?'

'Yes. Someone had been on there several times over the previous few weeks.'

'And you believed that that was significant?'

'It's my laptop. As far as I knew until then, nobody else had used it except me. I copied the link down from my laptop and put it into Josh's phone. I wanted to see what they had done on the site. It's all password protected but it was obvious from what came up that someone had set up an account with Willsonline on there. So I then filled in the thing on the login screen where it said, "Have you lost your password". I put my email address in and waited to see what happened.'

'And what did happen?'

'Nothing. The site said they had no record of that email address but to check to make sure that I hadn't made a mistake and signed up using another.'

'So what did you do?'

'On my laptop, in the history someone had been onto Hotmail and Yahoo Mail several times, over weeks. But I couldn't get into either of them.'

'You keep saying someone, Sarah. Do you mean Woody?'

'I don't know. I've got no proof it was him. There was a chance it could have been Ryan.'

'Your brother?'

'He could easily have used my computer. I mean, it was the kind of thing he would have done if he hadn't got his with him. Ryan always used to write his passwords down in a diary he kept in the kitchen. So I went downstairs to his flat. If he'd used my laptop to access those accounts with his passwords then I'd be able to open them too.

'The door of his flat was unlocked and it looked like someone else had already been through it.'

'What do you mean, been through it? Searched?'

'Yes. The drawers were open in the kitchen and the bedroom, and the cupboards too. There were things all over the place. Someone had definitely been searching for something. The police had said they wouldn't touch anything and they hadn't been down there long enough to have searched it like that. It had to have been Woody. And by the look of it, it hadn't been the first time. If he had found the place in a mess like that and it hadn't been him who had done it, surely he would have said something?

'There was a roll of rubbish bags on the kitchen table and another rubbish bag half full of what looked like the contents of Ryan's fridge on the kitchen floor, so – if you didn't know – it might look like someone had been clearing the place out.'

'And Woody had already told you he had been down there?'

'Yes, yes he had.'

'So did you look too?'

'Yes. I found his diary and got his passwords but I couldn't work out what else Woody would have been searching for. There was nothing obvious. So in the end I went back to the house and tried to log on with Ryan's passwords, but none of them worked. And then I went back up to the attic.'

'To Woody's room?'

'Yes. Josh had said he looked like he would be a while. I wanted to try and find out what it was he had had signed and witnessed. I went through the rest of the box files and there was nothing much in any of them until I got to the last one.'

Chapter Twenty

Sarah opened the file on the end of the shelf. It looked exactly the same as the others and appeared to be full of notes on the European Union and the Euro, but then, as she ruffled through the papers with her fingers she realised that there was a piece of card cut to the same size as the box sitting under the papers, not stuck in, just pressed home so that it formed a hidden compartment, obscured by the dry dusty notes on monetary union.

Very carefully, with an ear towards the door, Sarah lifted the papers out and pressed the card down along the side so it lifted along the other edge. Underneath were what looked like a cache of official documents, a couple of bankbooks, a chequebook, and a registered letter still in its envelope, all addressed to Woody. Inside the envelope, along with a letter confirming Woody's place on the MBA, was a passport. Sarah scanned the letter. It was from the college. It congratulated him on being awarded his place and thanked him for his passport, which, they assured him, had been returned along with his letter of acceptance. A second sheet of paper, folded up along with the first, was from the bank assuring him that he would be able to withdraw and manage his funds on the production of a suitable form of identification, and suggested he bring along a current passport or a photo driving license.

Sarah opened the passport. The photograph inside was of a good-looking Asian man with bright humorous eyes who bore more than a passing resemblance to Woody. But it wasn't Woody.

Sarah stared at the picture for a moment or two and let the thought sink it. *It wasn't Woody.* As she flicked through the pages a laminated card slipped out onto the floor. It was a photo ID, a student union card, with the same man's photo on it and underneath was his name. Woody's name.

Sarah turned the pages again just in case there was some possibility that she was mistaken, but she knew that she wasn't. And if this was the real Woody's passport and ID card then who was it she was married to? And what did he want?

Sarah sat very still, taking a moment or two to take stock, trying to piece it together, trying to work out what it all meant. Until now she had been terrified of what might happen if she went to the police, terrified of the consequences, but this was something else, bigger than anything she had imagined. Whatever it was that was going on, what was obvious was that she needed to tell someone.

There was nothing else in the box file that caught her eye; the other documents were written in a language she couldn't read, and though they might have told her much more about Woody or whoever it was who was masquerading as Woody, currently their secrets were locked tight. But someone else would no doubt be able to translate them. She looked over the things on the floor, trying to work out what to do next. Did she take them with her or leave them there, so that if Woody came home he wouldn't know that she had discovered his secret? If she left them she could choose her moment, catch him off guard. Maybe that was best, maybe, but she still needed proof of what she'd found.

Taking out Josh's phone Sarah took photographs of the letters, the passport, and the ID card.

Tucking everything back where she had found it Sarah started to search the room with renewed energy. She wanted to know everything, find everything. The bedside tables revealed nothing, the desk, the remaining things on the bookshelf; nothing gave her any more than she already knew. Finally, on her hands and knees, she peered under the bed.

Tucked up by the head of the bed was a biscuit tin. She slid it out. It was the one she usually kept in her bedroom. Sarah prised open the lid.

Sarah

'It's where I keep all my important documents. Mum always used to do it to keep them safe and all together. You know that question people ask about what you'd grab if there were a fire? For my mum it would have been her precious biscuit tin. I hadn't even noticed that it was gone.'

'And what was inside?'

'All sorts of things. There was the marriage certificate, my birth certificate, my driving license, and passport. Old bank statements that he must have got out of my bedroom drawer. Photos, letters from friends. My whole life. And then there were other things that I hadn't put in there. A photo of Woody and me together at the wedding. One Ryan had taken of us in the garden, standing side by side near the barbeque. Having them in there made it look like they were special. Like I was treasuring them.

'I felt sick, imagining him going through my things, searching through everything to find what he wanted. I kept wondering what else he had stolen.

And then I found a sheet of paper folded up, tucked down the side; it was like the one I had found in Ryan's coat pocket, except that it had my signature written over and over again down both sides of the page.'

'Are you saying you'd written it?'

264

'No. Woody hadn't just been practising his signature, he had been practising mine too. And it was good, anyone would think it was mine. Anyone.'

'Do you want to take a break, Sarah? I can see you're upset. We've been going for quite a while. If you just want to stop for a few minutes...'

'No, no I'm fine. Really. I took photos of the page with the signatures and then, in an envelope I found out why he needed to forge it. There were applications for credit cards and a loan. And there was a repeat prescription and a bottle of pills with my name on them.'

'Pills?'

'After Mum died I was finding it really hard to cope. I'd left college, more or less given up on my own life really so that I could take care of her. Ryan was playing up and I'd spent months nursing her, trying to keep her going, keep her pain-free. Not that I regret that but – anyway – after Mum died her doctor suggested anti-depressants for a little while till I got myself back together.'

'And did you have a repeat prescription?'

'I think I probably must have had one somewhere.'

'And was there anything else in the tin?'

'Yes, there was a copy of my will.'

'Your will?'

'Printed off from the website I was telling you about. Witnessed by Mrs Howard and someone I'd never heard of. It must have been what she signed the day that Woody told her that he was in a hurry.'

'You believe Woody wrote it?'

'I know he did. I don't have a will. I've never written a will.'

'And you read it?'

'Yes, of course I did.'

265

'Are you sure you don't want a break, Sarah. We can stop if you like?'

'No. I need to tell you what he had done. I need you to understand. It was all totally legal looking, all very efficient, all signed and sealed, all so plausible. The will – my will – left Woody everything. It said: To my loving husband – my loving husband. The house, my car, all my possessions, everything. Every last thing.'

'No mention of Ryan?'

'Yes, he was in there. It said in the event of Ryan predeceasing me that Woody would inherit it all. If I died first, under the terms of the trust my mum left for us, Ryan would get the house.'

'So it was convenient for Woody that your brother was dead?'

'Very.'

'So what happened?'

'I took photos of everything that was in there.'

'Did you take the biscuit tin?'

'No, I didn't want Woody to know that I'd been in his room. The only thing I did take was the page of signatures. It was the one thing that I thought would prove that he was committing fraud, maybe worse.'

'What do you mean by worse?'

'I wondered if he had the patience to wait for me to sell the house and pay him back, after all if I was dead he would have it all.'

'Didn't it occur to you to call the police then?'

'Yes, of course it did. But I wasn't sure where to start, or if anyone would believe me. I have been keeping quiet about the wedding and so many things for so long. It wasn't an easy step for me. In the end I decided it would be better to go to the police station and see if I could see someone. I was worried that they wouldn't believe me. And where

266

did I start to explain? "Oh and by the way my husband isn't who he says he is and I've entered in to a sham marriage?" I needed to talk to someone face to face.'

'You had proof that he was impersonating the real Mustapha Sid Ahmed, Sarah, and that he had forged your signature, and had stolen your documents.'

'I know, but I was still frightened. You don't know Woody, I can see him now telling the police that I had been depressed and that I wasn't myself and had imagined it all. The tablets were there to prove it. I'd already seen when they came round to tell me about Ryan how bloody good he was at persuading people that I was half crazy. And what if I told them and they didn't believe me, what would happen then?'

'It was cut and dried. You had all the evidence you needed.'

'So you say, but what proof have I got that you're right? I kept thinking about what would happen if no one would believe me. What would happen if you questioned him and then you let him go? What would happen then? I was frightened.'

'Okay, okay – so what did happen, Sarah?'

'I tidied everything away, left everything just the way I found it, then I locked the door, got dressed, went back downstairs and got ready to go into town.'

'And go to the police?'

'You want the truth? I wasn't sure if I could do it. I didn't know where to start. But yes that was my plan. Crazily it was the first time I had felt hungry in weeks. And I thought if Woody wanted a reason why I'd gone out without him, I'd got the perfect excuse, I needed to go out to get food. There was nothing to eat in the house, and I'd got no idea when *he would be back. Sometimes he stayed out for an hour, sometimes all night. I'd got no way of knowing. So that was it, I was going. I put my coat on, put the paper with the forged signatures in the pocket and then I realised I couldn't find my car keys.'*

'You'd lost them?'

'No, I'm certain that I'd left them on one of the hooks just inside the kitchen door. I was more or less sure that Woody had to have taken them. I was going to go and look in my room, but as it was I didn't get the chance. I'd barely got into the hall before I heard Woody unlocking the front door.

Chapter Twenty-One

Woody looked her up and down, taking in the details of her coat and her outdoor shoes. 'Where do you think you're going?' he asked.

'You said we need to go shopping. We need food – milk,' Sarah said, a little unsteady, unnerved by his return, unnerved at being caught.

'I've told you not to leave the house on your own; I said that we'd go shopping later.' He paused. 'What's the matter with you?'

Sarah shook her head, wondering what it was he thought he saw in her. 'Nothing. I'm hungry, that's all.'

He nodded, his gaze travelling around the hall. 'You haven't cleaned up.'

'No, not yet, but I was going to do it as soon as I got back,' she said, trying not to meet his eye, afraid of giving anything away. 'Have you seen my car keys? I don't seem to be able to find them.' She kept her voice calm and even.

He stepped closer. 'I've already told you I don't want you going out alone. We'll go in a little while. Why don't you make a start on the kitchen?'

Sarah nodded, the sound of her pulse banging in her ears. She tried hard to stay calm and still as if she didn't know the things that she knew, as if everything was right with the world. She slipped off her coat and hung it up, feeling Josh's phone tucked away in her cardigan pocket as she moved, aware of its weight and its contents and praying that it didn't ring.

'Did you make a list?' Woody asked.

'No, but I can do it now,' she said, glancing over her shoulder, as she headed into the kitchen. He nodded.

A moment or two later Sarah heard Woody

climbing the stairs and let out the breath she had been holding. It would be fine. It would be fine, as soon as he went out again, whenever that was, she would go to the police. She was glad now that she hadn't taken anything out of any of the boxes. It would be fine. She had put everything back where it had been. He would never know she had been up there. Never know. Never guess.

Sarah took a sheet of paper off the pad by the house phone and tried to concentrate on what she needed to buy. Her hand shook, her mind raced while upstairs she heard Woody moving around, going up the stairs, then down again and into the bathroom, back up, his footsteps and the creak of the boards oddly reassuring.

She closed her eyes. He didn't know. He wouldn't guess. Everything was normal. All she had to do now was choose her moment, make a plan. It would be all right if she could just keep it together. Sarah felt the tension beginning to ease in her shoulders. He didn't know – nothing had changed as far as Woody was concerned, nothing at all. She stared at the paper. What was important now was to carry on as usual so that he didn't suspect anything.

'Milk, cheese, eggs,' Sarah mumbled, the words spoken aloud like a prayer as she wrote them on the pad. When she had done the list Sarah started on cleaning the kitchen, every atom straining to hear what Woody was doing. A while later she heard his footsteps on the stairs and turned around.

'I've got the list,' she said, pointing towards the table.

She turned round to face him. He hadn't guessed. It was going to be all right.

'I don't want you going out on your own,' he said. 'Is that clear?'

'I've not told anyone about us if that's what you're

worried about and I'm not going to. And we need to eat. And you're not always here.'

He paused as if weighing up her reply.

'We're out of everything – milk, tea. What do you think I'm going to do? Run away? This is my home, Woody,' Sarah said evenly, and then in an effort to deflect him, said, 'Did the hospital ring about Ryan?'

Woody took her phone out of his jacket. 'I don't know.'

'I thought you told me that you would let me know if they called,' she said.

He grinned at her, a lazy knowing grin. 'I didn't have the phone on. I didn't want to be disturbed.' There was something unsettling about his body language. She watched him as he switched on the phone, waiting for it to power up, waiting for the familiar trill. He watched the screen and as he did, Woody said, 'Have you been into my room?' His voice was soft and even, apparently it was just a simple enquiry with no edge to it.

Sarah made an effort not to let the panic show. 'Why? Do you want me to clean up there too?' she said, wiping the sink down.

'No, I just wondered what you were doing up there.'

'Nothing. How long before we go shopping? ' she said, not meeting his eye, not stopping her tidying.

And then he stepped closer so that he was in her space. 'I know that you were up there, Sarah. I know that you have been in my room and if it was for something innocent you'd have owned up and not lied to me.'

Sarah felt her pulse lift. 'I don't know what you mean. Mrs Howard came round and then I had a bath and tidied my room and then I was going to go out get some shopping.' She was talking too much, her voice sounded high and thin.

271

Woody held out his clenched fist towards her, palm upper most, fingers curled around something. It was impossible not to look. Slowly he opened it to reveal a small blue foam ball around the size of marble. Genuinely baffled Sarah stared at it.

'Do you know what this is?' he asked.

'I haven't got a clue.'

'I put it into the lock of my bedroom door before I go out. Just in case you or Ryan got nosey. And then I check when I get back to make sure it's still there. Do you know where I found it today?'

Sarah's heart missed a beat. She had completely forgotten about having to push the key into the lock when she first went in. She had forgotten to look for whatever it was that had been blocking the keyhole and forgotten to put it back. Sarah made the effort not to let the realisation show on her face and instead shook her head. 'Not a clue,' she said. 'I've never seen it before.'

Woody grabbed hold of her arm. 'Don't lie to me. You were in my room while I was out. What were you looking for?'

Sarah shook him off. 'Get off me. I don't know what you mean,' she said, but she knew that Woody knew she was lying. There was something in his expression, something wolf-like and dangerous in his eyes that made her flinch.

He smiled grimly. 'I had hoped we might find a way to keep this going a bit longer, Sarah. Find a way to make it work, but I'm afraid this means that we're going to have to part company sooner rather than later.'

'You mean you're leaving?' she said.

He grinned. 'No, not exactly.'

As he spoke he grabbed her again, tighter this time, with real force.

'What are you doing?' Sarah yelped.

'You're going to come with me,' he said. 'I've got something I want to show you. Something you'll understand. It's a way out of the mess you're in. A way to make it all alright. You miss Ryan, don't you? I know you do. You've been so sad since he went, so very sad.' His voice was singsong, uncanny, unhinged.

Sarah froze and stared at him. 'Stop it,' she said. 'Please, Woody, just stop this; you're scaring me.' But he was having none of it. She tried to pull away, tried to break free, pushing and struggling, but he was too strong for her. 'Come on, you just need to do as I say,' he said.

'Or what?' Sarah hissed.

He laughed and as he did Sarah saw something in his face, something in his eyes and with it came the realisation that it was now or never. With fear pumping through her like molten lava, Sarah leaned in close and bit his arm as hard as she could. Woody shrieked and let go, back handing her across the face and as he did, instinctively she twisted away, pulling as hard as she could, trying to dislodge his remaining hand, trying to tear herself away from him, turning left and right. As he was concentrating on keeping control of her arms and torso, Sarah kicked him as hard as she could in the shins. Woody yelped in surprise and pain and let her go, bending double so that he could grab his leg.

Sarah glanced at the back door. It was locked and bolted, by the time she had got it undone Woody would be recovered and on her. So she ran out of the kitchen into the hall. It took her a split second to realise that the front door was locked and the key gone. With no way out Sarah had no choice but to run upstairs. He was behind her now and gaining fast.

Sarah glanced left and right, weighing up her

options. Her bedroom had a lock on the door but once she was inside there was no other way out. The bathroom on the other hand overlooked the kitchen extension. There was some chance she might be able to break the bathroom window and climb down onto the flat roof below, and some chance was better than none.

Scurrying inside Sarah turned and went to close the door. Woody was there outside, a step or two behind her, out on the landing and lunging forward to try and hold the door open, but she was on it and slammed the door shut behind her; turning the key in the lock and sliding the bolt across. She had barely pushed it home before Woody was banging against the door as hard as he could. Sarah leaned back onto it, feeling the force of the blows through the wood.

'You bitch,' he screamed, banging harder.

Praying the wood and the locks would hold Sarah turned round to tackle the window when she realised that the bathtub was almost full. The hot tap, not quite turned off properly drip-drip-dripped into the clear water. The sight of it stopped Sarah in her tracks. She looked round. It wasn't the only unusual thing. Propped up on the shelf above the sink was a plain white envelope addressed to Woody, in what looked an awful lot like her handwriting.

Sarah froze. Outside the door she could hear Woody trying to break in, hear him screaming and begging her to open the door, but in the bathroom it felt as if time had stopped still. She reached out, picked up the envelope and slid out the single sheet of paper that was inside.

'Dearest Woody,' it began. 'I'm so sorry, so very, very sorry, my love. I know how much you love me but I can't bear to go on.' There was more, but Sarah only needed the first line. There was no doubt now, if there ever had been, that Woody intended to kill her.

The forms, the will, the page filled with her signature. It all led to this.

Sarah glanced round the bathroom taking in the details. There were candles arranged along every ledge, a full bath, flowers, and there on the side of the sink was a razor blade. Now she knew exactly what Woody had planned for her, and he had her exactly where he wanted her to be.

Panic fluttered through her. This was it. She knew with an unshakable certainty that she was going to die here if she didn't find a way out. The bathroom window was far smaller than Sarah remembered, a foot across by perhaps two and a half feet high, the top third bisected by another smaller window. Realistically, unless she could push the whole frame out there was no way for her to squeeze out of it, and even if she tried, if Woody got into the bathroom before she got out and she got stuck Sarah could imagine him pulling her back inside, over the broken glass. Even if he couldn't explain her injuries, if Sarah was dead it wouldn't matter one way or the other, would it? The pulse was thundering in her ears. Think, think, there had to be a way out of this, there had to be.

Sarah took Josh's phone out of her pocket and rang the number for his business phone. He answered after a single ring.

'Sarah—' he began.

'Please listen, please help me. He's trying to kill me,' she said. 'If they find me dead I didn't kill myself, Josh. I didn't, I truly didn't. You have to believe me. I love you,' she gasped.

Behind her, Sarah could hear the wood splintering. 'I'm sending you the proof,' she said, her fingers working the phone, sending the images of the will, the signatures, the passport, everything, sending them one by one. It seemed to be taking forever. She tried hard not to panic, tried hard to ignore Woody screaming outside the door, tried hard to ignore Josh begging her to talk to him. When she was done she stood the phone up on the back of the toilet, wedged between the cistern and the wall, with the line still open. 'I love you,' she said. 'I've never stopped loving you.'

'Come on, Sarah, open the door,' Woody cajoled from outside on the landing, his tone softer now, more conciliatory. 'Just let me in. We can work this out. I can explain everything. Please, you have to believe me; just open the door. Open it. Come on. It doesn't have to be like this. We can find another way.'

'How do you explain not being who you say you are? How do you explain the passport?' she yelled. 'How do you explain the will?'

There was a split second's silence and then a terrifying crashing blow against the door.

'I knew you'd been in my room. I knew it. I'm going to kill you, you fucking lying bitch,' Woody screamed. 'Dead like your brother. Drowned like your brother, do you hear me. I'm going to push you under and hold you down. Just like Ryan. Do you hear me? Why don't you just let me in, let me in, and get it over and done with. Come on, Sarah. You know I'm going to get you in the end. There is nowhere for you to go, no one coming to help. Come on, don't make me come in there and get you. You want to be with Ryan, don't you?'

His voice was pleading and yet furiously angry. 'When the police come they'll find the door broken in, smashed down where I came home and couldn't find you. They'll see how desperate I was. How I tried to save you. You've been so depressed; so very, very depressed.'

Mind racing, Sarah tried desperately to think. She

felt sick but if she gave up now he would win. She had only one chance and she had to take it. Picking up the scales Sarah smashed the bathroom window. Although it was too tiny to get through she didn't think Woody would know that. She hoped it would make him think she was getting away.

Hearing the glass smash he wailed and renewed his efforts to break down the door, banging now, hammering, throwing himself against it again and again. Once, twice. Sarah pressed herself back hard against the door, managing to unfasten the bolt with barely a sound and then she eased herself to one side of the door and quietly turned the key. As he hit the door again, Sarah undid it. The momentum of the blow carried Woody forward and he tumbled head first into the bathroom.

Sarah was ready for him. He had barely hit the floor before she clambered over him, ran across the landing and up the narrow staircase towards the attic.

Woody was on his feet in an instant, scrambling after her, screaming with fury.

Sarah took the stairs two at a time, as she did she noticed that the biscuit tin and the box file she had found in his bedroom earlier were now out on the landing and standing on the floor by the balustrade. Maybe he had been planning to hide the documents more securely, maybe put the biscuit tin back in her room, so that whoever came once she was dead would find them.

Sarah was at the door to the attic room now. As Woody got to the tiny dog-leg landing he slowed. He was breathing hard, his expression was triumphant. Sarah was in the doorway apparently struggling with the handle.

'I've got you now, you bitch,' he said. 'This is it. There is nowhere else to go, no where for you to run.

The door's locked. You're all out of luck.'

But Woody was wrong. As he stepped up onto the landing Sarah turned round, braced herself against the locked door, and then launched herself forward as hard as she could, both hands outstretched, hitting Woody squarely in the chest, sending him backwards into the handrail. There was a noise, a great cracking splintering sound, and then the balustrade gave way under his weight and hers.

For a terrifying split second Sarah thought she might have failed. She saw the triumph on Woody's face and then something more quizzical and surprised as the balustrade unpeeled from the landing and then he was falling backwards, tumbling down into the stairwell, clawing at thin air, the biscuit tin and the box file falling after him, falling end over end, the lids coming open and papers and photographs floating down as Woody plummeted down onto the tiled hall floor below.

For one terrible moment Sarah thought she might lose her balance and follow him over the edge, but she managed to stop herself and stepped backwards, stumbling back onto the boards and banging her head on the wall behind her.

Below her Woody hit the ground with a sickening thud and then there was silence. Gingerly, Sarah got to her feet, hugging the wall, for a moment not daring to look over the edge in case Woody was on his way back up, wondering if the fall had been enough to stop him.

Fearing what she might see, Sarah edged her way across the landing and peered over into the void below. Woody lay below her on the black and white tiles, blood was already beginning to seep across the floor in a dark, almost black, puddle. He was folded at a peculiar, unnatural angle, his legs twisted so bizarrely that he looked more like a broken marionette than a man. Flurries of papers were settling around him like confetti, some close enough to soak up the blood, others fluttering away on an unseen draught gathering up into untidy drifts. It was obvious from his position that Woody was going nowhere.

Sarah took her time getting downstairs. She could hear him struggling to breathe. There was a bubbling froth of blood forming at the corner of his mouth while one hand grasped frantically, rhythmically at the air. She could see that each breath was an exertion, a great physical effort. He couldn't move, that much was obvious. His eyes were wide open and as she watched Woody blinked, as if he couldn't quite believe what was happening. Sarah moved in closer so that she was in his line of sight.

Woody was struggling to say something. She watched him, moving his lips, his tongue working frantically. She was shocked by how tangled and broken he looked, but at the same time felt no compassion, no pity, just a numbed relief that it was finally over.

'Help me,' he mouthed.

It surprised Sarah that he was still able to speak.

'Please,' he whispered. 'Help me.'

She shook her head.

His eyes widened.

'Who are you?' she asked.

He tried to smile, each breath wet, thick sounding and bubbling. 'No one you know,' he said, and closed his eyes.

Sarah waited until Woody had stopped making any noise before she went upstairs and picked up Josh's phone. The line had gone dead. She called 999 but barely had chance to speak before she heard frantic knocking at the door.

279

'Open up, this is the police,' shouted a loud voice from outside, and then there were more voices.

'Mrs Ahmed, Mrs Ahmed are you in there? Mrs Ahmed, it's the police. Can you open the door for us?'

Sarah walked to the door, skirting the pool of blood that was spreading across the floor and then knelt down and lifted the letterbox.

'I haven't got a key,' she said. 'He locked me in.'

'Are you okay? Where is he now, Mrs Ahmed?'

Sarah looked back over her shoulder towards the broken clutter of bones and brains, of body and blood on the hall floor. 'I think he's dead,' she said quietly.

They came in through the back door in the end. The police and the paramedics. They looked at her bruises and the finger marks on her arms, the bruising on her face that she didn't know she had where she had tried to fight him off in the kitchen. The ripped nails, the torn blouse. The look of terror in her eyes. They took away the note in the bathroom and the biscuit tin and the box files and all the papers, even the one in her coat pocket, and then they took Sarah away in an ambulance.

Sarah didn't see what they did to Woody or whoever he was. When she left, he was still lying there in the hall looking up at the ceiling and the landing above; he looked surprised.

Sarah

I've told the detective everything now, at least as much as I can remember, as much as I want to tell him, as much as he needs to know.

His expression is sympathetic. He knows that they have checked me over at the hospital to see if I had anything more serious than the bruises that over the last hours have flowered like thunderclouds on my arms, my face and my legs. He knows that they have taken photographs, taken my clothes, taken scrapings from under my nails, combed my hair. I'm lucky to be alive, they said.

The detective slides a photograph across the table from the file that he has alongside him.

'I'd just like you to take another look at these photographs.' He quotes the reference number so there can be no doubt later which photograph I'm looking at.

'Do you know this man, Sarah?'

'No. I don't know him. But I'm certain that this is a photograph of the man from the passport that I found in Woody's room.'

'You're positive?'

'Yes.'

'That's good. He's the real Woody. His name is Mustapha Sid Ahmed. Thirty-two. A Pakistani national over here on a student visa.'

I turn the picture towards the light. 'Where is he? Is he okay?'

'I'm afraid not, he's dead. We found a body in Soham, in a barn, that we believe may be Mr Ahmed. We suspect that the man you knew as Woody was responsible for Mr Ahmed's death and then stole his identity.'

'He killed him?'

'It would appear so, which is why Farouk, the man you knew as Woody, dropped out of college and cut off all contact with Mr Ahmed's parents.'

'But that can't be true; Woody can't be Farouk. Farouk was the man who Ryan borrowed the money from, the man at the Kirby Road house that Woody was afraid of.'

'I'm afraid that was probably just smoke and mirrors on Farouk's part. It's highly probable that your brother never actually met the man he believed was lending him the money. Farouk, masquerading as Woody, pretended to act as an intermediary when in fact it was him lending your brother the money.'

'But the money was real. Ryan bought a van, new clothes, tools.'

'Yes, it was taken fraudulently from Mr Ahmed's bank account. We've yet to ascertain exactly how much money was in the account before his death, but it was a considerable sum. Most of it missing, having been drawn out in cash. It appears that Farouk killed Mr Ahmed and took his passport and other documents, his bank account, his savings, his life.

'The two men bore a passing resemblance to one another, certainly close enough for Farouk to be able to pass himself off as Woody for the purposes of bank fraud. Farouk kept his old flat on in Kirby Road and the landlord thought the real Woody had moved out and come to live with you.'

'Because that's what I told him when I went to take the mail back?'

'That's right, although I'm sure Farouk probably told him much the same story, and as a result of that the landlord didn't bother to report Woody missing. He believed he had just taken his things and moved out.'

'To avoid Farouk who the landlord knew was bullying him?'

'Yes. And as Mr Ahmed, Woody had paid up front for his stay there; the landlord wasn't over keen to track him down in case he wanted his money back.'

'Are you sure he's dead? His parents will be devastated. They were so proud of him.'

'I'm afraid so, Sarah. We're waiting for DNA analysis to confirm it but Farouk kept a number of

Woody's personal possessions, his books, his clothes, a jacket, a hat – most of his wardrobe actually, to try and make the transition to someone who could pass for an MBA student, while he systematically drained Woody's bank account, and accessed and spent the allowance his parents were providing for him.'

'So who is he? The man I married.'

'His real name is Farouk Holbein although we believe this isn't the only name he's been using. He's a career criminal, petty theft, fraud, identity theft – until now we had no reason to believe that he was violent but this changes things obviously.'

'And did he plan all this? Woody, Ryan – me?'

'I can't say that for a fact, I think he just saw an opportunity and worked it. There is no doubt he was clever. When it looked like one revenue stream might be about to close he needed another and latched on to Ryan and then when he realised Ryan was a dead end, he saw the house and your inheritance and hooked into another cash cow.'

'Ryan and me?'

'Not just you. We've got evidence of benefit fraud on a large scale. Multiple claims, multiple identities. In your case he wanted your house, possibly even your lifestyle. Settled, respectable, in a nice house in a good area. You can see how that would play out to his advantage if he was hoping to dupe other people.

'As Woody Ahmed he was your next of kin, so with or without a will he would have been the sole beneficiary to your estate once Ryan was gone. I think he saw that one very clearly.'

'But what about being deported; his application for the right to remain?'

'Just part of the con to get you to agree to marry him. Farouk is a British citizen. His mother was

Algerian, married to a British national, although Farouk's biological father is unknown. He's been in and out of care since he was five. It would appear he was just using Woody's student status and vulnerability as a means of influencing Ryan and yourself.'

'But if he didn't need them why did he take all those photos, the wedding pictures.'

'He might have anticipated needing to use them to back up his claim, when it came to claiming your estate, you know "here we are as a happy family". And having gone through his possessions it would seem that he has nothing from his own past or childhood. Who knows, maybe he thought of you as his family. His next of kin.'

I stare at him and shake my head. 'I didn't want him as part of my family.'

'Obviously not, Sarah, I can understand that. We also found documents in his room and at his previous address on Kirby Road that indicated he was trying to raise a loan against your property, although I think he eventually decided it would be better for him to wait until he had the opportunity to sell.'

'You mean when Ryan and I were both dead?'

'I'm afraid so. He was happy to play the long game.'

'The long game?'

'He had his flat on Kirby Road where he could live the kind of lifestyle that he preferred, entertaining women, taking drugs – and he had you both where he wanted you. Although we can't prove it we believe he also may have been responsible for your brother's death. That just left you, and he had already inferred to our officers when they came round to inform you about Ryan's death that you were mentally unstable and having emotional problems long before your brother died.'

'Are you telling me that if I hadn't fought back he could have got away with it?'

The detective sucked at his teeth, taking his time to reply. 'I'd like to think not, but it's not impossible – which is one of the reasons why we're re-examining a couple of other cases with some similarities to this one.'

'He's done this before?'

'It's possible. Likely.'

Finally he turns off the recorder and looks at me. Really looks at me.

'I think we're done here, Sarah,' he says.

When I get to my feet my whole body aches. I stretch but it doesn't help, it just makes the pain more intense.

'Is it all right if I look at them again?' I ask, nodding towards the things on the table.

'Yes, of course,' he says.

I get up and walk over to the table, and look at the things arranged there. I take a long look at the stain on our marriage certificate. It's about the same size as my hand, shaped like a flower and mahogany brown and I know now that it's blood. And now, looking more closely, I can see that there is blood on everything.

These are the papers that were on the floor in the hall where Farouk died. There are little droplets on letters, splashes on the papers, something crusty and dried on the corner of the tin, and smeared over the receipts and the bills.

I put the certificate back where it came from, very carefully, back on the table, back in its place, and move it with my fingertips till it is square with all the other things. Although everything is in plastic bags I can clearly see what's inside. There are the box files and the biscuit tin and then, alongside each one, the contents are set out, inside evidence bags, all numbered, all neatly arranged, evenly spaced: passports, some photographs, letters and bills. Lots of envelopes. And my old mobile phone, not lost after all but stolen by Farouk and hidden.

The room is very quiet. Dust motes spin in a shaft of afternoon sunlight.

'It's over now, Sarah,' says the detective. 'You should go and get some rest. We'll need to see you again. There will probably be more questions, and I'm afraid you can't go back to your house at the moment. Have you got somewhere you can go and stay until we release it back to you?' The detective speaks in a soft voice.

I'm not sure, but I don't say that. Maybe Anessa or maybe a hotel. Maybe somewhere anonymous would be better, somewhere I can sleep.

'There will still be some formalities to go through; but for now you need to have a rest, get something to eat.' He's smiling as he puts the photographs from the table back into his folder. 'It's going to take a while,' he said. 'There are people you can talk to. Victim support.'

I stare at him.

He smiles grimly. 'Don't try to rush it. You've been through a lot, you're lucky to have got out of it alive. You might like to know that we've got statements from Farouk's associates who have confessed to beating your brother up and threatening you. Are you okay?'

I look up and nod. 'I'll be fine,' I say.

I don't tell him that I meant to kill the man I knew as Woody. I don't tell him that I don't care what he was called, or that in the bathroom I had made my mind up, that I made a plan, that I wanted him dead, that I planned to lead him upstairs, that I intended to kill him, that it was him or me. I'm not sure if he guesses. If he does he doesn't say anything.

The uniformed female constable is still standing watching us. She smiles at me now as the detective indicates the door and then opens it for me.

'I think we're done here for the time being, Sarah,' he says. His tone is conspiratorial and gentle, as if I'm a child. 'If there is anything else you can think of, anything at all, then all you have to do is call me. This is my direct line.' As we walk along the corridor he hands me a business card from a little case he has in his inside jacket pocket. 'We've arranged to have some clothes brought in for you. And I'll be in touch if we need anything else. Are you sure you're okay?'

I nod, but unsatisfied, he waits until I look him in the eye.

'Yes, really, I'm fine,' I say. Which is a stupid thing to say because we both know I am anything but fine.

Then it occurs to me that I don't really care anymore what he believes or understands, or even, really, what happens to me now, because it is finally all over and the man I married is dead – whoever he is or was – and I am free, and nothing can touch me now, and nothing can be worse than where I've been. Nothing.

The officer smiles. 'I believe Josh is waiting for you outside,' he says.

I look up at him. 'He's here?'

He nods and then he opens the door into an office space.

Josh is sitting on a bench. He has a hold-all by his feet. As I step outside he stands up. He hasn't shaved and he looks tired and drawn as if he hasn't slept.

As our eyes meet I feel my pulse quicken and I'm filled with something like delight and relief and joy, and a hundred other things that don't have a name, and I feel my eyes fill with tears.

We stand for a moment. I think he is nervous, I know I am. And then Josh smiles and opens his arms and the tension I have been holding in my spine eases and I step into his embrace, letting him hold me.

'I brought you some clothes,' he says, holding up the bag.

But I don't want to be away from him, instead I relish the heat of his body and the smell of him and the way my body moulds into his, it makes me want to stay in his arms forever and forget everything else. I can hear sobbing and it takes me a moment or two to realise that I'm the one crying.

Josh holds me tight up against him, pressing his lips to my hair. And then he takes my hand and the policeman guides us through a maze of corridors, and then Josh leads me out of the police station.

It is dark outside, and cold. The glow from the streetlights is reflected in the puddles, a taxi goes past and on the other side of the road a young couple stroll by, hand in hand, chatting to each other under the shelter of a blue and white umbrella.

For some reason I'm surprised that ordinary life is still going on.

I start to shiver again and my teeth start to chatter. Josh pulls me close and, taking his jacket off, wraps it around my shoulders; it is only then that I realise I'm still wearing the police tracksuit and the beach shoes.

'I need to explain,' I say to Josh.

He smiles down at me. 'There's plenty of time for that. The truck is just round the corner,' he says.

'I've lit the fire. Let's go home.'
And we do.

Acknowledgements

I'd like to thank everyone who has helped me get Next of Kin written, edited and out into the world.

Huge thanks to the dream team - Susan Opie, Jane Dixon-Smith, Maureen Vincent-Northam and Rebecca Emin for helping sort out all the practicalities of copy, cover and content as well as offering lots of encouragement, advice and support!

A really big thank you too, to the amazing people who volunteered to read Next of Kin when it was just a draft - especially Lisa Garwood and EM Dawe who not only read it, but went through it with a fine tooth comb and picked out all kinds of bloopers, typos and errors – Thank you! Your thoughts, comments and input have been absolutely invaluable.

Thanks too to Janet Reynolds-Spark for her advice and Phillipa Ashley for letting me tell her the story over the phone while she drank coffee and ate toast, and her amazing work on the blurb, which is an art form in itself.

Any errors or sins of omission are entirely mine.

And finally I need to thank Phil and Jake & our much anticipated new rescue dog, Daisy, who don't seem to mind living with a woman who spends most of her days talking to her imaginary friends.

Sue Welfare
June 2015

47649361R00161

Made in the USA
Charleston, SC
13 October 2015